NAKED FOR MISTRESS

NAKED FOR MISTRESS

ALEX JORDAINE

Published by Accent Press Ltd – 2010

Print ISBN 9781907726569
Ebook ISBN 9781907726576

Printed and bound in the UK

Cover design by
Zipline Creative

To my beloved Mistress G, always and for ever

Xcite Books help make loving better
with a wide range of erotic books,
eBooks, adult products
and dating sites.

www.xcitebooks.com

Sign-up to our Facebook page
for special offers and free gifts!

Part One

A NEW MAN

'The moment of change is the only poem.'
Adrienne Rich

Chapter One

THE NIGHT WAS AS black as pitch, moonless and starless. Peter Lane stood at the edge of the tall, jagged cliff and heard rather than saw the surging waves of the ocean, which was itself as black and deep as the sky that stretched above him to infinity. Peter listened to the pounding of the waves as the night breeze tugged at his clothes. He stared into the dark and thought about how easy it would be to simply step out over the edge of that cliff and yield once and forever to the infinite darkness of the sea and the sky. Peter also thought about his wife. When he had first met Christine he'd fallen in love with everything about her: the look of her, the sound of her voice, her scent, her charisma, her spirit, her *aura*. She'd put him under a spell then. He was still under her spell now despite all that had passed between them.

Peter walked away from the cliff edge and climbed back into his car, the sound of the ocean still pounding in his ears. He clutched at the steering wheel as he drove back into the resort, to the villa, wondering who his wife would be bringing home to fuck that night.

It was ironic, Peter thought ruefully as he pulled the car into the villa's large garage, that Christine and he had honeymooned not only in this same resort but in this very property just six years ago. They'd discovered soon after they met that they both loved the same part of Southern France, and the upmarket coastal town of Dauge, steeped as it was in antiquity and charm, turned out to be a particular favourite of them both. It seemed an ideal place to go for their honeymoon, with its ancient stone buildings and its mediaeval churches and cobbled streets; with its shaded squares and fishing piers and restaurants and bars. And that great long sandy beach. *Remember that beach at midnight, Peter?* How could he ever forget it? But, things had been different between Christine and him back then, very different. Images from that time were never far from his consciousness, as if they were playing on a screen at the back of his eyes. They came back to Peter now, as sharply poignant as ever...

He first met Christine Steele at a swish West End art gallery. He'd been pleased to receive his invitation to attend the opening of an exhibition of the latest collection of works by Martin Rolf, an artist he particularly admired. As it turned out Peter didn't take any notice at all of the striking abstract paintings hanging on the walls of the modish gallery. Nor did he take any notice of the other wealthy patrons gathered there at that fashionable venue. Except for one, that is, although to say she caught his attention would not be doing justice to the experience in the least.

As soon as Peter arrived his eyes were drawn immediately to the ravishing dark haired beauty. She was standing a little apart from that select crowd, nursing a glass of champagne. He fell in love with her completely and in an instant, simple as that.

He acted on it immediately too. Completely in the grip of the *coup de foudre* of all time, he went straight up to her and announced, 'You're the loveliest woman I've ever

4

seen.'

He wasn't exaggerating either. Christine really was stunningly beautiful. Her strong, angular face was perfection, softened as it was by lips that were full and delightfully sensuous and by large blue-green eyes that were so luminous they were hypnotic. Lustrous dark hair fringed her forehead and trailed on either side of her lovely face, falling loose to just above her shoulders. Her figure was perfection too, softly curved with shapely breasts and rounded hips. It was shown off to splendid effect by her stylish black mini dress, which was low cut, daringly short and close fitting in all the right places.

And what did Christine make of her impulsive admirer? She let her eyes linger on Peter for a long moment, wandering over his face and up and down his body. She gave a husky little laugh that made his spine tingle. 'You're not so bad yourself,' she said.

Which indeed he wasn't. He had dark shiny hair, a handsome, intelligent face with sculptured features, bright blue eyes, and a seductive lopsided grin that he was beaming at her right now. He was tall and lean too, looking good in his cream button-down shirt, tailored dark blue jacket, chinos and loafers.

Peter grabbed a glass of champagne from a passing waiter and raised it in a toast. 'To us,' he said, still smiling that seductive smile, a direct look in his eyes.

'To us,' Christine replied, meeting Peter's gaze, and clinking glasses with him.

Right from the start the sexual chemistry between the two of them had been electric and one thing led to another rapidly – very rapidly. Within one hour of that champagne toast they'd arrived at Christine's plush apartment nearby. Within one hour *and one minute* of that toast they were in her bedroom, they just couldn't get there quickly enough. Both of them were so consumed by desire that they were barely in control, their sexual anticipation so intense it hurt.

As soon as they got through the bedroom door they started undressing together in a fever of mutual longing. Christine had more than a head start, it transpired. She pulled her little black dress over her head to reveal that she had not been wearing any underwear. She had an all-over tan, beautiful breasts and her nipples were dark and enticingly erect. Her pussy was entirely free of pubic hair, her mons silky smooth.

Christine kicked off her high heeled shoes and that was it, she was done. Peter shucked his jacket off his shoulders in double-quick time. She unbuttoned his shirt for him and pulled it off, virtually tore it off.

His breath coming ever more quickly, Peter took off his loafers and his socks and his chinos. When lastly he removed his briefs, his cock sprang out, stiff and urgent with need.

Christine laid herself down on the bed and Peter joined her. They lay for a moment, facing each other and gazing rapturously into one another's eyes. Then Christine rolled onto her back and Peter put his lips to her mouth. They kissed with great passion, their tongues flicking together, and then Peter brought his mouth to her throat. He licked a warm trail down her collar bone to the swell of her breasts. He began sucking them greedily, taking her erect nipples into his mouth.

At the same time Peter ran his hand over Christine's stomach and down to caress her quivering thighs. He began to rub the opening of her vagina, his fingers sticky in her sex. Christine soon became very wet indeed, soaked with the sap of desire. Peter started to roll his fingers over her stiff clitoris and she groaned with pleasure. Then he pushed his fingers in further, digging them in deep, plunging into all her juicy wetness over and over.

Christine then reached for his now achingly hard cock and started to pull and stroke it. The feeling of sex rippled through Peter and he groaned with her movement as she stroked and pulled at his hardness, jerking more forcefully at it all the time.

Peter could smell the scent of sex everywhere in that bedroom now – his sex, her sex, their sex; it was intoxicating. He knew that he couldn't wait any longer. Nor could Christine. 'Fuck me. Fuck me now,' she whispered urgently, staring into his gleaming blue eyes. Her breath was coming quickly, her cheeks flushed.

Peter placed himself between Christine's legs and pushed his cock inside her, filling her tight wet pussy with its thickness. She sighed with delight and turned her head to one side. Peter laid himself on top of her, fucking her deep and hard. Christine hugged him close and grasped his hair, wrapping her legs around his waist, her athletic limbs supple and pliant, as he forged deep into her.

Peter pushed into Christine even harder and she moaned and cried out with his movement. He began to fuck her faster and faster, his whole body shaking, his groin crashing against hers, his cock thrusting deep inside her sex. Peter could feel himself building to the peak of excitement. Then the pleasure tightened and exploded through him. He climaxed long and hard, spouting spurt after spurt of warm seed deep inside her, and grunting again and again as orgasmic spasms ripped through him like a sound wave.

At the same time, fighting for breath, Christine began to rock and buck and moan. Then she shuddered to a violent orgasm, crying out deliriously as her own climax exploded and wave after wave of ecstasy washed over her.

Afterwards they lay together panting and gasping. Christine was the first to speak 'That was fantastic,' she said, looking at Peter with shining eyes. 'Let's do it again.'

They did.

Three months later they did something else. They got married.

Chapter Two

PETER WAS IN MANY ways the archetypal whizz kid at that time in his life. He was a very successful entrepreneur who was making a lot of money for the development company he worked for and plenty for himself too in the process. He was a man brimming with energy and imagination. He was incredibly busy too. It went with the territory, naturally, but he was a prime candidate for burnout at some stage if he wasn't careful, and he knew it. Peter became determined to ease off on his workload after meeting Christine and he got on with the process. But such things take time and his busy work schedule kept the couple apart far too much of the time before the day of their wedding.

Once they were on their honeymoon, *nothing* could keep them apart. Peter and Christine were constantly together during that magical fortnight. They held hands everywhere they went, not that they ventured far from the villa, far from their bedroom in fact. Their lovemaking was such a constant enveloping delight it left them amazed. They felt as if they had entered some kind of sensual paradise, one they never wanted to leave.

In the mornings they'd wake curled around each other. They would luxuriate in the warmth of the Mediterranean sunshine as it streamed through the shutters, breathe in the balmy pine-scented air and lay in each other's embrace.

They felt happy beyond words.

They'd head for the shower together, this inseparable pair, where they would soap each other's bodies, and towel one another dry. They'd have some juice and a cup or two of that full-bodied coffee the French love so much, perhaps a bite to eat. This was a prelude to … to what? To simply falling back into bed to make love and laze around together all day, that's all. But what better activity has ever been devised than that?

On the rare occasions they ventured out it was usually in order to sample some of the excellent local cuisine for which the town was justly famous. They'd throw on some clothes and go and find a restaurant where throughout their meal they'd gaze into each other's eyes and hold hands across the table. Other diners would glance at them knowingly and smile with approval (*Ah l'amour!*). Afterwards the romantic pair would return to the villa and to their bedroom, pulling at each other's clothes on the way and laughing as they stumbled into the room. They would tumble onto the bed, where they'd make love some more – just by way of a change.

And when they weren't making love, they talked and talked: of books and films and art, of childhood and family and friends, of good times and bad, of dreams and fantasies. Their talk turned inevitably to sexual fantasies.

Like fucking each other's brains out at night time on the beach under the moon and the stars.

So that's what they did at midnight one night, taking the descending cobblestone street that took them to the seafront and then rushing down to the beach. Once there, they threw down their towels and stripped naked. Christine got onto all fours and told Peter to take her right there and then. Her pussy was hot and wet and tight as he pushed into her from behind, his cock forging deep into her. He pushed and pushed into the hot warmth of her sex, slick and oozing for him and she pushed and pushed back They thrust together hungrily on the warm sand, before plunging into the ocean itself and making love in the water in hopeless abandon as the waves crashed over them again and again, their only audience a crescent moon and the stars that glimmered above them in the endless sky.

And when they finally drifted back to the edge of the shore and back to their villa and back to their bed Christine had wanted more. She said she couldn't help it, he'd made her insatiable. She had fallen onto Peter, grabbing his shoulders and making him lie on his back. She had raked her fingers over his smooth, hard body and then, her thighs pressing wetly against his, had guided him inside her. They went on to devour one another feverishly again. But eventually, inevitably, the fever turned into something else and their lovemaking became ever more languid and drowsily sensuous until sleep took them at last. And when they woke in the morning, locked in each other's arms, it started all over again. They couldn't resist going back to the beach at night either, most nights actually, to become one yet again with the elements in all their naked, uninhibited passion.

Chapter Three

SIX YEARS AGO THAT had been the pattern, with one day slipping blissfully into another like the waves of the sea. But that had been then. This was the way it went now:

Peter and Christine would both rise mid-morning and go straight outside to the villa's pool that shimmered invitingly in the clear sunlight. They'd swim a few laps together, their nude bodies, warmly brown from the Mediterranean sun, glistening with rivulets of water.

They'd towel off and, still naked, would seat themselves at a shaded metal table on the lawn and take a light breakfast of juice, croissants and coffee. They were completely private in the garden as the neighbouring properties were screened from view by the villa's high wall. As they sat together breakfasting, shaded from the bright sunshine, the nearby pool glistened and rippled, and solid beds of flowers presented a bright swathe of colour on the smooth lawn around them.

They barely exchanged a word during their repast. Instead, as they sipped their juices and drank their coffees and munched their croissants, Peter would absently scan the headlines of the daily paper, his French a bit rusty but still quite serviceable, while Christine would bury herself in her novel. The silence between them was companionable enough but slightly awkward too, unnatural somehow.

The couple would then go indoors to complete their ablutions, dress casually, and go off together to do the tourist bit. Strolling side by side, they'd visit the resort's fine churches, museums and art galleries, shop for gifts, explore the maze of cobblestone streets and squares.

Christine enjoyed these excursions, had always been a bit of a dabbler, a dilettante. But Peter didn't enjoy them, not even the visits to galleries, his interest in art these days negligible. He supposed their touristy wanderings passed the time well enough. Even so, there were occasions when he could hardly conceal his boredom. He'd look at his watch and let out a muted sigh of exasperation that would prompt Christine to gaze irritably in his direction.

The couple would invariably end up at the same restaurant, one they'd always especially liked when they'd come to Dauge for their honeymoon. It was situated on the town's main thoroughfare and was not far from their villa; easy walking distance, a mere stroll. They'd take a seat at an outdoor table under a substantial awning, thankful for the shade it afforded at that time of day, and give their order to the waiter when he arrived with the menu. They usually had one of the restaurant's superb salads, accompanied by bottled water and a little white wine.

As the meal went on they would converse rather than talk. Their conversation was superficially affable yet there was something peculiarly cool about it, distant. They did not hold hands across the table; they never held hands these days. They seldom caught one another's eye as they forked their salads and drank their water and sipped their wine.

Then, as the town drowsed lazily in its afternoon torpor under the burning Mediterranean sun, they'd go back to the villa for their own siesta, this never but never involving sex. After their nap, they'd go out to the pool area to swim and soak up some late afternoon rays, the sun still high in the clear blue sky and the pool's rippled surface shining with its reflected light.

Nearing sunset when the sky was starting to glow pink and the air was becoming slightly cooler, the almost silent pair would go indoors. They'd shower separately, dress with studied care and then go downstairs to have a light meal as they waited for the sun to go down completely... waited for the cover of darkness.

And when daylight had finally gone for good to be replaced by the thickness of night, by that darkness they had both been waiting for all day, truth be told, Christine went her separate way. The couple exchanged kisses, the merest grazing of cheeks, as she departed. Sometimes Christine would give Peter a short wave when she left, sometimes even a little smile which he returned.

Peter usually settled in for the night after that although he was far from relaxed; he was still waiting, waiting... Sometimes, he'd get the car out of the garage and go for a bit of a drive to kill some time, as he'd done tonight.

Christine, on the other hand, *always* went out. Night after night she would venture out into the warm evening air all on her own, to find a good bar, to find some good wine, to find a sexual partner to bring back with her to the villa.

They never stayed till morning, these one-night stands of hers, that was one of the rules the couple had. One of the other rules was that, while Peter never had anything whatsoever to do with these fleeting guests, he did get to watch what they did with his wife.

Chapter Four

HE WOULD BE WATCHING very soon now; he would be being the complete voyeur, but at the moment he was listening. And very intently too, from the open door of their unlit bedroom on the first floor. Not long to wait now, he was sure of it, and he was right. Peter could feel tremors of excitement shiver through his body as he heard the sound of a key being worked in the front door, followed by the sound of that door opening and then an emphatic bang as it was shut. *Honey, I'm home!* He trembled some more when he heard the click of Christine's heels and the echo of male footsteps on the marble floor downstairs. *Soon, soon.* He heard the drinks cabinet behind the bar being opened. Indeed you could have heard a pin drop at that time of night. He'd have to make sure he was exceptionally quiet himself, he always was.

'Vodka?' he heard Christine say. There was perhaps a nodded assent from her companion, Peter surmised. He heard the metallic twist of a bottle top and the splash of liquid in a glass followed by the clink of ice cubes.

He heard Christine's voice again, 'Enjoy your drink, Pierre. I'm going for a skinny dip.'

'OK,' the man said. The reply sounded deceptively flat. Peter could only imagine what lubricious thoughts must be racing through his namesake's mind.

15

They were certainly racing through his own head. Peter was naked and already fully aroused. He felt his cock harden even further as he moved gingerly through the inky blackness towards the bedroom window, which was widely open. He leaned against the wall at its side, taking the weight of his body on his left arm and his stiff shaft into his right hand.

Peter looked down at the pool, which was illuminated by the lights at its side. It was further lit up suddenly when Christine switched on the external lights. She obviously wanted him to see it all, he thought, didn't want him to miss a thing.

He saw a breeze ruffle the still water of the pool. And then he only had eyes for his wife. His mouth was dry with excitement as he watched Christine, naked as nature intended, stride towards the pool, the palms of her hands flat on her thighs. Peter watched and admired anew the seductive sway of her hips and the way her shapely calves tapered to her slender ankles, watched as she walked bare foot, bare arsed, to the pool's shallow end.

Peter watched Christine sit by the edge of the pool for a moment, watched her step into the rippling water and then turn and begin swimming on her back. He watched as she kicked her feet and let her hands propel her body slowly across the pool to the deep end. He watched her turn again and, lifting her arms, swim back to the shallow end. He looked admiringly at her lovely face and beautiful breasts and shaven mons. *She wants me to see everything*. He watched her turn once more before standing up. He looked at the way her hair dropped down like shiny black satin when she did this. He watched as she stepped, graceful as a nymph, out of the pool.

He watched her drag the excess water from her hair and bend down to pick up a towel that was on one of the sun loungers. He watched her fluffing her hair with the towel and using it to dry her body too, rubbing at the back of her neck and under her arms and along her legs.

Peter was looking down at Christine but she, his nymph, his nymphomaniac, was not looking up at him. She wouldn't have been able to see him in that darkened bedroom even if she'd tried. No, she was looking at her companion, this Pierre person, who had come to join her now in the pool area. He was, Peter noted, tall, dark, well-built and good looking, just the way his wife liked them. He could also not fail to notice that he was buck naked and displaying an impressive erection – just the way she liked them too. He had evidently taken a leaf out of Christine's book and had shed his clothes before coming outside.

Peter watched as that darkly handsome man took a step towards Christine, watched as he held her in his muscular arms in a powerful embrace, her full breasts flattened against his chest. She lifted her face to his and Pierre began kissing her passionately on the mouth, holding her even harder to him. Peter watched this too. He could only watch, watch as Christine took control now, watch as she got hold of Pierre's right hand and pushed it between her legs, watch as he masturbated her. He watched too as his namesake took one of her nipples first between the thumb and forefinger of his left hand and then into his mouth as he continued to masturbate her harder and harder with his other hand, rubbing it all over her hot pussy.

Peter watched as Christine pulled away from Pierre and moved over to one of the sun loungers. 'I want you to fuck me now,' he heard her say as she lay wantonly back, her thighs spread. The Frenchman moved on top of her and pushed himself inside as she arched her back and wrapped her legs around him. While he thrust

17

rhythmically in and out of her sex, Christine held him tightly and looked over his shoulder and, yes, she did look upwards then. She looked up into the dark, right in the direction she knew her husband was standing. And she knew just what he was doing, knew that he was watching, watching it all and masturbating.

Peter trembled increasingly with excitement and pulled rhythmically at his erection as he watched his wife being fucked ever more energetically by this complete stranger while she in turn looked, or appeared to look, straight back at him, her ever-loving husband.

Peter's tongue flicked lasciviously in his mouth, his heart pounded wildly, and his cock flexed and throbbed within his fist. He was almost coming but not yet, please not yet. He stopped masturbating all of a sudden, wanting to hold back his imminent orgasm before it was too late. Then it was too late. He watched Christine climax, heard her animal-like moan carry into the night, which was joined almost at once by the strangled cry of her companion, joined almost at once too by his own stifled gasping. Peter closed his eyes and convulsions shook his body as warm creamy cum spurted from his throbbing cock.

He went to bed soon after that and it was not too long afterwards that he felt his wife slip in beside him. She brought with her an aroma of chlorine and sex. Pierre had been sent on his way, of course. Like they all were. Christine always made it clear that this was going to be a once only experience. That was the deal, take it or leave it. Pierre, like all the others before him, had taken it.

Chapter Five

THE DAY WAS TAKING a familiar course – an extremely familiar one once you knew the way it was going to end. It was post-siesta time now and Christine and Peter were both naked in the pool area as was their usual routine. It was another fine day too, like all the others had been so far this vacation. The sky above was clear, not even the hint of a cloud, and reflected sunlight danced on the shimmering blue water of the swimming pool.

Christine, her shapely body tanned all over to a honeyed brown, was laying on her front on a sun lounger, basking in the late afternoon sunshine. She was resting her chin on her arms, and her eyes, which were shielded by sunglasses, were turned in the direction of the pool by her side where Peter was swimming. She watched as he dived to the bottom of the deep end for the umpteenth time and swam underwater, holding his breath even longer this time. What a peculiar thing to be doing, Christine thought. Why couldn't he just *relax* for God's sake?

He finally broke surface near the edge of the pool right next to Christine's prone body. She looked directly at him and he could see himself reflected in her sunglasses. 'Put some suntan lotion on my back, would you,' she said.

'Sure,' Peter replied. He liked that about Christine, the way she just told him what to do sometimes. It seemed to meet some strange need in him, although what it was he didn't know. He preferred not to think about it, to blank it out of his mind, merely enjoy the squirmy little thrill it gave him each time she did it. On occasions she could be a bit too abrasive of course, he reminded himself.

'Come on,' she said impatiently, as if to prove his point. 'Get a move on.'

'OK …OK …OK,' he chanted and hauled himself out of the water, rivulets of water running down his tanned skin. Reaching out for a towel, he dried himself in a perfunctory way, rubbing quickly at his face and torso.

He dried his hands more thoroughly before picking up the bottle of suntan lotion. He poured some of it onto the palm of one hand and got to work. Folding his hands around and over Christine's shoulders, he kneaded the suntan lotion into her skin, smoothing her flesh with it. What a magnificent body she had, he thought as he worked his way down her back; her narrow waist, that gorgeous curvy rear, perfection.

Peter had thought once that he could never have enough of that wonderful voluptuous body. They had made love as much as they possibly could when they had first met, he reminded himself, and that had been just the beginning. They had made love *all* the time when they'd been on honeymoon, lost to themselves in sensual delight. They'd shared sexual fantasies too, hadn't they, like that one about fucking their brains out on the beach at midnight. They had lived that fantasy as well – over and over – while they were in Dauge that first time together, and it had been fabulous.

Their honeymoon had been a tough act to follow, needless to say. Even so, their lovemaking had carried on being almost as abandoned, almost as all-consuming, for a long time afterwards. They'd continued to trade sexual fantasies as well, fantasies that seemed to come from out of some murky dark nowhere in the mind. Christine said she fantasized about masturbating in front of him while he jerked off at the same time, and so they did just that, frequently.

Peter told her on one occasion – about two years into their marriage, it was – that he'd started having a recurrent fantasy of actually watching them making love. So, at his suggestion, they'd started fucking in front of their wardrobe mirror.

That was how it started, with that wardrobe mirror, innocuous really judged by all but the most puritanical of standards. But then things got more elaborate and they arranged – Peter's idea again – to have a mirror fitted to the ceiling above their bed.

What used to happen was this: Christine would straddle him – she liked that, she told him, being on top – and they would make love, with him watching her in the ceiling mirror and her looking down at him. She said she liked that too, loved it, said it gave her such a feeling of power over him, such a feeling of control.

Peter remembered her saying that. Christine remembered it too. She remembered it all. She remembered how he would sigh and let his body collapse into submission as she straddled him, pressing her groin on his, and how she would moan with pleasure as she felt the thickness of his cock slide into her pussy, so tight and moist. She remembered how Peter would reach up to her and she would grab his arms and pin them above his head. She remembered how he would groan with her movements as she pushed her hips down, fitting them around his hardness. She remembered the short, throaty cry Peter would let out, looking up at the mirror in the ceiling as he watched her grinding into him. He could see it all in the mirror.

Christine could see it all too now in her mind: the expression on Peter's face when she looked down through half-drawn lids at him, the wonder in his eyes and his slack, open mouth. She could hear it all too, and feel it: how when she shoved herself down on him with force, he gave out a soft groan and whimper and would stiffen even more inside her.

Then Christine would grip his arms more tightly and push her weight forward, falling down on him, while still moving her hips, so that the pressure on them both remained unabated.

And she could smell it now too, smell the scent of his excitement and sweat as he began a long drawn-out moan and started to thrust his hips up rhythmically, pulsing with a climax she knew he'd do his very best to restrain until she'd had her own orgasmic release.

Christine remembered that at this point she would begin to moan and flush and rock back and forth, so conscious of Peter's stiffness rock hard inside her and ready to burst, and her hand would start to rub out a complementary rhythm, sticky and frantic, over her stiff clitoris. Then she would let go of herself altogether and shudder frenziedly as exquisite oscillations began to pulse through her. And as she climaxed she would watch his mouth widening in exaltation as, taken along by her orgasm, he allowed himself his release. He would begin to spasm uncontrollably beneath her before shooting his liquid, spurt after vigorous spurt, deep inside her sex.

Peter finished massaging Christine's back with suntan lotion and plunged back into the swimming pool with a splash. When he surfaced he took a really deep breath and dived right to the bottom again, started repeating that strangely edgy, obsessive routine.

Christine stayed where she was on the lounger, alone with her thoughts once more, and her memory leapt back three years almost to the day. That was when Peter had told her he had another fantasy, one he just couldn't get out of his mind: a fantasy, now don't be shocked Christine, of seeing her fucking someone else.

But surprise, surprise, she hadn't been shocked, far from it. The idea turned her on too, she had to admit it, turned her on a hell of a lot. And they were a broadminded couple, a liberated couple, a couple that made their fantasies a reality, weren't they? You bet your sweet life they were.

Christine and Peter got rid of the ceiling mirror, bored with that now anyway. They arranged to have another mirror rigged up – a large one-way mirror this time, between their bedroom and the one adjacent to it.

Everything was all set for the big event.

They say you always remember the first time. Christine certainly remembered the first time she picked up a stranger to have sex with, knowing that her husband would be watching it all from the next room and jerking off.

What had been his name now, that first one: Jay was it, Jake? Fucked if she could remember. But she could remember the fuck. In fact she could vividly recall the sharp, nasty thrill of the whole experience from start to finish.

She remembered what she'd been wearing, or nearly wearing, when she'd picked him up at the bar. It had been a diaphanous little dress that was cut indecently high on the thigh and low over her breasts. She wasn't wearing any underwear either, as was her wont. She had on strapped black sandals with very high heels as well, to complete her fuck-me ensemble.

Christine couldn't remember what he'd been wearing, this Jay, Jake whoever, only that he'd been tall and handsome with black hair and brown eyes. She remembered, too, that he used his hands a lot when he spoke – and when he made love – and that his drink had been vodka on ice, just like Pierre last night. But unlike the way it had gone with Pierre, she'd been on top when they'd fucked.

She remembered kicking her shoes off, pulling her miniscule dress over her head and telling him to get naked too. She remembered pushing him down onto the big bed and straddling him, positioning herself so she could manoeuvre the head of his cock against her pussy lips, against her clitoris. She remembered rubbing herself against his cockhead gently at first and then more vigorously. She remembered sliding herself onto his shaft right up to the hilt, and then up and down, up and down, on and on, riding him in a mounting frenzy of lust until she was completely absorbed in the pleasure she was giving herself and the pleasure she was giving to the man behind the one-way mirror.

'Was it good for you?' she'd said when it was all over.

'The best,' sighed her companion as he lay spent and damp on the rumpled sheets. But Christine hadn't been talking to him, the sex machine she'd just used, the human dildo. She'd been looking in the mirror, *through* the mirror to the person she'd really been making love to.

That had been three years ago. Since then she'd let Peter watch a host of other strangers have sex with her. It was what he said he wanted, *all* he wanted. But Christine had wanted it too, make no mistake, wanted it in her imagination and wanted it in reality too. That was another of the rules, you see. She had to really want it, had to be in control, that was crucial. But Peter said he liked to be in control as well, and he got his wish also for, as he was fond of saying, what person is more in control than the masturbator?

Which was what Peter became from that first time, because from then on he and Christine never made love together. It was always this kinky surrogate ritual they played out instead and they both came to crave it like a powerful drug, enjoying it immensely too, each time they did it. And Christine simply *loved* to give Peter something really worth watching – worth wanking over. She would always put on as good a show as possible for him. The threesomes were often the best. One in particular stuck in her mind...

When Christine walked into the bedroom with the two hunky blond guys she'd picked up not half an hour ago in a nearby bar, she knew one thing for sure. She knew that Peter would have already started stroking his cock with practiced ease behind that one-way mirror.

She knew – and the knowledge of it made her clit twitch, made her sex feel slippery – that he'd be masturbating with a little more vigour now that she was peeling off her tight top and micro-mini skirt and slipping out of her high heeled shoes. It obviously really turned on the two blond hunks she was with to discover that she hadn't been wearing a stitch of underwear beneath that sexy outfit and that her breasts were soft but firm and her nipples stone-hard and that her pussy was completely shaved. Christine knew the fact that she was clearly turning them on would have turned on her husband as well. She knew that he would be masturbating more vigorously still at the sight of her as she cupped her breasts and rolled her stiff nipples between her fingers.

'Strip for me,' Christine said and she knew that *he* knew that instruction *wasn't* for him, knew that she knew he was already stark naked and wanking. The two blond guys were also naked now, their cocks thickly inflated. Christine saw herself in the mirror as she knew her husband could see her at this stage of the show, her head back and her full lips parted as the two men fed hungrily on her breasts, suckled her engorged nipples.

She knew that Peter would be stroking his cock even more energetically by now, pulling and gasping, as he witnessed the three-way scene unfolding before his eyes. She knew that he'd be working his fist up and down ever more insistently as he watched his raunchy wife drop to her knees and grab a cock in each hand. Christine stroked the guys' hard-ons, glancing lustfully from one stiff cock to the other, then into the mirror, imagining that all-important third cock being pulled up and down, up and down, faster and faster.

Christine's eyes gleamed and she smiled a salacious smile to the man behind the mirror before putting one of the hunky strangers' cocks into her mouth. She sucked on it for a while, as she held onto the man's buttocks, at one moment pulling him in, at another controlling the movement so that it was smooth and fluid. And then she did the same to the other cock. Christine alternated between the two cocks, sucking expertly on each in turn, before jamming both of them into her mouth at once. She bet Peter almost shot his load when he saw her do that. But she knew that a highly experienced voyeur like him wouldn't have actually ejaculated. She knew that Peter would be wanking away hard, without doubt, but that he would make damn sure that he didn't spill his seed until he'd seen all there was to see.

Christine finally disgorged the two cocks, withdrawing

them slowly from her mouth, and got back to her feet. She pushed one of the men down onto the bed and climbed on top of him, steering his swollen cock into her pussy and making him groan with pleasure. And as he started sliding his erection in and out of her dripping sex, forging deep into her, she reached back and spread the cheeks of her backside. Christine looked at the second man. 'There's a bottle of lube on the bedside table,' she said. 'Lubricate your cock and my arsehole and then fuck me in the arse.'

'Will do,' the man replied excitedly, thoroughly dousing his cock and her anus with lube and then climbing into position. Christine reached back again, this time to take his hard cock in her hand. She rubbed the slippery head against the equally slippery opening of her anus and then let the man ease his shaft into her until it ground at the back of her rectum. And her anal hole was so tight around his cock that she felt her pussy tighten too around the other guy's cock, which was pounding into her humid sex. Then the man behind her really started pounding too, ramming into her anus hard and fast.

It felt so good to Christine to be fucked front and rear like that, felt even better to know that her voyeuristic husband could see it all and would be pulling at his cock furiously now, his fist working up and down faster and faster. Christine loved being fucked in both holes at the same time, loved it all the more knowing that she was being watched by Peter as she was being fucked that way. She knew that as he witnessed the three-way spectacle she'd laid on for him he would now be jerking away at his cock like a jack-hammer.

Christine decided that it was time to bring the show to its grand finale. She ground her hips down, churning her pussy back and forth on the throbbing cock of the guy beneath her until he suddenly opened his mouth, let out a moan and came hard. His body shook as he grasped Christine's waist and shot his sperm deep inside her pussy, and that brought even closer the impending orgasm of the man hammering into her anus. He speeded up his thrusts, arse-fucking her in a frenzy as she pushed herself back on him. Finally he was jolted by an orgasm that filled her anus to overflowing with hot, creamy cum.

Then Christine was overcome herself, and her glistening body quivered uncontrollably as she came right along with her husband. Because she knew, just *knew* that he was shooting warm, silky sperm all over his fist at that very moment as he joined in the climax of the *four*-way fuckfest that had been her gift to him and her gift to herself.

So, Peter and Christine were both getting what they wanted from these steamy surrogate sex sessions; great, wonderful, fantastic. Except that it wasn't great, it wasn't wonderful, it wasn't fantastic – not any more it wasn't. Because somewhere along the line the whole arrangement had gone more than a little sour and their relationship was now in deep trouble.

Christine was acutely aware of that fact, which was why she'd organized this vacation in Dauge. She'd thought that being back here might rekindle some of the old magic between Peter and herself that had been there in such abundance six years ago. It patently wasn't working, though; that couldn't be clearer. All Peter wanted from the holiday was for Christine to go out every night and pick up strangers to fuck out in the pool area while he watched from the darkened bedroom and masturbated.

No, there was no sign of the old magic, no sign of the old Peter either. In his place was this one-track-minded voyeur. That might have been just about OK, Christine thought, if it actually made him happy as it once seemed to have done. But it definitely wasn't doing that these days. What had happened to the old Peter? Where was that charming man she'd married six years ago? Where was all that good humour, that flippancy, that *joie de vivre*? It was all gone, seemed now like the most distant of memories.

Peter had once been a decision maker too, as you'd expect from someone who'd built such a successful career for himself. But in the last few years that quality had morphed slowly but surely into nothing more than a kind of surly stubbornness. Christine had long been the decisive one in the marriage, ever since Peter had thrown in his highly lucrative job and started to turn inward on himself. Well, she'd be decisive now. Christine decided there and then to do something about this whole skewed situation.

She'd put an end to the now thoroughly jaded routine they'd got themselves into back in England. And the first thing to go when they got home would be the fucking one-way mirror; she was determined about that. But she wouldn't wait until they got home. She'd quash the variation of that routine they'd been pursuing day after day while on this travesty of a vacation. She *wouldn't* go out tonight or any other night from now on and leave Peter on his own, waiting pensively for her return with a good-looking stranger or two and for his own voyeuristic, masturbatory release.

It would be a case of out with the old and in with the new, a completely clean break, Christine decided firmly. Tomorrow they'd have a day on the beach, try to behave like a normal couple on holiday. Jesus, they hadn't even *looked* at the beach yet this holiday; it was ridiculous. And what about after that, in the evening? Christine knew: she'd book them a table at *Ma Maison*, which was not only no more than a ten minute's walk from the villa but was also the best restaurant in town. There they'd enjoy a marvellous dinner and toast their new clean living lifestyle in the best champagne that excellent establishment could offer.

Christine would tell her husband all this right now, that's what she'd do. There was no time like the present, she told herself.

Peter broke surface again from one of his strange and ever lengthier underwater sojourns.

'Get out of the pool and come over here, would you please,' Christine said, turning over and adjusting the sun lounger so that she could sit up. 'I've got something I want to say to you.'

Peter didn't reply and his face registered no expression, but he did what she said and clambered out of the pool.

Chapter Six

PETER'S FIRST RESPONSE TO Christine's proposals was short and less than sweet. 'So, we're going to become Mister and Misses Average,' he said caustically, threading his fingers through his wet hair. 'Are you quite sure we're capable of that, Christine? Are you quite sure *you* are?'

Not waiting for an answer, Peter took two quick steps and plunged back into the pool, disappearing once more into its blue depths. He reappeared a few moments later at the far end of the pool, only to plunge right down to the bottom again, where all he could hear was the drone of the pool filter. And where he didn't have to listen to what he didn't want to hear.

Christine sighed heavily but not in resignation, quite the reverse. She wasn't going to let this go, *no way* was she, and if Peter thought she was going to capitulate, compromise even, he was in for a big surprise. Christine rested her head back on the sun lounger and closed her eyes against the sun that glinted brightly on her sunglasses. She'd soon find another opportunity to tackle her obstinate husband. This was all too important to let lie, way too important.

Christine found that opportunity once they'd gone indoors and showered, just before they got dressed for the evening. They were in their bedroom, which was large, white walled and uncluttered. Peter was sprawled naked on the four-poster bed. His shoulders were resting on two pillows he'd piled against the headboard and his arms were above his head. He was staring up at the high ceiling, looking sulky. Christine was equally nude and was sat at the mirrored dressing table, drying her hair with a towel. The resolute, not to say downright confrontational expression she was wearing on her face suggested that she was a woman who knew she was going to have a battle on her hands and was more than ready for it.

'So, you don't think much of my new approach,' she said, glaring at her husband in the mirror in front of her.

'You could say that,' Peter replied, turning his eyes to hers in the mirror and meeting her glare with his own.

'Tell me something,' Christine asked, continuing to rub at her hair with the towel. 'Do you like anything at all?'

'What do you mean by that?' he bridled.

'Well, let's look at the evidence,' she said, putting the towel down beside her. 'You decided you didn't like working so you packed it in, didn't you?'

'Yeah, I did,' Peter replied. He added, chuckling under his breath, 'But only after making a fortune, be fair.'

'I'll give you that,' Christine smiled in spite of herself. And he'd worked damned hard for his fortune, he could have said, whereas she'd inherited hers.

'Also I was burned out.'

'If you say so,' she muttered, picking up a hairbrush. He'd been a bit young to be burned out, she'd always thought.

'I do say so,' he reiterated. 'I was burned out good and proper.'

'Yeah, whatever,' Christine drawled, giving him an ironic look. She looked back at her own reflection in the dressing table mirror and started to brush her hair with short, deliberate strokes. 'You never read much of anything these days,' she went on, 'and your interest in art, which used to be something of a passion of yours I recall, seems to have gone right out the window.'

'What can I say?' Peter replied with a shrug. 'Interests wane.'

'Yes, I know, but …'

'Anything else?' he interrupted.

'You don't like your family.'

'My brother, you mean,' he said, turning his head to face the ceiling again. 'He's the only one of my family left.'

'OK, your brother.'

'Dave's an arsehole,' Peter announced bluntly. He was, too. When Peter's parents had died in a boating accident a little over a year after Peter and Christine had married, he had been devastated but his brother Dave couldn't even be bothered to come to the funeral. Dave was five years Peter's junior and they'd never been close at the best of times. Since their parents' death they'd become positively estranged.

Christine was obviously on a loser with this particular subject. She decided to switch tack, without really thinking.

'We've got that big house all to ourselves back home,' she said. 'But you're adamant that you don't want kids.'

'Nor do you,' Peter said. 'You told me once you thought you'd make a lousy mother.' Touché again, Christine thought. She decided that, never mind about making a lousy mother, she'd certainly make a lousy barrister. Still, press on regardless, she told herself stoically.

'You don't seem to have any love for your fellow man,' Christine continued. 'You've turned your back on all your friends.'

'What friends?' Peter looked directly at her reflection in the mirror again, meeting her gaze.

'You said it,' she replied. 'You've become as near as makes no difference a complete recluse.'

'True,' he acknowledged with another shrug.

'We never make love.'

'Undeniably true also.'

'I repeat my question,' Christine said, with a note of triumph. 'Do you like anything at all?'

She pinned him with her gaze in the mirror and stared him down during the long silence that followed.

'Yes, there is something I like,' Peter finally replied.

'And what might that be exactly?'

'I like watching my wife fucking strangers,' he said, staring her right back in the mirror.

'Bastard!' Christine hissed, waving a hand in disgust.

'I'm only speaking the truth.'

'Fuck you!'

'That's not an option,' he said with a dry laugh.

'Ha bloody ha. Isn't that funny.'

'I thought so,' he said, still meeting her hostile glare.

'Shut up,' she hissed. 'Just fucking shut up.'

'All right, all right,' Peter said and looked away from her. He pushed his pillows down on the bed and rested his head on them, staring up at the high ceiling once more.

'Jesus, you're exasperating,' Christine said. She gripped the handle of her hair brush tightly in one hand while starting to tap the bristles onto the open palm of the other. 'I've a good mind to put you over my knee and take this brush to your stubborn hide.'

'You and whose army?' Peter retorted scornfully. But to his surprise he felt his cock start to harden as images of what she'd just said flashed across his mind. He quickly manoeuvred himself onto his stomach to disguise his growing tumescence. He was winning this argument in his view, even if he'd had to resort to barbed comments and sarcasm to do so. He didn't want his wayward cock to lose it for him at the eleventh hour.

Peter was as quick as anything in getting himself onto his stomach, but he wasn't quick enough for Christine. That's interesting, she said to herself. She stared at the reflection of his taut, well-shaped backside in the mirror (*Oh, the temptation to give it a really good walloping!*) and then looked back at her own reflection. And then at nothing at all as her eyes clouded over and she remembered one specific occasion that now seemed particularly relevant to what she'd just observed.

It went back to the days when she and Peter had been in the habit of sharing sexual fantasies with each other, and living out those fantasies too. That is, back before Peter decided to fix on their living out essentially just *one* fantasy over and over again ad nauseam.

Peter had returned from a business trip that had lasted over a week and Christine had told him excitedly that she had a new erotic fantasy to share with him. She'd been fantasizing about blindfolding him with her red silk scarf, tying his arms behind his back and his legs together with the half dozen black leather belts she possessed. Well, with five of them actually, retaining the sixth, the thickest one, to whip his arse good and hard. It was now her favourite masturbation fantasy, Christine told him. She'd pleasured herself all the time while he'd been away, luxuriating in the images of it that had suffused her mind as her fingers had worked at her stiff clit and wet, wet pussy. So, Peter darling, she'd said seductively, how about making this onanist's dreams come true? How about letting me become your dominatrix?

'Forget it,' he'd said unequivocally, clamming right up straight away. 'Not interested.'

'Not even once?'

'Nope.'

'Why, for goodness sake?'

'I'll tell you exactly why,' Peter said, and went on to count out the reasons on his fingers like some pedantic schoolteacher.

'Number one,' he said, 'I'm frightened of the dark, and so blindfolding is out. Two, I don't like pain.'

'You're a devout coward, right?' He was always saying that.

'Right,' he laughed. 'So the beating's out. Three, I have to be in control, you know that, so tying me up is a no-no as well. Lastly ...'

'There's more?'

'Lastly, four,' Peter said, not missing a beat, 'I don't like bullies and surely S&M is just bullying under another name. That's what I reckon, anyway. So, like I said, not interested.'

Yes, thank you, teacher, she'd thought. Please forget I spoke.

But they carried on with the conversation anyway. Frightened of the dark? That had been a new one on Christine, so she'd asked Peter to elaborate. It all went back to a night in his early childhood, he told her. He must have been about four or five at the time. He'd woken up alone in the blackness of his bedroom and had been frightened. He'd called out and called out, but no one had come. He'd been left all alone, it seemed, and suddenly he felt surrounded by that darkness in his room, terrified by it. He'd cried out even louder, loud enough to wake the dead; certainly loud enough to wake his parents, who'd been in the house all along as it turned out, fast asleep in their bed. It may have been a false alarm but his fear of the dark had stayed with him ever since.

Or so he said. Thinking about it now, though, Christine was sceptical. After all, on the face of it, it had hardly been a really traumatic incident, just a false alarm as Peter had acknowledged. And this supposed fear of darkness hadn't ever really evidenced itself when they'd been together, not that she'd ever noticed in any event.

And focussing specifically on this vacation, his apparent fear of the dark hadn't been stopping him from creeping about in their darkened bedroom with his cock in his hand, waiting for her to start fucking one or another stranger outside in the pool area. Had he somehow gradually got over his fear of the dark in the years he'd been with her, that was certainly a possibility, or had it all been bullshit in the first place?

Here was something else. Peter liked to be in control, he said. Well, whichever way you looked at it, jerking himself off while watching her fucking strangers was a very strange way of being in control. In fact it was a uniquely passive activity when you thought about it. Then there was his purported fear of pain. Why, then, the growing erection at the mention of having his arse tanned by her with a hairbrush?

Peter liked Christine bossing him about, too, liked her being a bit of a bully to him, you could say. He tried not to show it, but he couldn't fool her. She picked up on the little frisson of pleasure it gave him every time she went all dominant on him.

It made one wonder, it really did. Somewhere deep inside Peter, Christine strongly suspected, he had a craving for precisely the thing he said he abhorred.

But enough of such thoughts, Christine told herself. She was getting sidetracked here, which wasn't helpful at all given that Peter didn't seem prepared to budge an inch in this conversation. If he was going to be as stubborn as this, she would be even more stubborn. And she would win. She and Peter were going to clean up their act and that was that.

'Christine?' She seemed distracted, miles away, Peter thought. He had to call her name again.

'Yes.' She turned from the mirror to look directly at him, noting that he was still lying on his front and was addressing her over his shoulder.

'Are we done here?'

'For the time being,' she replied. There was a hard, neutral edge to Christine's voice, now that she'd returned to planet earth from wherever her thoughts had taken her, and Peter recognized that tone all too well. It was the one she used when she'd made up her mind about something and was determined not to be swayed from her chosen path, come what may. Maybe he'd have to go along with what she wanted after all, he thought momentarily. And then he thought again: over my dead body, he said to himself.

An uneasy silence settled in around the couple once more. Christine fixed Peter with a penetrating gaze. Next time, husband of mine, she thought, next time … And it's interesting, by the way, that you're *still* lying on your stomach.

Chapter Seven

CHRISTINE WAS RESOLUTE IN her determination to win this battle of wills with her obstinate spouse. There was too much at stake to leave it now. In her mind it was essential that her viewpoint should prevail; the survival of their marriage depended on it. But she knew she wasn't doing very well. It had been rounds one and two to Peter, no question. She was determined to make it 'third time lucky' this time as she stared silently out of the open French window of the living room, going over her strategy in her mind.

It was a clear night and a full moon was shining in a sky filled with stars. The air was slightly cooler than it had been of late and a light breeze was making the living room curtain move slightly against the French window. It was still more than warm enough, though, and Christine was perfectly comfortable in the little she was wearing, which was a thin white cotton dress that was low-cut and short. It showed off both her tan and her curvaceous figure wonderfully well. She also had on strappy red sandals with high heels.

Peter was a little more casually dressed: loose-fitting denim cut-offs and a crisp white T-shirt, espadrilles. Standing at the bar that was set up near the fireplace, he moved to fix himself a scotch. He unscrewed the bottle cap and poured out a substantial measure into his glass, not his first that evening or his second or even his third, it has to be said.

But, what the hell, Peter told himself. He deserved the hefty belt or four of the hard stuff he'd already granted himself before Christine had even come into the room and he had a taste for more. Just look at his wife, standing over there by the French window. She was so drop-dead gorgeous it was enough to blow your mind. And you could tell she wasn't wearing any underwear. When did she ever?

Christine shouldn't be here at this hour, he thought, that was the problem. She should be out on the prowl, picking up some hunk to have sex with, that he could watch. Or perhaps it would be a couple this time, so they could enjoy a threesome, all *four* of them. *Heh! heh!* He'd be the silent partner, of course, as always. Or maybe she'd visit a lesbian club, bring home a girl to make love to. That was far from unknown, too – very far from unknown. Just think of what she got up to with that horny little redhead she brought home with her the other week. His more than slightly inebriated brain flooded with the memory of what they'd done, what he'd seen them do …

Peter was in his usual position: standing on his side of the one-way mirror, naked and ready, cock in hand. He had a half hard-on and felt himself stiffen further within his fist as he watched his wife and the other woman pad into the bedroom. Both of them were bare footed but otherwise still dressed, if you could call it that. Christine looked lovely, as usual, incredibly sexy. She was wearing a semi-transparent black blouse and an extremely short tight leather skirt, also black. The other young woman appeared to be in her early twenties, a petite girl with short red hair. Christine had a bit of a thing for red-headed women, Peter had noticed. This one was clad in a body-hugging mini-dress, bottle-green in colour, which displayed to great effect her slim but shapely figure. She had small high breasts, her nipples stiff and sticking out underneath the thin fabric of her dress.

Christine suddenly grabbed the redhead in her arms and kissed her full on the lips. She responded by wrapping her arms around Christine and kissing her right back. *Showtime,* Peter said to himself salaciously, squeezing his cock, which was now rock hard, and beginning to pull it up and down.

He gazed intently as Christine momentarily broke the kiss, only to grab the other woman's head in her hands, and press her mouth against hers again, kissing her even more passionately. She painted the girl's lips with her tongue, then shoved it inside her open mouth quick and tight. The two women kissed passionately as Peter began masturbating in earnest. He pushed his fist up and down on himself in a regular rhythm, all the while keeping his voyeuristic eyes peeled on the developing action on the other side of the glass.

Christine finally broke the kiss to lick her way up and down the other woman's slender neck, her pink wet tongue travelling all over her soft throat. The redhead responded this time by unbuttoning and removing Christine's semi-transparent blouse to fully reveal her gorgeous breasts with their hard jutting nipples. She wasted no time in going to work on those breasts, fondling them with her soft hands and teasing their swollen nipples with her tongue. Christine then unfastened her tiny leather skirt and shimmied out of it, and the redheaded girl pulled off her own dress and the flimsy g-string she'd been wearing under it.

Peter pressed his face to the glass and jacked away at

his erection, stroking and pulling, as Christine and the redhead climbed naked onto the bed. They kissed passionately some more, the redhead on her back, Christine on top of her, their breasts pushed heatedly together. Then Christine moved down the bed and fastened her bright lips to the girl's pussy, drinking her. The redhead bucked and tried to move her sex more rapidly against the regular licking of Christine's tongue. She jerked her hips forward again and again towards the point of her tongue. Christine then turned round and positioned herself so that her and the other girl's thighs were scissored together, their pussies rubbing up against each other excitingly.

Peter stood back from the glass a little. He stared hard and stroked his cock harder, pushing his fist up and down on himself even more forcefully, as Christine and the redhead ground their glistening slits together. The other girl panted and moaned in delight as Christine desperately fucked her with her pussy.

Then it happened. Christine's undulating body suddenly shook with orgasmic tremors, as the hot pussy friction built to boiling point and beyond. At the same time the redhead let out a long drawn-out moan as she too was consumed by ecstasy. That brought Peter to the boil as well and, jerking frenziedly at his cock, he built to a climax so powerful that he coated the glass of the one-way mirror with spurt after spurt of pearly cum.

No, Christine certainly wasn't the slightest bit averse to a bit of horny girl-on-girl action, Peter said to himself. Or girl-boy-girl action or boy-girl-boy action or whatever damn permutation you cared to conjure up. Admittedly it was usually lone guys or lone girls she brought home for sex, but not always by any means. Hell, some of those threesomes … He never knew what to expect, that was the point. The kinky routine they'd got themselves into these last few years wasn't *samey*, for crying out loud, nothing like it. So, what was her problem?

All this shit, Peter laughed to himself, it was enough to drive a man to drink. Picking up his full glass, he downed half its contents in one swallow. The spirit burned his stomach but it felt good, just like all the other glasses of liquid fire he'd enjoyed before Christine had come into the room.

He picked up the bottle of scotch from the bar and went and sat down in a black leather armchair, taking another gulp from his glass as he put the bottle on the marble floor by his side.

Christine moved away from the French window and took several determined steps in Peter's direction, her high heels clicking on the marble floor. Here it comes again, Peter said to himself resignedly, the fucking Spanish inquisition. He topped up his drink liberally from the whisky bottle to fortify himself against the onslaught he knew was coming his way.

'You really don't want us to clean up our act, huh?' Christine said.

'No, I like it nice and dirty, just the way it is,' Peter replied, curling his fingers around his glass and taking another swig.

Christine stepped in closer, shifting her weight from one high-heeled foot to the other. She looked at Peter for a long moment, her expression stony.

'And it makes you happy, does it, our lifestyle?' She strained the words through her teeth.

'Yeah.' He looked at her blankly, then took another long swallow from his glass. He relished yet again the burn of the whisky in his throat, the small fire in his belly.

'That's so, is it?' Christine said. 'You're perfectly happy with the way things are between us?'

'Sure,' Peter said blithely. 'I mean, if it aint broke, you don't fix it.' He downed some more scotch in a big gulp and immediately topped up his drink again.

'You're priceless, you really are.' She let out a bitter laugh. 'If it aint broke … Christ!'

'I think things are fine as they are.'

'No shit.'

'Yeah well.' Peter's lower lip quivered. He couldn't keep up this façade much longer, he knew that, especially as the surfeit of hard liquor he'd taken into his system in such a short space of time was really starting to kick in now. Boy, was it ever.

'Things are fine, you really think that?'

'They're fine,' Peter repeated, not meeting her gaze, his own vision starting to blur.

'You could have fooled me,' Christine said, emitting another dry, humourless laugh.

'What's happy, anyway?' he said suddenly. He sucked at his bottom lip to try and stop it quivering and gave her a desperate look, then quickly looked away.

Peter topped up his glass of whisky from the bottle, held the glass to his lips and drank deeply once again. He's certainly caning the sauce tonight, Christine thought. He's knocking it back like there's no tomorrow.

'What's happy?' Peter said again, his voice decidedly slurred now. 'That's what I'd like to know.'

'What's happy? I'll tell you. It's the opposite of what you are,' Christine said, leaning down and shouting in his face. 'Goddammit, the very opposite. Don't you see that? Can't you accept it? Can't you see what you've become, what *we've* become?'

There was a long silence that seemed to stretch for

ages.

'How'd we ever end up like this, Christine?' Peter said quietly, finally breaking the silence. His voice was even more slurry. 'How did everything get so fucked up?'

'I don't know, love.' Her voice was soft. Maybe they were getting somewhere at last, she thought, if he wasn't already too drunk, that is.

'Oh fuck, what am I going to do?' Peter's voice cracked as he blurted the words out. He drained his glass. He went to refill it but the bottle was empty. My God, Christine thought, he's polished off the lot.

'… need to open another bottle …' His voice was thick now, almost incoherent, his blue eyes glassy.

'You need to do nothing of the sort.'

'… thirsty …'

'Let's get you to bed,' Christine said. 'You're smashed out of your head.'

She helped raise Peter unsteadily to his feet. His knees buckled and for a moment Christine thought he might pass out on her.

'Keep awake, damn you,' she demanded loudly, her tone as incisive as she could make it, and her command had the short-term effect she'd hoped for. She led Peter's wavering body up the stairs and helped him get undressed and into the bed, where she left him to sleep off his drunk. Peter was perfectly fine with one or two stiff drinks inside him, Christine reflected. But he certainly couldn't handle the hard stuff in any quantity. On the rare occasions that he did hit the bottle the effect was always the same. It ended up knocking him flat out, after which he would remain utterly dead to the world for hours and hours on end.

And so it was that night. Nothing would have budged the drunkenly comatose Peter; he was completely out for the count. Christine, by contrast, didn't sleep at all well. All night long she could feel anxiety pressing in on her like a fog. Just before he'd become non compos mentis there had been something so heart-achingly desperate in the way Peter had spoken to Christine that it had really alarmed her. She'd known her obstinate husband had been unhappy. She hadn't realised until then quite how unhappy. It troubled her greatly.

Chapter Eight

THE FOLLOWING DAY PETER awoke just as Christine
entered the bedroom. She was carrying a long glass of
orange juice. He yawned elaborately and sat up, plumping
his pillows around him as he did so. The blinds were
drawn but sunlight was bleeding into the room around the
edges of the window. Christine opened the blinds but only
slightly, anxious not to aggravate the thumping great
hangover she assumed her husband would be suffering
from, and the room remained in semi-darkness.

'Good morning,' he said.

'Good *afternoon*,' Christine said pointedly, handing
him the glass of orange juice.

'Huh?'

'Look,' she said, gesturing in the direction of the
luminous clock on the bedside table.

'Oh my God!' Peter exclaimed, registering the time.
'I've been asleep for bloody ages.'

'That's right,' Christine replied, taking a seat near the
bed.

'Amazing,' he said, shaking his head in disbelief.
'When did you get up?'

'Hours ago,' she replied. 'How are you feeling?'

'Fine thanks.'

'Not even a headache?'

'No,' he replied. 'Although I must admit that my

mouth feels a bit like the inside of a bird cage.'

'It would do after the industrial quantity of scotch you got through last night,' Christine said. 'Drink some of your juice. It'll give you a much-needed injection of vitamin C.'

Peter picked up the glass and drank thirstily from it, gulping half of its contents down in one go.

'Good?' she asked.

'Just what the doctor ordered.'

'Hungry?'

'Now you mention it, yes I am,' he replied.

'I'll rustle up something for us both in a moment,' she said.

'Great.'

'By the way, do you remember anything about last night?' Christine asked, folding her arms against her chest.

'Sure,' Peter said blandly. 'Of course I do.' But did he, Christine wondered. She suspected that he couldn't remember much of anything about last night and was just bluffing, trying to brazen it out.

'What do you remember?' she asked.

Peter took his time before answering. He drank the remainder of his orange juice, his throat working slowly as he swallowed it. He set the glass down on the bedside table. 'You said we needed to clean up our act and I ...'

'Yes?' Christine said, watching him intently from the chair in the half-darkness.

'I ...eh ...bowed to your superior judgement.'

'I'm not sure I'd sum up your response quite like that,' she said, her voice dripping with incredulity. What was he playing at here?

'Look, I know I was under the influence of the demon drink last night,' Peter said in a conciliatory tone. 'If I said anything to offend you as a result of that, I apologize.'

'You didn't,' Christine replied. He hadn't said anything to offend her, no; disturb her, yes; worry the hell out of her, certainly.

'Good,' he said hurriedly. 'Now, didn't you say something about our going to the beach today?'

'Yes I did but ...' Don't change the subject, she was going to say.

'Well, we'd better get a move on then, hadn't we,' he said, throwing back the bed sheets. He pulled himself to his feet and moved swiftly towards the louvered doors that led to the en-suite bathroom.

'But Peter...' Christine said to his retreating form.

'If we leave it too much longer there'll be no more of the day left,' she heard him say from behind the door. A moment later she heard the shower start, followed by the steady cascade of water. End of conversation.

Christine got up from the chair and left the bedroom in order to go downstairs and prepare them both a bite to eat. As she descended the stairs she shook her head and let out a frustrated sigh at Peter's evasiveness. Still, she'd achieved something she supposed. They'd go to the beach today like any ordinary couple, that's what she'd said; they'd go to the beach, he'd agreed. So, off to the beach they'd go. It might not do any good, but it couldn't do any harm either.

And the sooner they got to that beach the better, Christine thought when they were about halfway there, going by foot. It would be a great relief to get the benefit of the sea breeze, because on the streets it was insufferable, absolutely blazing hot. The blue sky was blinding, the sun much the fiercest she'd known it this vacation. The sunlight was over-bright, fuzzing the outlines of everything in its glare like a badly exposed film. Humid heat filled the air, making her perspire uncomfortably. But, be grateful for small mercies, Christine told herself as she and Peter got ever closer to the beach. At least the walk there was relatively brief and downhill. It was quiet too. The steep cobblestone street that led to the beach, so full of tourists and townspeople when it wasn't so unspeakably hot, was almost deserted.

Not so the beach when they got to it, which was crowded with oiled sun worshippers from end to end, all sweltering under the ferocious orange sun. But where was that sea breeze? The ocean's rippled surface gleamed like fire in the sun and only the most listless of breezes pushed the small ruffles of foam at the water's edge.

Nudity was *de rigueur* on the beach and Christine and Peter were relieved to remove their sticky clothes and get naked. They stood together and quickly applied suntan lotion to the parts of their bodies that had previously been clothed. It would be even more of a relief, they both agreed, to find somewhere to park themselves, preferably as close to the water as possible. They trudged along the shore over the heavy sand past the crowds of sunbathers until at last they found a suitable space a few feet from the water's edge. They settled themselves down, spread their towels side by side, and lay down on their stomachs, facing away from the sea. Peter immediately shut his eyes and began to doze in the hot sun.

Christine rested her face sideways on her hands and looked idly to her left. A pretty young blonde woman in designer sunglasses was sunbathing nude some feet away, her pale face to the sun. The sight of the girl gave Christine a sharp jolt of *déjà vu* since she appeared to be a dead ringer for one of her more recent assignations back home. Leslie had been the girl's name, she remembered, and she'd been one half of an attractive young married couple that she'd hooked up with at a singles bar. Alan had been the husband's name, she also recalled. You quite often used to get that at singles bars in Christine's experience: couples on the look out for someone to prove that two's company and three's … a threesome …

The three of them were naked on the bed. Alan, well built and handsome with close cropped dark hair, was lying on his back between the two women, his thick cock erect. He leaned over to kiss his wife but she cupped his face and turned him towards Christine. 'No, kiss her while I suck your cock,' demanded the beautiful blonde. Alan's mouth was warm and wet and he probed Christine's mouth with his tongue. While he was doing this, Leslie slipped down the bed and between his legs. She began sucking his shaft, her head bobbing up and down.

As his cock slid in and out of his wife's mouth Alan carried on kissing Christine. 'I want to eat your pussy,' he murmured against her lips.

'Do it,' Christine whispered back.

Leslie slid her mouth from Alan's cock and slithered back up the bed. 'Yes, do it,' she said. 'I want to watch.'

Alan trailed his lips down Christine's body and she spread her legs around his wide shoulders as he nuzzled her pussy with his mouth. Christine looked over at Leslie. As she watched her husband go down on Christine, Leslie worked her fingers between her pussy lips, masturbating feverishly until her palm and wrist were soaked. Before long she tensed, gasped and clamped her thighs around her hand. Her breath came in quick little pants as she climaxed.

Leslie smiled wickedly at Christine as she took her

soaking wet fingers out of her vagina. Then she kissed her softly on the mouth, making her shiver and moan at her gentle kiss combined with Alan's mouth as it worked tirelessly on her pussy.

Leslie stopped kissing Christine and said, 'Fuck her now, Alan.' And suddenly he was above Christine, driving his thick cock into her aching sex. Over and over, he thrust into her, his shaft filling her as his body pinned her to the bed. She could hear Leslie's soft whimpers and moans and knew she was watching them and touching herself again. Christine rocked her hips up to meet Alan's thrusts and with a loud groan he came. And so did she, and so did Leslie. Alan's cock twitched, throbbing inside Christine as she squeezed her pussy around him, drawing out everything he had to give. She stroked his shoulders and back softly, holding him to her.

Leslie then spoke. 'That was great,' she said. 'I've just had a marvellous wank, watching you two fucking.'

You're not the only one, Christine thought wryly, smiling over at the one-way mirror.

Christine gazed again at the blonde girl sunbathing to her left. The girl had taken her sunglasses off now, making her resemblance to Leslie far less pronounced. Her eyes were smaller than Leslie's and a different shape too, slightly slanted. She had the same lovely porcelain skin as her, though. And goodness knows what she's doing to it in this sun, Christine thought. She was thankful for her own darker complexion, which responded well to sunshine in relative moderation. Although there wasn't anything moderate about the sun today, it was as fierce as could be.

Further along the beach, a group of teenage boys and girls sat in a circle chatting and flirting in a lazy sun-drugged way, apparently unselfconscious about their nudity. Christine thought what a healthy, natural thing nudism was. If you considered the matter logically, what was the sense of bathing costumes? They were just a throwback to more puritanical times. You certainly didn't want to be wearing *anything* on a day like today. It was *hot*.

The sun continued to hammer down out of the sky and Christine began to feel thirsty. She turned and sat up, reaching into her beach bag for the bottle of water she'd brought with her. She sipped the bottled water with slow deliberation, drinking deeply as she watched the blue waves of the Mediterranean roll lethargically in and listened to the rhythmic sound they made as they lapped the shore. There were a few people in the sea, splashing about half-heartedly, but not many of them. It was almost too hot to move, even in the water.

'Drink?' she said to Peter, touching his arm with the bottle.

'No thanks,' he replied sleepily, his eyes still closed.

She screwed the metal top back on, returned the bottle of water to her beach bag and sprawled back on her elbows, looking out again at the ocean, letting her eyes stray to its hazy blue horizon. Christine was starting to feel very tired in that oppressive heat. She shifted her gaze from the sea and turned to look at Peter, whose eyes remained closed. He appeared to be sleeping, his breathing even. Despite her fatigue, she felt full of love for him at that moment.

'You're so beautiful,' she whispered almost imperceptibly.

'Sorry?' he mumbled. He half opened his eyes. 'I nearly dozed right off there.'

'I was just admiring you,' she said. 'Actually, you

know, your shoulders are starting to get a little bit red. Do you want me to put some more suntan lotion on them?'

Peter grunted his assent. She took hold of the suntan lotion and rubbed some of it on his shoulders and all over his back too, for good measure. He rolled over slightly to thank her.

'You're welcome,' Christine said, stifling a yawn. Last night she had not slept at all well, unlike her drunkenly comatose husband, *because* of him, and it was really catching up on her now. She felt exhausted. She also felt absolutely stunned by that relentless sun. It really was murderously hot.

'Let me do your back for you now,' Peter said. He rolled over further and sat cross-legged on his towel.

'OK,' Christine said, handing him the bottle of suntan lotion as she got on to her stomach again. Peter ran his fingers over her back, massaging in the oil, which just made her even more tired. She was on the point of drifting off when she heard him say something. 'What was that?' she said.

'I said, it's so damned hot,' Peter repeated. 'I'm going for a dip.' He stood up and walked slowly towards the water's edge.

Christine glanced sleepily over her shoulder and watched him wade out a few yards before floating effortlessly in the water. She'd join him shortly, she decided, if she could muster the energy to shift herself. It sure looked refreshing. But she'd get the benefit of that recently applied suntan lotion first, soak up the sunshine for a little while. She was so hellishly tired though, really sleepy. She was just nodding off when she was jolted awake by the sharp cry of a gull, or was it a cry from inside her head?

Christine sprang to her feet and looked at the spot in

the water where she'd last seen Peter. He wasn't there. She gazed out further into the sea, shading her eyes against the glare of the sun, and saw him almost immediately. Panic over, Christine thought with relief. Peter had swum out a little too far for comfort as far as she was concerned, but he'd turned now and was facing the shore. She waved to him and he waved back.

Not waving but drowning, Christine said to herself. Now, what had brought that particular line of poetry into her mind? Stevie Smith, wasn't it? For a moment she lost sight of Peter's head. It sank and reappeared, and once again there was that movement of his arm. Not waving but drowning. Once more his head disappeared and he sank into the waves. When his head reappeared, there was no waving of the arm. He disappeared from view again. There was no sign of Peter for far too long this time and Christine got worried again. Then his head surfaced once more, no movement of the arm this time either.

What did this remind her of? She knew – it was that peculiar obsessive thing Peter had been doing in the pool yesterday, diving to the bottom of the deep end over and over again for increasing lengths of time. Christine felt a rising anxiety and then it came to her, the awful truth. Her body tensed and she let out a gasp. Suddenly she was petrified, her heart beating wildly. Peter had been practicing drowning himself, that's what he'd been doing, and now he was going to do it for real, she was certain of it.

Christine had to get to Peter before it was too late, every second counted. She sprinted into the water until she was waist deep and then threw herself into the waves and began to swim furiously in his direction. Completely oblivious now to the blazing heat of the day, all fatigue gone, she powered forward on adrenalin and blind terror in the fastest crawl her body could manage.

Christine strained every ounce of her energy as she cut through the waves, not letting up for even a fraction of a second until she'd reached Peter. And when she did, frantically trying to catch her breath, while treading water before him, she knew without a shadow of a doubt that her instincts had been right.

The look in Peter's eyes, wide and wild, was enough. Christine looked right back into his eyes, willing him desperately not to do this awful thing, telling him without words that he couldn't do it now that she was here.

Her eyes remained fixed on his and the two of them floated there in the bobbing water, just staring at each other, not saying anything, for an endless, agonizing moment. Then he turned away from her and began to swim back to the shore and she followed him in a slow crawl.

Chapter Nine

'IT WAS JUST A touch of cramp,' Peter lied when they got back to the beach. And *that's* just a bunch of crap, Christine thought. 'Had me worried there for a moment,' Peter added before closing his eyes to the sun and to Christine's probing gaze.

'It's just a touch of the sun,' Peter lied that evening, when they should already have been at *Ma Maison*, seated at the table for two that Christine had booked. It goes without saying that she'd have been more than willing to cancel the dinner reservation given what she was convinced had so nearly happened that afternoon in the sea. She certainly would have done so if Peter had said anything. But that was the problem. She couldn't get a sensible word out of him.

What Christine wanted more than anything was for Peter to talk to her honestly, so they could start to work things out. Fat chance of that. She was getting nowhere with him, *nowhere*. He was completely impenetrable; it was like talking to a brick wall. Christine felt a jumble of unpleasant emotions: acute anxiety most of all, utter frustration, and – in the ascendancy at that precise moment, and with every good reason – seething annoyance. 'A touch of the sun?' she repeated his words through clenched teeth.

'Un huh,' Peter mumbled. 'Sorry about that.'

Like hell he was sorry, Christine thought with a great surge of anger she could not hold in check any longer, and like hell was it a touch of the sun. You didn't need to be a genius to work that out; a halfwit could have managed it. While she'd gone off to have a shower and get dressed for the evening he'd remained naked in the living room – and got himself quickly and comprehensively plastered.

Peter was now slumped on the black leather couch and looking woozily at Christine with rheumy eyes. One of his hands was dangling near the ground next to an almost empty bottle of scotch and the glass tumbler he'd just drained in front of her eyes. He was too drunk to make an even halfway plausible attempt to cover up what had been his second major drinking binge in as many days.

Christine gave Peter a long withering look. 'How could you?' she said.

'I'm sorry,' Peter mumbled drunkenly.

'Yeah, sure you are.'

'… am …'

'No, you're not,' Christine spat out in infuriation. 'What you are is a selfish, self-obsessed bastard. I've been worrying myself sick over you, as I think you're very well aware, but you obviously don't give a damn about me. Well, the fuck with you. I'm going on my own.'

'Out on the prowl again, huh?' Peter slurred with a ridiculous drunken grin.

Christine gave him her most vitriolic look yet, but it was wasted on him. The stupid grin slipped from his face and the look he gave her back was blank and uncomprehending. Christine continued to gaze at Peter angrily, not that he noticed in the slightest, and she eventually looked away. 'Goodnight and good riddance,' she said in a final burst of angry exasperation.

A sigh came out of Peter. He did not look up and didn't reply, couldn't reply. He was as near as makes no difference completely out of it now and he just curled up naked where he was.

But Christine didn't go, not immediately, of course she didn't – not after what had come so terrifyingly close to happening that afternoon. She was almost sure that Peter was as totally comatose from whisky by this time as he'd ended up making himself the night before and he would doubtless remain that way all night long. That was always the way after he'd had a real skinful of the hard stuff. But she wanted to double-check – *treble-check* – on his condition. It was vitally important that she should do so, absolutely critical.

'Peter,' she said, shaking his shoulders as vigorously as she could, but she got not the tiniest reaction. She tried again, nothing. And again, the same. She tried one last time just to make absolutely certain, zilch.

Peter did not hear the sound of Christine going out, didn't register the sound of the front door shutting. He did not stir at all, lay perfectly still and soon all that was audible in the room was the rasp of his heavy breathing as he slept the deep, stupefied sleep of the utterly, profoundly inebriated.

The walk to *Ma Maison* did Christine good and by the time she got there she had calmed down quite a bit. But had she, she wondered, arrived too late? It certainly looked like it. She could see very clearly that the popular restaurant was crowded, absolutely packed. The head waiter, a tall patrician-looking man of about fifty with slicked back greying hair, welcomed her courteously before giving her the bad news. They had held her table booking for as long as possible but after more than half an hour it had been allocated to another couple.

It was only to have been expected, he explained to her. There was a virtually never-ending stream of people who arrived trying to get a table at *Ma Maison* at this time of the year, and the restaurant couldn't afford to let one stand empty. They had assumed that Madame and Monsieur had made other arrangements and they'd reallocated the table, he hoped she understood.

Christine said that of course she understood entirely, but it was such a shame. She explained that the table would now only be required for one person, herself. Did that make any difference? The head waiter considered for a moment and then said there was one possibility, he wasn't sure. He asked her whether she would mind sharing with another woman, an American, who was there on her own. I wouldn't mind, Christine said, but would the other woman?

He asked her to wait while he went and found out. Christine saw him approach a very attractive woman with short dark hair who was seated on her own in a corner of the restaurant. The woman looked in the direction the head waiter was gesturing and nodded agreement, smiling a warm hello to Christine across the room. The head waiter quickly produced an extra chair, and escorted Christine to the table. He then smiled at her and the other woman and turned briskly on his heels; busy, busy, busy.

The woman's name was Claudia and, after they'd made their introductions, Christine apologized for breaking in on her privacy. Claudia laughed away her apology, saying that she was only too pleased to have some company and such beautiful company too.

'What's a lovely-looking woman like you doing dining alone anyway?' she asked in slightly accented English. More than likely a New Englander, thought Christine who had quite a good ear for dialect.

'I could ask you the same thing,' Christine said. And meant it as well, because close up Claudia was even more attractive than she'd appeared to be when she'd looked at her from across the room. In fact she was nothing less than ravishingly beautiful, with high cheekbones, very dark almond-shaped eyes which were arched with black brows, and a generous sensual mouth. She was graceful and elegant in her movements also, and carried with her an air of authority that Christine could certainly relate to, because it matched her own. She also had genuine sex appeal, something a person either had or didn't have, in Christine's view – and this woman had it in spades.

'You're here on vacation I assume,' Claudia said.

'That's right,' Christine replied. 'You too?'

'No,' she replied. 'I'm originally from the States but I've lived out here for the last few years, love the place. My mother was French and her family's traceable to these parts a couple of generations back so I guess it's in my blood.'

The conversation continued in a similar superficial but friendly manner for a while longer and Christine found herself really warming to Claudia. They had only just met but with her open infectious smile and good humour she had managed to set Christine at ease in a remarkably short space of time – no mean accomplishment under the circumstances. She could not have been more cordial and yet Christine was conscious that there was something extra between them, a real rapport evident almost the first time they'd spoken to one another.

Their corner table was quite small and set apart from the other tables, ideal for a private conversation. It was spread with a starched and spotlessly clean tablecloth on which Claudia's cutlery and glasses were set.

The waiter, plump and cheerful and wearing a white shirt and black bow tie, came up to lay a place for Christine and take their orders, drinks first.

'Christine, do you like champagne?' Claudia asked.

'I love it.'

'Then, this is my treat.'

'But we've only just met,' Christine protested.

'True,' she said. 'But I simply know we're going to be the best of friends. Don't you feel it too?'

'Yes, Claudia, but even so …'

'Well, there we are,' she said and ordered a bottle of Dom Perignon.

Christine thanked her warmly for her generosity. She said that she would pay for the wine they had with the meal, it was only fair, and when the time came she made sure she ordered a particularly good white wine. They both decided to dispense with starters and ordered the same dinner, fresh grilled shark with a green salad.

The two women fell silent for a while and looked around them, enjoying the hubbub of activity of a busy, well-run restaurant: the laughter of other diners, the chiming of ice in glasses, the dash of the efficient waiters as they scurried around, their heels click-clicking across the floorboards.

'Ah, our champagne has arrived,' Claudia said and flashed a smile at the plump little waiter as he removed the gold foil and the wire cage from the neck of the bottle in his hand. The cork popped and he filled their two champagne glasses before leaving the bottle on the table and rushing off to serve some other diners.

'To us,' Claudia said, closing a hand round her champagne glass and lifting it.

'To us,' Christine replied in surprise, lightly clinking glasses.

'What's up?' Claudia said, noticing the wide-eyed expression on Christine's face.

'That was just the weirdest thing,' Christine explained. 'My husband used exactly the same toast, also with champagne, when we first met six years ago.'

'Maybe it's some kind of omen,' Claudia said. 'Are you two still together?'

'Yes we are,' Christine replied and sipped some champagne.

'I assume he couldn't make it on vacation with you,' Claudia said. 'Don't tell me, let me guess. He's too busy with business commitments.'

'That would very likely have been my answer a few years ago, but not now,' Christine said, taking another sip of champagne. 'He's here with me. He's just indisposed this evening, shall we say.' Yeah, as indisposed as a fucking newt, she thought.

'My husband is indisposed tonight too,' Claudia said, her eyes narrowing with amusement. 'You could say that he's all tied up at the moment.'

'Not literally, I hope,' Christine said with a smile.

'No, actually, although it wouldn't be too wide of the mark,' Claudia said, her mouth also curling into a smile. 'You see, he and I have a very unconventional relationship.'

'Tell me about it!' Christine exclaimed. You want unconventional, she thought; you should try my relationship with Peter for size.

'I will tell you about it, if you like,' Claudia said, pouring them out some more champagne.

'No, I meant …'

'I know what you meant, my dear,' Claudia said dryly. 'I'd like to tell you about it, I really would. I just hope you won't be shocked.'

'I assure you I won't be,' she said.

'I am a dominatrix,' Claudia announced simply. 'And my husband, Simon, is my sex-slave.'

Christine spluttered into her champagne in surprise. 'Now, that's what I call living the dream,' she said.

'You're serious?' Claudia asked.

'You bet I'm serious,' Christine enthused. 'That's my number one sexual fantasy *bar none*.'

'So, what's stopping you from making it a reality?'

'My husband.'

'Really?'

'Yes, unfortunately,' Christine replied. 'Peter insists that he's not interested in that sort of thing, I mean absolutely *insists*, but you know what, Claudia?'

'What?'

'I think he protests too much, I honestly do.'

'You think he's a closet submissive?'

'I'm virtually certain of it,' Christine said. 'Although how one would ever get him to admit it to himself I just don't know.'

'He's seriously in denial, huh?'

'And how,' Christine said. 'That's not to say our lifestyle isn't decidedly kinky – because it certainly is.'

'So, what are you two into if it's not BDSM?' Claudia said. 'You've got me intrigued.'

Christine breathed deeply. 'Not to put too fine a point on it,' she said, 'I pick up strangers I find attractive and fuck them.'

'And what does your husband do?'

'Peter watches us through a one-way mirror and masturbates.'

'I can see the appeal of that from your point of view,' Claudia said, not batting an eyelid at Christine's revelation. 'I'm certainly not monogamous.'

'Do you let Simon watch when you have sex with other people?' Christine asked.

'I *make* him watch, yes,' Claudia said. 'Whether I let him masturbate is another matter. Sometimes I do. Sometimes I don't, just leave him drooling.'

'My heroine!' Christine laughed.

Claudia poured some more champagne for both of them and they sipped silently for a few moments.

Claudia then said, 'These strangers you pick up, are they always men?'

'Sometimes more than one man, actually,' Christine replied. 'But no, not always men. Sometimes it'll be a couple or a woman on her own. I like those types of scene a lot, I must say. I'm bisexual, you see.'

'You and me both,' Claudia said, looking at her meaningfully. If looks could thrill, Christine said to herself with a shiver of excitement.

The meal arrived then, causing their conversation to pause at that point, and no bad thing as what they had just revealed to each other had given the two women more than enough to think about for the time being.

In fact they said very little to each other while they ate, just the occasional bit of chatter of no real consequence. The fish was delicious and so was the salad, and as for the light white wine that Christine had selected, it accompanied the dish to perfection.

Christine kept looking over at Claudia during the course of the meal, thinking how sexually attractive she was and what an excellent dominatrix she must surely be. She found that her eyes had a particularly powerful allure. They were a very dark blue, almost black. Several times she caught herself gazing only at those eyes.

But then her own eyes went inward as her thoughts returned inevitably to Peter. How could they not? Her anger towards him earlier in the evening had completely disappeared now, to be replaced once more by great anxiety.

As the meal went on, Claudia could not help but notice that Christine had withdrawn into herself and that her expression was becoming increasingly troubled. It was obvious that her new friend was seriously upset about something.

Claudia finished eating and wiped her mouth. 'Christine, there's something really worrying you, isn't there,' she said, gazing at her with a look of concern.

'Yes,' she replied, meeting her gaze. 'I won't deny it.'

'It can't be a matter of life and death, surely.'

'Now, there I'd have to disagree,' Christine said, her eyes darkening.

'Ahh,' Claudia said. 'Look, I think you'd better tell me all about it, don't you.'

And that's exactly what Christine did. Maybe it was the alcohol that loosened her tongue, made her open up the way she did, or maybe it was the real sense of fellow feeling she had developed very quickly for Claudia, or maybe she was so desperate about the situation with Peter that she needed someone, anyone, she could voice her fears to. Or was it all of those things? In any event she told her about it in great detail and Claudia listened very attentively indeed.

It was a tremendous relief, Christine found, to have poured it all out, or most of it, to this most sympathetic of listeners. But now she'd got to the worst part and it was not easy to get the words out. Her voice quavered as she spoke. 'I believe he wants to end it all,' she said. 'He'd have done it today – drowned himself in the sea – if I hadn't been there to stop him.'

'Are you sure?' Claudia asked in alarm.

'I've got no absolute proof that he'd have done it, it's true,' Christine acknowledged. 'But I'm convinced of it in my own mind, utterly convinced.' Her hands shook as they fluttered up to her face.

'Then why aren't you with him now?' Claudia asked with a bewildered frown. 'I'm sorry but I don't get it.'

'Oh, he'll be in no fit state to do anything for many hours, believe me,' Christine said. 'He's completely out of it courtesy of his drinking binge earlier this evening, I mean *completely*. I don't think even an earthquake would shift him out of the drunken coma he was in when I left him. No. It's not tonight I'm worried about. It's tomorrow or the next day.'

'The situation's urgent huh?'

'It is.'

Claudia looked away, pondering for a while and then turned back to her companion. 'So, your husband wants to die, does he,' she said, catching hold of Christine's hands. She brought them down on the table and gripped them tight. 'Do you know what you need to do?'

'What's that?' Christine said, looking at her hopefully.

'You need to hand him over to me.'

Christine was bemused. 'What do you mean?'

'What I say.'

'And what will you do with him?'

'Kill him, my dear,' she replied. 'Kill him.'

Chapter Ten

'I'M SPEAKING METAPHORICALLY, I hasten to add,' Claudia added hurriedly.

'I'm relieved to hear it,' Christine said, looking directly into her dark eyes, searching them. 'But what on earth are you talking about?'

'Well, I've been listening carefully to everything you've said and clearly the situation is very serious.'

'You can say that again.'

'Only a truly radical course of action will resolve it.'

'I'll grant that it was a bit spur of the moment on my part,' Christine said. 'But, as I explained to you, I came up with one yesterday.'

Claudia gave Christine a look that suggested she was far from convinced. 'Listen,' she said. 'There's an old Chinese proverb that goes, "If you don't change the direction you're going, you're likely to end up where you're headed." Where do you think Peter's headed if he doesn't change direction?'

'To the morgue,' Christine replied starkly. 'And some time very soon.'

The two women fell silent as the waiter brought them their coffees. Neither of them had wanted dessert, the general drift of their conversation having finished off their appetites completely.

'Now, be honest,' Claudia said once the waiter had

moved away out of earshot. 'What are the chances of the radical change of direction you came up with yesterday being successful?'

Christine lifted her cup of coffee, took a sip, put the cup down again and replied, 'Not good on my track record so far, I have to admit.'

'I'll tell you why that is,' Claudia said. 'It's because your proposal is fundamentally flawed.'

'I don't see that.' She sipped at her coffee again.

'OK, tell me something,' Claudia asked. 'What was your first impression when you met me?'

'I liked you a lot.'

'Likewise,' Claudia said. 'What was Peter's first reaction when he first met you?'

'He fell in love with me.'

'And you fell in love with him.'

'Sure did.'

'First reactions count for something, then, don't they,' Claudia said and took a quick sip of coffee.

'Agreed.'

'Right,' Claudia said. 'Do you remember what you told me was Peter's first reaction to your proposal that you clean up your act, become a "normal couple"?' She did the quotes in the air thing with her fingers.

Christine did not say anything. She stared silently into her coffee.

Claudia went on, 'He was highly sceptical that you could pull it off, that's what you told me, wasn't it?'

'Yes.'

'He was highly sceptical that you *personally* could pull it off.'

'Uh huh.'

'Don't you think he had a point?'

'Well, yes,' Christine admitted.

'Why's that?'

'I guess it's because I'm exceptionally highly sexed,' Christine said. 'I also love variety, I can't pretend I don't. But I can go straight, I know I can. If it will save Peter's life I'll *make* myself go straight, believe me.'

'But Peter doesn't want you to go straight, as you put it,' Claudia said. 'He likes you being a sexual desperado. It's not you he's so dreadfully unhappy with, is it, it's himself.'

'I suppose.'

'Tell me something else,' Claudia said, her eyes lingering on hers for a moment. 'Do you find me sexually attractive?'

'Yes I do – very,' Christine said, feeling a tremor of excitement squirm through her body despite herself.

'Well, I feel the same way about you,' Claudia said and Christine could feel her hand touching her thigh beneath the table cloth. It was an electric touch, quite amazing. It almost made her climax there and then, she could hardly believe it.

'And given that we are so sexually attracted to one another,' Claudia went on, 'I'm sure you won't mind me doing …'

'Doing what?'

'This,' Claudia said and pushed her hand between Christine's legs. 'Very nice,' she added, 'no underwear – just like me, no pubic hair – just like me, and a nice moist pussy – *moi aussi*.' She pushed down hard on Christine's clitoris and then started rapidly working two, then three fingers in and out of her ever more slippery sex. She masturbated Christine furiously until, her blood singing in her veins and her vision flashing, she climaxed with a frantically stifled groan. Claudia then removed her sticky fingers and licked them slowly, one by one.

There was a long silence between the two women during which Christine struggled to recover her composure. Finally she spoke, 'So, we've established that I'm a sex-mad slut.'

'No we have not,' Claudia said emphatically. 'What we have established is that if Peter carries on as he is he's likely to commit suicide some time very soon. We have also established that your proposed solution – cleaning up your act, as you put it – is doomed to failure. It would be going totally against the grain for you, which you *have* just proved, and would make Peter even more miserable.'

'Which leaves us where?' Christine said in dismay. 'Precisely nowhere.'

'You're wrong,' Claudia said and swallowed what was left of her coffee. 'There is, you see, a third way.'

'A third way?'

'That's right,' Claudia said. 'We can discuss it as we take a short walk to my home.'

Claudia signalled to the waiter for the bill. 'I'm paying for all of this meal, Christine, and I'll brook no argument about it,' she said. 'I'm taking over your problem, too, and I shan't brook any argument about that either. You're a very dominant woman, my dear, that's plain to see. But you're not as dominant as me.'

Claudia locked her arm in Christine's as they left the restaurant and the two women started up the sidewalk beneath the muted glow of the streetlights, going in the opposite direction to which Christine had come. The click of their narrow heels echoed off the buildings. The night was mild and a nice cool breeze was blowing, a welcome contrast to the excessive heat and humidity of the day.

'So, what's this third way of yours?' Christine asked.

'I'm going to kill off the old unhappy Peter and bring

71

to life the person he really wants to be.'

'Which is?'

'Your sex-slave,' Claudia replied. 'He wants to be your slave. He just doesn't know it yet.'

'I'm not sure about this,' Christine said, shaking her head.

'Don't you believe that deep down inside that's what he wants to be?' Claudia said. 'It's just a version of himself he can't bear to contemplate for various spurious reasons.'

'That is true,' Christine said. 'It *feels* true.'

'So, what's the problem?'

'The problem is that those reasons may be spurious, all right *are* spurious, but they are extremely entrenched with him.'

'So entrenched he'd rather die than allow his true self to come to the surface?' Claudia asked.

'I think that's right, I honestly do,' she said. If Peter had succeeded in drowning himself that afternoon, God forbid, Christine knew one thing. She knew that even as the briny water had been filling his lungs he would *still* have been clutching to himself the leaden weight of his obstinate, self-deluding convictions. It was just the way he was. When Peter fixed on an idea, it tended very much to stay fixed that way. Conversely when he closed his mind to something, it stayed closed – like a steel trap. It was a fatal weakness in his character. Fatal. 'I do think he'd rather die than allow his true self to emerge,' Christine added. 'Which means that whatever you've got in mind for him, he won't wear it. Believe me, he just won't wear it.'

'My dear, he'll have no say in the matter,' Claudia replied with a soft chuckle, 'no say whatsoever in any aspect of the outlandish ruse I have in mind.'

A ruse, huh, Christine thought. 'Will he fall for it then?' she said. 'Put it that way.'

'Oh, he'll fall for it all right,' Claudia laughed. 'Like all the best dommes, I'm a consummate actress.'

The two women continued to stroll along together, arm in arm. 'My place is this way,' Claudia said, motioning with her free arm, and they crossed the cobblestone street, their stiletto-heeled footsteps resounding noisily. They turned right into a smart little square that led to a prosperous looking street. Claudia pointed at an imposing residence, set back behind iron railings, with a sizeable garage at its side. The property itself had high-arched windows and its grand entrance door was flanked by marble pillars and approached by wide steps. 'There it is,' Claudia announced, going on to open the front gate to the residence by pressing in a security code to the panel next to it.

They walked up the steps to the main entrance and Claudia went through a similar security code process to open the door. She turned to Christine and invited her in. The front door opened directly into a lengthy room with a very high vaulted ceiling and a floor of shining marble. Christine let out a little gasp of appreciation at the elegant splendour that met her eyes: all soft dark leather, highly polished woodwork, fine old oil paintings, and cut-glass *objets d'art*. Claudia was obviously a woman of consummate taste and no little wealth.

'You like?' Claudia said.

'I like very much.'

'Well, I like you very much,' Claudia said, 'very much indeed. And I'll sort out your Peter for you, have no fear.'

And Christine thought Claudia would sort him out, she really did think that. Why else would fate have brought this extraordinary woman into her life at this time? They had only met that evening and yet it felt as if they had known each other all their lives. Christine knew instinctively that Claudia felt the same way about her too. And, of course, there was the palpable sexual chemistry between them, stronger still now that they were alone together at last, overwhelmingly strong.

It was Claudia who made the first move, suddenly drawing Christine close to her. Slipping a hand behind her neck, she pulled her face to hers and kissed her on the mouth, her lips pressing hard against hers. Christine felt the tip of Claudia's tongue probe her lips. Claudia moved her mouth away for a fraction, and then brought it back. She kissed Christine's open mouth again, this time pushing her tongue into hers, sliding it over and over. As she kissed Christine, she pressed her body against hers and it turned her on even more than the smoothness and insistence of her tongue and the warmth of her lips against hers.

Then everything happened very quickly. Claudia brought a hand up beneath Christine's short skirt; she reciprocated urgently, and before they knew it they were masturbating one another in an increasing frenzy. They plunged fingers between pussy lips, rubbing fast and hard, feeling sticky wetness, the heat of their bodies, the thrilling pulse of their clits. The two women finger-fucked each other in a delirium of lust, both breathing heavily, both as wet as anything, their fingers now as gentle as ramming rods. And then the two of them climaxed simultaneously, spasms of carnal pleasure rocking their bodies; it was absolutely delicious.

They kissed again after that, losing themselves in the kiss, and that was delicious too. They broke the kiss eventually, breathless, and pulled apart.

Claudia suddenly became all business. 'Time for you to meet my sex-slave,' she announced.

'Right,' Christine replied.

'I said earlier that he was all tied up, didn't I,' Claudia said.

'Yes, you did.'

'Actually, to be precise, I've got him locked in a metal cage in my dungeon.'

'Thanks for the clarification,' Christine replied with a sardonic smile.

'It's important that you like Simon for my plan to work as well as I would wish.'

'Why's that?' Christine asked.

'Because you'll be taking him away with you,' Claudia said. 'Peter needs to learn to become a sex-slave. But you need to learn to be a dominatrix. For that you'll need a well-trained slave to practice on, which is where Simon comes in. OK?'

'OK,' Christine said. She'd gone this far, she thought, might as well see this thing all the way through. 'But how do I get Peter to you?' she asked.

'Simon will do that and, when the time comes, he'll get him back to you as well,' Claudia replied. 'I'll put him in the picture and give him his instructions shortly. Speed is clearly of the essence here, otherwise you're going to have a dead husband on your hands. It is vital that we move fast. I'll go into exact details in a moment and you will of course be the one that has the final say, all right my dear?'

Christine looked at her and nodded silently. She followed Claudia through that big palatial room, along a wide corridor lined with more fine old oil paintings and down a flight of marble stairs at the end of which was a big oak door.

Chapter Eleven

PETER, SHOCKED ALL OF a sudden out of his drunken stupor and yet not really awake, was gripped by a mixture of confusion and blind fear. Who was the sinister man in the leather hood standing over him? His head reeling, Peter tried to cry out, started to struggle. But the man clamped a vaporous rag over his nose and mouth and held it there firmly. Then everything went as black as it had been before, as black as a dreamless sleep.

He was awake now – barely – but was disorientated again. This was partly because everything remained blackness. He blinked several times, trying to get his eyes to adjust to the total dark. Apart from moving his eyelashes Peter did not move at all because he was still half asleep. He hadn't come back to his senses yet, not by any means. His memory was painfully slow and uncertain. What he'd *thought* had happened had felt horribly real at the time but it had to have been some kind of ghastly drunken nightmare, Peter told himself. Perhaps he'd had a touch of the DTs, he thought. He'd be seeing pink elephants next!

What time was it, Peter wondered vaguely, still not stirring. Everything was completely dark, so presumably it was still night time. How long had he been sleeping? Seven or eight hours, much more, much less? It was impossible to know in this blackness.

Where was Christine, was she back yet? If she was back she wasn't lying by his side, that was for sure. He'd have been able to hear her breathing if she'd been there. Was she still mad at him, Peter wondered. He wouldn't blame her if she was after what he'd done, deliberately screwing up her dinner-for-two plans like that by getting completely shit-faced again. It had been inexcusable.

Where was he, for that matter? Was he still on the couch? If so, that would explain why he was on his own. Or maybe Christine had helped him upstairs and into bed as she'd done the previous night. If so, he had no recollection of it at all and, if she had, why couldn't he see the luminous clock like he always could when his head was turned in this direction? No, he concluded sleepily, he must still be on the couch.

Peter remained motionless in the darkness, didn't feel like moving a muscle, still so drowsy. But he couldn't see a damn thing, which was slowly starting to get to him. Perhaps he could hear something, some movement elsewhere in the villa that might indicate what sort of time it was. Peter continued to lie as still as ever but concentrated on listening for a moment. Nothing. Oh fuck it, he thought, I'd better make a move. He went to get up but found he could not.

Because his wrists and ankles were manacled.

They weren't manacled together but attached in some way to chains, or so it appeared from the clinking noise he heard.

Suddenly all Peter's drowsiness had gone. He was wide awake.

And terrified.

He felt beneath and around him in the blackness to the extent his restraints would allow. He was lying on the couch; no, that wasn't right. He was lying on some other article of furniture, a large rectangular bench or table or the like that was covered in a similar kind of soft leather. But where was he? Was he in one of the other rooms in the villa? No, that couldn't be the case because, when he edged himself backwards – which his relatively slack chains allowed him to do – behind him was not the dappled surface that was common to all the villa's internal walls, but what felt like, indeed what must surely be, a brick wall. Was he in the garage, perhaps? No, he'd be able to smell engine oil. Anyway, there was nothing remotely like this leather-covered table in there. Come to think of it, there was nothing like it anywhere on the property, that he could remember.

His chains, four of them attached one each to the steel manacles on his wrists and ankles, were anchored to the side of whatever it was he was lying on, Peter identified by touch again. They clanked and clattered as he pulled at them, trying to free himself. Because each of the chains was quite loose Peter had reasonable room for manoeuvre. That was a bit of a plus, he supposed, but not much of one given that he couldn't get free of them, try as he might. He pulled as hard as he could at each steel manacle but soon realised that his efforts were having no effect at all and the pain of struggling against them was cutting into him too much. All in all, it was a hopeless effort.

Peter slumped back down, panting, and tried to take stock of his situation. It was grim, very grim. He was completely naked, chained up in the dark, someplace. But where? And why? And what was his captor, that man in the leather hood, going to do to him? Who could he be, for God's sake? Was he one of Christine's one-night stands who'd turned out to be a psycho? Was it that Pierre guy, maybe? The hood he'd been wearing made it impossible to say. What had this madman, whoever he was, done with Christine, *to* Christine?

Or was this some sort of sick joke Christine herself had perpetrated, to get back at him for his atrocious behaviour of late? But that made no sense either. She was considerably more worried about him than she was angry with him, he knew that perfectly well. Perhaps she was somewhere there in the blackness, though, that had to be a possibility.

'Hello, Christine,' Peter called out loudly. 'Are you there, darling?'

Silence.

'Christine.'

Silence.

'Hello,' he called out again, louder still. 'Hello. Is anybody there?'

Nothing. The only sound Peter could hear, and it was becoming deafening, was the sound of his heart beating in his temples.

Panic was mounting rapidly within him now and tears started to sting at his eyes. Then he began to sob, he couldn't stop himself. Tears streamed down his cheeks and his hands quivered against his manacles.

'Please,' he blubbered, sobs wracking his shackled body. 'Please, I'm so frightened. Please help me.'

Numb silence again.

This is no good, Peter chided himself, you're being pathetic, a wimp. He wiped the tears from his cheeks and tried to get a grip, work things out. *Think Peter, think.*

He must have been drugged by the man, the intruder, when he put that rag over his mouth. It had been wet with something, chloroform maybe. So, was all this a deluded hallucination on his part, a nightmare trip brought on by the drug or perhaps – here was a possibility – brought on by a mixture of that drug with all the alcohol sloshing around in his system? Would he come round soon and find ... what would he find? ...that the place had been ransacked, worse, that Christine had been abducted, raped, murdered even? Christ Almighty, it was too awful to contemplate.

Then again, was all this taking place in his cranium for a different reason? Had he gone stark staring mad? That was another possibility, a much more acceptable one to contemplate under the circumstances than the idea of something ghastly having happened to Christine. His behaviour lately had hardly been that of a rational man; it had been very far from being that. Had it been the start of a serious mental illness? Was he now certifiably mad?

Or was he actually dead? There was an even grimmer thought. Perhaps he'd died and gone to hell. He'd been wishing himself dead recently. He'd almost taken the plunge too, quite literally; would have done as well if Christine hadn't intervened the way she had. They say: Be careful of what you wish for, it might come true. Was this some form of hideous poetic justice? Was this what the death for which he had wished away his life of late actually amounted to – being chained up in the dark for an eternity of damnation?

But no, Peter decided, he wasn't hallucinating as a result of the drug that lunatic in the leather hood had forced upon him, nor from the copious amount of booze he'd consumed, nor from a combination of both. He wasn't insane either, nor was he dead. He was alive.

He was alive all right.

Alive and living a nightmare.

Naked and locked in chains.

In the pitch black.

Peter had thought that over the last few years he'd pretty much got rid of that childhood fear of the dark from which he'd suffered for so long, had convinced himself that he'd finally outgrown it, not before time. That fear was certainly back again now, with a much greater force than he'd ever experienced before. Who or what was lurking in that darkness, Peter asked himself, quivering from head to toe with fear, his chained restraints rattling and shaking. What were they going to do to him?

'Please don't hurt me,' he called out piteously into the blackness that surrounded him. 'Please let me go.'

Answer, yet again, came there none.

And it dawned on Peter then. Oh God. The realisation finally hit him. He could call out and call out as many times as he liked but it was futile. He'd never get any answer. Because there was nobody there. There was nobody and nothing lurking in the darkness. There was only silence. He was all alone. He'd never been so completely alone in his life.

Then Peter became conscious of something else, something worse still because of where it took his terrified imagination next. Crying out was futile, he knew that now, but he couldn't do it any more in any case. This was because his mouth and throat had all of a sudden become incredibly dry. He was beginning to feel thirsty, extremely thirsty. He ran his tongue thickly over parched lips, thinking he would do anything, *anything*, for a little water. But there was nobody to ask, nobody to beg.

He'd been left here all alone in the dark with a chronic thirst, his dehydration made worse by his drunken binge, and made worse still by the drug that had been forced on him. How long would he survive without water when he was in this state already? Not very long at all, he suspected.

Peter didn't want to die of thirst. He didn't want to die period; he realised that all too clearly now that it was probably too late. I don't want to die, he whimpered to himself desperately, and then louder, also to himself, I don't want to die, then much louder. '*I don't want to die, I don't want to die, I don't want to die!*' he screamed inside his head over and over.

Chapter Twelve

TIME PASSED SILENTLY AND interminably. It felt as if it had been many hours since he'd woken from his drugged stupor to find himself in darkness and in bonds. But how long had it been really? Peter had no way of knowing. All he knew for certain was that his mouth was so dry, his tongue so thick, his thirst for something, anything, to drink so excruciating that if he didn't get it soon he'd die of thirst that very day. Or was it night? There was no way of telling in the midst of such total darkness.

Then he heard something at last. It was the sound of a key scraping in a lock. It must be that madman in the leather hood, he thought as he sat up.

But when the door swung open, it was not a man in a hood standing there silhouetted in the rectangle of light. It was a woman in a hood. And some sort of tight all-in-one outfit, a cat-suit maybe. The first thought that came into Peter's mind was that it was Christine, and that thought made his heart lurch inside his chest with relief.

The woman entered and the door closed once more. Was it Christine, though? He so much hoped that it was, prayed with all his soul that it was. But what was she doing, getting her revenge? OK, fair enough, he'd deserved to be taught a lesson for behaving like such a complete prick. But enough was enough.

Then suddenly there was a sharp click and he was

dazzled by the glare of a powerful spotlight. Its sudden beam was so violent it was like the stroke of a sword. He blinked in the abrupt white light, trying to adjust his eyes.

Peter made out the silhouette of the woman in the blackness behind the light. She was now seated about ten feet in front of him in what looked from the shape of it to be a grandiose chair of some kind, a throne even.

'Is that you, Christine?' he asked and squinted into the fierce whiteness of the light, only to see the woman shake her hooded head negatively.

'All right,' he said. 'Then what have you done with Christine?'

No response.

'I'm so worried about her,' Peter went on urgently. 'Look, if she's all right, not harmed in any way, just nod … please.'

The woman nodded decisively. *Jesus, the relief.*

'Thank you for that, Madame. Thank you very much,' Peter croaked. 'But, listen, I desperately need something to drink.'

No response.

Peter got onto his knees on the leather-covered table or whatever the hell it was, his chains rattling. 'Please let me have something to drink.'

The hooded woman still did not reply or make any further movement.

'Please, Madame, I beg of you,' Peter pleaded, his voice even more hoarse. He stretched his manacled wrists out towards her, his hands palm to palm in an attitude of prayer, of supplication.

Nothing.

Tears sprang to his eyes and he began to weep, his shoulders shaking. 'Please, please, Madame, I'll do anything you want, anything,' he coughed the words out between tears. 'But please let me have something to drink, I'm begging you.'

The woman still did not respond. Instead she got up abruptly and departed in silence, locking the door behind her and leaving her captive in despair.

… And *still* in the glare of that relentless spotlight. The darkness that had engulfed Peter for so long had given way now to this blinding artificial light, the incessant glare of which hurt his eyes and tormented his being.

Could the hooded woman have been Christine, Peter wondered as he tried unsuccessfully to shield his eyes from the glare. He knew she'd indicated not, but then again perhaps it was all part of some elaborate trick she was playing on him. But couldn't she see that the time for tricks had long passed? His thirst now had become unendurable. It would be life-threatening before too much longer, he was sure of it.

Another stretch of time passed, mercifully brief this time, before Peter heard the sound of the key in the lock again and saw the door swinging open.

Once again the hooded woman entered. She did not sit down this time. Instead she walked towards him, her arms behind her back, taking measured steps in her skin-tight cat-suit, if that's what it was, and her high-heeled boots that clicked against the floor. She was head to toe in tight black leather, Peter realised, the closer she got to him, and the closer she got the more afraid he felt. He could tell from the way she carried herself that she wasn't Christine. She was just as voluptuous, though, he couldn't help noticing in spite of his fear and disappointment.

For disappointed Peter most certainly was. His heart had sunk like a stone at the realisation that this frightening woman was not his wife. But then it suddenly lifted as he saw that she was presenting something to him with one of the leather-gloved hands she'd previously been holding behind her back and that the something in question was a glass of water.

She handed it to him and he held it to his mouth avidly, gulping the water down and swallowing it in two quick draughts. It felt indescribably good passing down his throat. Refreshing didn't even come close to describing the feeling. It was like nectar.

Peter wiped his lips with the back of his hand, his chains rattling, as she took the empty glass from him.

'Thank you, thank you, Madame,' he gasped. 'Thank you so very much.'

The woman's only response was to turn round sharply and leave the room again, walking with rhythmic strides that snapped her high heels down hard on the floor. But this time she switched off the spotlight as she went. The door shut resoundingly behind her, there was the sound of the key scraping in the lock again and suddenly all was darkness and silence once more.

Peter sighed in the blankness, in the blackness. He felt genuinely grateful to that mysterious woman. He had begged her to let him know that Christine was all right and she had. He'd begged her to take pity on him and let him have a drink of water, and she had taken pity on him. He felt beholden to her, he couldn't help himself, and couldn't wait to see her again, couldn't wait to see her face for the first time.

But when would that be? It could be ages from now. Peter tried to make the time pass by imagining what she might look like. He had a strong feeling she was going to turn out to be a real beauty, a cruel one though no doubt.

He felt a tingling in his loins at the thought of it. Then there came the beginnings of an erection, a slow luxurious rush of blood to his cock. Peter became very conscious of his manacles now, how they dug into his flesh. To his surprise, he felt his penis harden still further at the thought that he was in bondage like this, and completely at the mercy of that mystery woman clad from head to toe in tight black leather.

He must be one very sick bastard, he decided, because there was something about this whole nightmarish experience he was actually starting to enjoy in a perverse way, in a perverted way. Peter lay back down and brought his right hand to his cock. He began to masturbate, his manacled wrist moving rhythmically, the lengths of chain that held him in bondage clinking and rattling, adding to his pleasure. He pulled himself up and down into a lascivious state of sweat and sex and grip. He then began pulling faster, grunting and rubbing harder and harder all the time.

Then his arousal tightened into something desperate, frantic, as he stroked away feverishly until he was ready to burst, nearly ready to come. And then he did come. His manacled body shaking without control, he groaned and tightened his fist and shot out his semen. It sprayed out in warm bursts over his torso. Peter continued to shudder uncontrollably for a while longer as his orgasm subsided. And he then felt strangely peaceful, more peaceful than he'd felt in a very long time. He soon drifted off to sleep. He slept deeply and did not dream.

Chapter Thirteen

MEANWHILE BACK AT THE villa Christine and Simon were getting properly acquainted. In his leather hood, Simon had struck a sinister figure indeed as, acting in accordance with Claudia's instructions to him, he'd drugged Peter with chloroform, thrown him over his muscular shoulders and abducted him. And what a slick operation that had been, Christine reflected: from living room to garage to boot of car to brief drive, to garage to removal from boot of car to dungeon; the whole process taking no more than about twenty minutes.

Without the hood Simon still looked physically strong, yes, but he struck anything but a sinister figure. Christine discovered an almost immediate compatibility with her handsome blond-haired guest, not only because of his highly submissive nature, which she found very appealing, but because he was genuinely likeable, intelligent and articulate. He was a kind and thoughtful man too, with a gentle charm about him that was most engaging. He was also proving to be a good teacher when it came to passing on to her the essential skills and rituals that underpin the arcane world of BDSM. And he was a sympathetic listener.

'I'm extremely concerned about Peter,' Christine had told him about an hour after they'd made the switch. She had felt her stomach churn as she'd walked away from her comatose husband, shackled naked to that bondage table in the dungeon, and she hadn't stopped thinking about him for a moment since. 'Have I done the right thing, Simon?' she'd asked, looking anxiously into his pale blue eyes. 'I know desperate circumstances call for desperate measures and all that. And things don't get any more desperate than having a husband hell-bent on committing suicide at the earliest opportunity. Even so, I'm terribly worried that I've made the most dreadful mistake. Jesus, I've just conspired in the drugging, abduction and imprisonment of my husband. It's madness when you think about it.'

Simon had smiled kindly at her in reaction and said, 'You – *we* – have done the right thing, I'm sure of it. You've already said what the alternative would be, which is so dreadful it doesn't bear thinking about.'

'What we've done was ultimately my decision. I could have put a stop to it,' Christine had said. 'I take full responsibility.'

'From everything I've heard about the nightmare situation you were in, you made the right decision,' he'd replied. 'And now the deed's been done Peter's in the safest of hands with Claudia, believe me.' And somehow Christine had believed him. Those reassuring words voiced with obvious sincerity by such a thoroughly nice man had given her all the comfort she'd needed and her crisis of confidence had evaporated like dew in the morning sun.

Christine and her new friend, her new *slave* for goodness sake, were in the main bedroom and were surrounded by an accumulation of the bondage equipment that, at Claudia's insistence, Simon had brought with him to his temporary home. There was bondage rope and bondage tape and leather utility straps and metal trigger clips; and strewn everywhere there were various kinds of whips, paddles, canes, clamps, pegs, weights, gags and other instruments of correction.

Simon had attached four of the leather utility straps, one to each of the corner posts of the bed to demonstrate how they could be used to hold a submissive in a spread-eagled position. He had shown Christine how all the other disciplinary equipment he'd brought with him should be correctly used also. This was all part of the crash course in BDSM he was giving Christine, he was finding her to be an exceptionally quick study.

Christine was already very easy with Simon as evidenced by the fact that she was completely naked as she padded around the room with him, soaking up the knowledge he was imparting to her. Simon was as close to being naked himself as makes no difference, wearing only wrist and ankle cuffs and a slave's collar, all of black leather. His cock was not hard but then again it wasn't soft either. That was understandable given that he had been explaining a subject – how to use various items of disciplinary equipment – that spoke to the very core of his sexuality.

Christine gazed at Simon, thinking how good he was to look at: with his aquiline features, his gentle eggshell-blue eyes, his mop of blond hair, his athletic frame – entirely devoid of body hair, Christine noted with interest – his large semi-tumescent cock, his firm arse, and his long muscular legs. He wasn't just good to look at, she thought, he was gorgeous, and a very nice guy as well. And she wanted to know more about him.

'Tell me a bit about yourself,' Christine said conversationally.

'What would you like to know, Mistress?' Simon

asked.

'How about telling me how you first got into S&M,' she said, settling down gracefully on the edge of the bed and gesturing for him to join her. 'Was it with Claudia, before you moved here from the States?'

'Yes to both questions, Mistress,' he said, sitting down beside her. Christine liked the way Simon kept calling her Mistress. It gave her a distinct thrill, made her pussy moisten a little more each time he did it.

'When did it all start?' she asked. 'Can you remember?'

'Yes, Mistress,' he replied. 'I can remember it as if it was yesterday. It happened the first time Claudia put me over her knee and gave me a spanking.'

'Was this early in your marriage ... or before that even, perhaps?'

'Actually, no,' Simon replied. 'It was quite a few years after we'd got married. It was a major new excitement for both of us and it happened just when we thought we'd about reached the end of novelty and experimentation in our sexual relationship. It was Claudia's idea, she initiated it and it was obvious straight away that it turned her on in a big way. For my part I had to admit that, although that first spanking hurt quite a bit – enough to make me cry out – and was a very humiliating experience, I liked it, liked it a lot. I wanted more of the same and the sooner the better.'

'Why was that, do you think?' Christine asked.

Simon cleared his throat softly. 'It was for a whole number of reasons I guess, Mistress,' he said. 'I got off on the pain itself, all those endorphins it released, but also the feeling of being punished because I was guilty.'

'Guilty of what?' Christine asked. 'Had you done something wrong? Was that why Claudia spanked you in the first place?'

'Not at all, Mistress,' Simon replied. 'With respect, you misunderstand me. I felt guilty because I'd discovered that I liked being beaten. And because I liked it, it made me feel guilty and ashamed and yet that shame itself made me sexually excited. I was doing something that was forbidden, shameful, and yet loving it for that very reason.'

'It was a vicious circle,' Christine suggested.

'You could say that, Mistress,' Simon replied. 'But it was wonderful too, for Claudia as well, I know. She wanted to beat me harder the next time, use a whip, and I wanted it too. It was as if I was discovering the real me at the same time that Claudia was finding out the person she really was. We found that the more Claudia hurt me, the more I wanted it, the more we both did. It was soon very clear that I wasn't just a masochist but was deeply, profoundly masochistic, a real pain-slut, and that Claudia wasn't only a sadist but was extremely sadistic.'

'Didn't you get frightened, though, Simon?' Christine asked. 'All that escalating pain.'

He paused before saying, 'Yes, I did get frightened, Mistress. But the fear and the excitement were all one and the same sensation really, two sides of the same coin, so to speak. And the greater the fear I felt, the greater the excitement I felt too.'

'I see,' Christine said. 'And Claudia kept pushing your limits more and more, presumably.'

'That's right, Mistress,' Simon replied. 'As time went on she progressed from disciplining me with her hand and with a whip to every type of paddle, cane, crop and flogger imaginable – studded paddles, fibreglass canes, riding crops, braided floggers … She also started using nipple clamps on me, torturing me with hot wax, sodomizing me with a strap-on dildo, and subjecting me to various forms of cock and ball torture. And if all that weren't enough,' he added with a wry smile, 'we found that another fetish had kind of crept up on us.'

Simon went on to explain that the penchant for leather that Claudia and he had always had in common had grown over time into a positive fetish. 'We'd both come to adore the look, the smell, the feel of leather,' he said. 'We found we simply couldn't get enough leather – clothing, fetish-wear, instruments of correction, furniture, you name it.'

'I can relate to that,' Christine said, gazing around at all the leather disciplinary instruments that currently festooned the bedroom. 'I've always loved leather myself. What is it about leather that's such a turn-on, do you think?'

'It's dark, sensual, and … I don't know … *pagan,* somehow, Mistress,' Simon replied. 'It always makes me think of sex.' It made him think of sex right then, sex with Claudia. He recalled one particular occasion when she had stood before his nude form, entirely naked herself except for a miniscule leather thong she'd just bought. He remembered what happened next …

'Orally service me,' Claudia told him. 'Worship my pussy with your lips and tongue.' Simon made to respond to this by now familiar command by starting to remove the thong from her hips. 'No, while I'm still wearing it,' Claudia said, pushing his hands away. She sat down on their dark leather couch and then sprawled back wantonly on it with her legs apart. Simon got onto his knees and began with great energy to lick and suck and probe her sex with his tongue. Claudia's pussy was soon absolutely soaked, her wetness seeping through to saturate the tiny leather thong which was pulled tightly between her swollen labia. Simon pushed the thin strip of leather further into her body with his sinuous tongue. He pressed his tongue against the wet thong, forcing her pussy lips open although the tautly stretched leather stopped his tongue from penetrating any further.

'Come on, you can do better than that,' Claudia urged him. 'Lick it as hard as you can, really move that tongue around.' And Simon did, using his tongue to force her thong yet further into her pussy. It was now pulled even deeper between the lips of her sex. Simon kissed Claudia's pussy lips. He pressed his tongue directly at the opening of her sex, pushing the leather material deeper still into her pussy. The harder Simon had to work, he knew the better it felt to Claudia, that the leather really intensified the incredible sensations she was experiencing. Claudia began to tremble uncontrollably. She climaxed, and climaxed again and again, her body shuddering with waves of ecstasy as the pleasure went on and on...

'OK, you and Claudia had got heavily into S&M and had developed a leather fetish as well,' Christine said. 'So, how did things develop from there?'

'We began to feel a real need to come out of the closet, Mistress,' Simon replied, adding with a laugh, 'even if it was by that time full of leather!'

'Out of the closet?'

'Yes, Mistress. Claudia and I wanted to meet other people who shared similar deviant sexual tastes to our own. We decided to go to a fetish club that wasn't far from where we were living at that time. We'd read about the club – *Submission* it was called – in a bondage magazine we used to buy. The club enforced a strict dress code, as all the good ones do, and had an excellent reputation. We went to *Submission* intending to meet some fellow sadomasochists and generally enjoy ourselves, and so we did. But going there that first time also changed our lives in a way we couldn't possibly have expected.'

'In that case, I think you'd better tell me all about your first visit to *Submission*,' Christine said. And that's what he did.

Chapter Fourteen

CLAUDIA AND SIMON DECIDED that the outfits they would wear on the occasion of their very first visit to a fetish club would be of black leather; no surprises there. Claudia, foregoing underwear as was her usual practice, chose a figure-hugging dress, minute in length, and a tight-fitting pair of tall boots. She told Simon to wear only a leather collar, tiny g-string and wrist cuffs. The idea of wearing so little at the club gave him a feeling of incredible vulnerability. But, what could he do? Claudia had *told* him it was what she wanted; there was no more to be said. Thinking of it in this way gave Simon a tremendous feeling of exhilaration as he anticipated the delicious embarrassment to come

Submission did indeed prove to be an excellent choice of club. Claudia and Simon could not help but be nervous about this initial foray of theirs on to the fetish scene and yet their feeling after the first few moments there was one of comfortable familiarity. The organizers, Mistress Kay and her partner/slave Tony, went out of their way to be welcoming to the newcomers. The couple were very pleasant and it was obvious in talking to them that they were passionately committed to BDSM. Their staff were equally friendly, and the club's ambience and décor were fantastic, with great attention to detail. The lighting was subtle and atmospheric, designed as much to leave large patches of darkness than to illuminate.

Claudia had decided that she and Simon would simply observe rather than participate this first time at the club while they were finding their feet. But now that they were there, she remarked to him, she couldn't help feeling that it might have been a good idea to have brought along, say, one of her riding crops. That was because the dungeon equipment was just so tempting. It was superb – lots of polished wood, shiny metal and soft black leather – and seemed to be crying out to them to use it. But it was the people that made that club, that gave it its style and raw erotic energy, no question about it. Two people in particular as it turned out.

'We'll just watch and learn,' Claudia reminded Simon, their eyes gazing around the dark, crowded play room as sex music pounded in the background. The room was packed with serious players and, looking around, it made for a highly erotic tableau: nearby, a naked man grovelled on the floor at the feet of an Amazonian blonde in a leather bikini and pointed-tipped high heeled boots. He was kissing and licking her boots as she stood above him, the expression on her face positively regal. Another naked man, numerous metal pegs attached to his genitals, was being led around on all fours by a dominatrix in a tight leather cat-suit. A male wearing a rubber latex outfit was strapped on his front over a whipping bench and before him stood a highly attractive elfin-faced woman with a completely shaven head. She was also tightly clad in rubber and the male was vigorously sucking on the strap-on dildo that jutted from her crotch.

Making their way towards the centre of the dungeon playroom, Claudia and Simon noticed a handsome man with sensitive features, short dark hair, eyes that were even darker and skin that looked almost olive in the muted light. He was naked apart from a slave's collar and wrist cuffs, had his head bowed and arms to his side, and was sporting a powerful erection.

There were a number of people standing watching as a strikingly beautiful woman openly played with his cock. She had shiny black hair that hung to her shoulders and large electric-blue eyes. The woman was evidently a leather mistress, dressed very similarly – almost identically in fact – to Claudia, in an extremely short, figure-hugging dress and long high-heeled boots. She stopped masturbating the man and told him to stretch his arms above him, after which she used trigger clips to attach his wrist cuffs to either end of a metal spreader bar hanging by chains from the ceiling. The woman then took a length of black bondage rope, which she wrapped over his naked shoulders and torso and up tightly between his legs, causing his jutting erection to throb.

It was the first time Claudia and Simon laid eyes on Mistress Mandy and her slave, Mark. They could not have realised it at the time but their lives were never to be the same again.

The stunning dominatrix turned to her audience, which was continuing to steadily grow. 'I'm looking for a volunteer,' she said, holding up a large roll of clear plastic wrap. 'I want to shrink wrap Mark here up against another sub.'

'I'd like to volunteer my slave,' Claudia called out almost without thinking and for a while all eyes were on her and Simon. But she'd said they were just going to watch, Simon thought, although that wasn't what really addressed his mind. Her *slave*, that's what she'd called him. She'd never called him that before. He liked the sound of it very much indeed.

'I want him to take this off,' Mistress Mandy said,

pointing to Simon's bulging leather g-string, before turning her glistening blue eyes back to Claudia. 'That OK?' Claudia nodded her assent.

'By the way,' Mandy added with a wonderful wide smile, 'I think you're gorgeous.'

'So are you,' Claudia replied, returning her smile. Their eyes met and lingered for a moment.

When Simon took off the tiny leather garment that had been struggling to contain his growing erection, his cock sprang out stiff and erect. The two women held him in front of Mark so that their two stiff cocks rubbed together excitingly. Mistress Mandy used two more trigger clips to attach Simon's wrist cuffs to either end of the metal spreader bar from which Mark was suspended. The faces of the two men were inches from one another.

'Hello,' said Mark, a twinkle in eyes that were the deepest brown Simon thought he'd ever seen. 'I don't believe we've been introduced.' The half-grin he gave showed a set of white, even teeth.

'Hi, Mark. I'm Simon,' he replied with a smile. 'Is this the beginning of a beautiful friendship, do you think?' God, Simon thought, did I actually just say that out loud? He wondered why on earth he had said it. It sounded positively flirtatious, for Christ's sake, which was absolutely crazy. He wasn't interested in guys at all, not one little bit, right? OK, there'd been those couple of times with his cousin Paul back when they'd been teenagers, a bit of mutual masturbation and some imaginative by-play but ...

Before Simon could pursue this confused line of thought any further he was distracted by a ripping noise. Mistress Mandy began to walk around the two men in circles, pulling the transparent plastic from the roll, covering them with wrap from the top of their chests to their knees, and in the process pinning their hard cocks even closer together.

'Would you care to join me?' Mistress Mandy said to Claudia, reaching into a long black leather hold-all, extracting two rattan canes and handing one of them to her.

'Don't mind if I do,' Claudia replied, giving the other woman a mock-courtly bow of the head.

'You beat your slave and then I'll beat mine,' Mandy said and stood back to give Claudia the floor. Claudia gave a practice swipe with the cane and then ...nothing. Simon waited, his heart pounding with excitement. An intoxicating combination of anticipation and shame was making him breathe faster, making his erection pulse like crazy against Mark's stiff cock.

Simon wanted the punishment to begin, wanted to feel the cane lash his body painfully. He was tremendously aroused, his body aching with desire. That he was pressed up tight against another naked man and was being watched by a growing audience of the club's perverati only added to the sublime humiliation of the experience. He could not conceivably be making a more shameful exhibition of himself if he tried, and he loved it. But how could that be so? He was an introvert; there was nothing of the exhibitionist about him at all, never had been.

Then it started, snapping Simon out of this bewildering reverie. Claudia sliced the cane through the air in a graceful arc that cracked hard across Simon's plastic-wrapped backside. It really hurt, a white flash of pure pain that caused him to inhale sharply and left a red track across his backside, visible beneath the clear plastic. The second stroke whistled through the air, cracking hard against Simon's rear and he clamped his teeth tight to suppress a cry of pain. There was that white flash of sensation again and then a second track to join the first. A third stroke of the cane followed the second one before Simon had time to recover. Strikes four and five came down in even swifter succession, harsher and sharper still. The sixth stroke bit hardest of all, a flash of agony that made him cry out. Claudia stopped then and the pain Simon was suffering started to dissolve, becoming a suffuse red heat that seeped through his body, connecting with the hardness of his cock as it throbbed against Mark's own pulsing erection.

'I want to cane my slave now,' Mistress Mandy announced and it was Mark's turn for six of the best. Each time Mandy caned him he winced and squealed and bucked against Simon. Then it was Simon's turn for the cane, and then Mark and then Simon again. Then both together. On and on the two women caned their slaves until excruciating pain burned like twin flames into their flesh. Their eyes, now wet with tears of agony, met for the first time since their punishment had begun and, as soon as they did, intense mutual desire shot through them. It was a kind of madness. Pain suddenly turned to pure lust, throbbing and hot. Their nerves were on fire, the heat of desire swept through their bodies and blood pulsed in their aching cocks. Mark suddenly kissed Simon on the mouth, a hard passionate kiss, precipitating them both instantly to orgasm. Their shafts pumped thick waves of cum over their stomachs that were pressed so closely together as they writhed helplessly in their plastic-wrapped bondage.

At the same time, Claudia and Mandy dropped their canes to the floor and kissed, bringing their lips together tightly, tongues flicking. They then began masturbating one another furiously, plunging fingers between labia, feeling all the hot wetness, the throbbing of their clits.

101

The two women both climaxed as one, spasms of erotic delight rippling through their bodies … and bringing forth a burst of spontaneous applause from the audience that had grown even more in number as the quartet's highly stimulating performance had unfolded.

And so it was that at the very first fetish club they ever attended Claudia and Simon started a close friendship with Mistress Mandy and her slave Mark in just about the most dramatic, most erotic way possible. It turned out that the couple were in a twenty-four seven Femdom relationship, and the more Claudia and Simon got to know them and got to know themselves, the more such a relationship began to feel right for them as well.

Chapter Fifteen

CHRISTINE AND SIMON REMAINED seated together on the side of the bed. 'So, your friends, Mistress Mandy and slave Mark, became your role models,' Christine said. 'They showed you the way forward.'

'That's right, Mistress,' Simon replied. 'We had so much in common with them anyway but they were a little ahead of us. They'd decided to go twenty-four seven in their relationship not long before they met us. They made the decision once it dawned on them that their love of sadomasochism had gone beyond being a strong passion and had become an addiction. Claudia and I realised a while later that we'd become addicted in the same way and ...'

'Addicted?' Christine interrupted.

'Yes, Mistress,' Simon replied. 'I know it's a strong word but it's appropriate. As time went on I'd grown not to just love being punished but, yes, to actually be addicted to it, addicted to all that exquisite pain and humiliation. And Claudia couldn't resist being the one to administer my punishment, had found herself longing for it too. We found that neither of us could get enough of our deviant new way of life.'

'You didn't ever have doubts, think you ought to stop?'

'Never,' he said. 'We looked at what Mandy and Mark

had, the way they now lived their lives, and we concluded that that's what we wanted too when the time was right. We realised that we'd ventured down a one-way road, that there was no turning back, but more importantly, that we never *wanted* to go back. We knew that it was only a matter of time before I'd become Claudia's full-time slave, that it wasn't a case of whether but when.'

'It was a mutual decision when the time came?' Christine asked.

'Very much so, Mistress,' Simon replied. 'And that time arrived soon after we'd decided to move from the States to France and found that the house here in Dauge we'd fallen in love with had a huge basement. We bought the house and Claudia suggested that we arrange to have that basement converted into a fully equipped dungeon where I'd stay – naked or semi-naked at all times – and where, she informed me, I'd be disciplined constantly. I agreed wholeheartedly with her proposal and all that it implied as far as my complete enslavement to her was concerned.'

'Really?' Christine sounded a little sceptical.

'Oh yes,' Simon insisted. 'Claudia keeps me in that dungeon most of the time nowadays. I am her naked prisoner to all intents and purposes. And do you know something, Mistress?' His pale eyes were spiked with tears.

'What, Simon?' Christine said softly.

'I've never been happier in my life.'

Simon became silent, his tearful eyes fixed on the ground. There may have been tears in his eyes, Christine thought, but they were tears of joy and the expression on his face was content, serene. She wanted more than anything else to see that kind of softness, see that level of contentment, on Peter's face.

Which reminded her. 'How do you feel about being seconded to me while Peter takes your place in the dungeon?' she asked.

Simon gave a slight shrug. 'Whatever Claudia wishes me to do, I must do without question, Mistress,' he said. The tears had stopped and his face now registered zero. 'I am her creature. I always do exactly what she tells me without question.'

'Being with me is a matter of indifference to you, then?' Christine said, arching an ironic eyebrow. 'You can take it or leave it alone.'

'I wouldn't exactly put it like that, Mistress,' he said. There was a dry sense of humour underneath that subservient demeanour, Christine thought, and it made him even more attractive to her. 'No,' Simon added. 'I wouldn't say that I was indifferent to you at all.'

'I see what you mean,' she said, eyeing his growing erection.

'Yes, Mistress,' he smiled shyly, slyly.

'I am in the process of learning how to be a dominatrix,' Christine said. 'And, may I say, I'm being very ably assisted by a slave "topping from below", I believe is the correct expression.'

'It is, Mistress,' he said. 'And thank you.'

'How do you think I'm doing so far?'

'Very well indeed, Mistress.'

'And do you think I have a lot to learn?'

'Absolutely not, Mistress.'

'Why do you say that?'

'Because a true domina is born not made, in my view,' he said.

'And you think I'm a born domina?'

'I'm certain of it, Mistress,' he said. 'I think you're a complete natural.'

'Well, let's put that supposition to the test, shall we?' Christine said.

'How, Mistress?'

'You'll see.' Christine gave him a sidelong look, a little smile twitching at the corner of her mouth. 'A typical disciplinary session with Claudia, how would it start?'

'Let me think, Mistress,' Simon replied. He reflected for a moment and said, 'She usually puts me over her knee and gives me a sound spanking, just to warm me up, as she says.'

'What, like this?' Christine motioned for Simon to bend over her knee.

'Yes, Mistress,' he said. 'She sometimes pretends to be shocked that my cock is erect,' he added with a grin before positioning himself over her lap.

'It certainly is,' said Christine, using one hand to stroke Simon's erection as she caressed the curve of his backside with the other. 'Now, for that spanking.' She lifted her hand and brought it down. The cracking sound of her first smack reverberated around the bedroom, as did the second and the third. Christine spanked Simon quite lightly at first but soon built up to much harder smacks. She kept spanking him and stroking his erection until Simon felt the painful heat burning into him ignite the growing fire that was also being stoked in his loins and he very nearly climaxed.

But he didn't. Simon was a modest man by nature but one of the things he did pride himself on was his orgasm control, which was formidable. It was something Claudia was extremely strict about and it was very rare indeed for him to give her any cause for complaint on that score.

Christine then told Simon to move off her lap and bend over the bed. 'Does Claudia switch to a paddle at some stage, by any chance?' she asked as she stood up.

'Yes, at about this stage actually, Mistress,' Simon replied, turning his face towards Christine and giving her another grin. She was going to wipe that grin right off his handsome face soon, Christine thought gleefully. My, but this was so much *fun*.

'Play with your cock yourself now. Pull it hard,' Christine instructed as she took hold of a leather paddle. She used this to beat Simon's backside vigorously, delivering one hard stroke after another with the implement until his flesh quivered and burned a glowing red. The robust beating and his own energetic masturbation caused Simon to get perilously close once more to climaxing. His strong willpower prevailed again, though – but only just.

'These typical disciplinary sessions you have with Claudia,' Christine said, putting the paddle to one side. 'There's something else I'd like to ask you about them.'

'What's that, Mistress?' he asked, looking up over his shoulder at her.

'Do they involve any grovelling foot worship of the kind you were describing for me earlier with such obvious relish?' The guy had been virtually salivating, she remembered.

'Yes, Mistress,' Simon replied. 'They do.'

'Then, get onto your knees on the floor facing me, slave,' Christine said, taking hold of a leather whip. Ooh, she liked saying that word, *slave*. She thought she'd say it again. 'Now put your arse in the air and spread your legs, *slave*.'

'Yes, Mistress.'

'Worship my feet.'

They were beautiful, those feet, with soft fragrant skin and freshly painted toes. Simon licked and kissed her toes, soles, arches, insteps, ankles and shapely calves. It was a delightfully sensuous experience for Christine.

But it could be improved upon, she was sure. So, as Simon continued to kiss and lick her feet as if his very life depended on it, Christine used the leather whip to rain blow after searing blow onto his rear until the burning red heat spread to his shaft again and its head began to trickle with pre-cum.

'I assume your sessions typically involve a very harsh caning,' said Christine next, adding in an ominous tone, 'I would be very disappointed if they didn't.'

'Your assumption is correct,' Simon replied hesitantly, looking up at her.

'Sorry, I didn't hear that,' Christine said. He wasn't smiling now, she noticed.

'I said, yes, you're right,' he replied, wetting his lips uneasily.

'You're right, what?' said Christine, putting down the whip and picking up a cane. She began ostentatiously flexing the pliable rattan rod.

'You're right, Mistress ... Sorry, Mistress.'

'I should think so too, slave,' said Christine sternly, very much the strict dominatrix now, and revelling in it. 'Stand up, turn your back to me and reach towards your toes.'

'Yes, Mistress.'

'Tell me, *slave*, does Claudia often tantalize you like this by first running the tip of the cane up and down your spine?' Christine asked.

'Yes, Mistress, she does,' Simon replied.

'And do you find'

Swish!

'That when she starts caning you'

Swish!

'She punctuates what she says to you'

Swish!

'With vicious stripes from the cane?'

Swish!

'Yes, Mistress,' Simon gasped.

'And does her caning become incredibly hard, leaving your backside …'

Swish!

'Red'

Swish!

'Bruised'

Swish!

'And covered in stripes?'

Swish!

Swish!

Swish!

Swish!

Swish!

Swish!

'Yes, Mistress, yes …oh mercy, Mistress, please …' came the agonized reply.

Christine stopped beating Simon then and threw the cane clattering to the marble floor. She told him to stand upright and turn round, after which she took him tenderly into her arms. She pulled him close, her fingers seeking out the worst areas of pain she'd inflicted on him and gently stroking them as trickles of pre-cum from his erect cock smeared her warm thighs.

'So, Simon, answer me this question,' Christine said, pushing him away from her slightly and looking into his gleaming eyes. 'Do these typical disciplinary sessions Claudia has with you finish when you can take no more extreme pain and have begged her for mercy?'

'No, Mistress, they don't.'

'They go on?'

'Yes, Mistress.'

'Tell me what happens next then,' Christine said. 'How do they usually finish?'

'Well, I often end up blindfolded, gagged and trussed up on my back.'

'Really?'

'Yes, Mistress,' he said, warming to his theme. 'Sometimes I'm strapped to the horizontal torture chair, sometimes to the leather-covered bondage table that doubles as my bed at night time.'

'And where we left Peter manacled to those chains?'

'That's the one, Mistress,' Simon replied. 'I am held in bondage, the chains no longer slack but winched really tight, my hard cock rearing in the air.'

'Your hard cock *rearing* in the air, huh, slave?' Christine drawled, raising her eyebrows.

'Yes, Mistress,' he smiled.

'Sit on the bottom of the bed,' she instructed. Simon instantly obeyed and she covered his eyes with a blindfold of soft black leather.

'Now, lie flat on your back ... that's it ... spread your arms and legs ... Mmmm, your cock's very, *very* hard now and it's pulsing too – *throb, throb, throb*.'

Christine clipped Simon's wrist and ankle cuffs to the leather utility straps that were belted to the four corners of the bed.

'Oh, slave,' she said softly, her voice full of sex now, *oozing* with sex.

'Yes, Mistress.'

'What usually happens next?'

'Claudia gags me and clamps me and ...and ...' he hesitated.

'And what?'

'She uses my cock to pleasure herself, Mistress.'

'Do you, by any chance, want *me* to do that, slave?' Christine said cajolingly. 'As part of my *training*, you understand.'

'Yes, Mistress.' Simon's voice was raspy with passion. 'Please, Mistress.'

'I mean, if it's what *you* want.'

'... Mistress ...'

'Well, all right then,' Christine said. 'But you are not to climax unless I give you permission.' And that's not going to be any time soon, she thought, smiling to herself. She added, 'Is that perfectly clear, *slave*?'

'Yes, Mistress.'

Simon stared into the blackness of his blindfold as Christine put a ball gag in his mouth. He lifted his head slightly to assist her as she buckled it into place. Simon gasped beneath the gag as she attached nipple clamps to his chest and gasped again as he felt her start to play with the head of his cock, moving her palm around the top of his slit, spreading pre-cum over its head. He gasped once more as she straddled his thighs and eased his throbbing erection into the humid wetness of her sex.

Christine looked down at the blindfolded, gagged, naked Adonis spread-eagled beneath her in his bondage. She could definitely get used to the life of a dominatrix, she thought. Oh yes, oh yes. As she rode Simon's body she pulled at his nipple clamps, not excessively hard, but hard enough. Just the way he'd shown her.

Chapter Sixteen

PETER WOKE UP IN the darkness, not knowing where he was and feeling like he'd been sleeping for eons. He lay trying to make sense of where he was and how he felt. The first thing he realised was that he was still incarcerated and in chains, which remained just about the sum total of what he knew about his location. The second thing that came into Peter's mind was the realisation that – inexplicably, as far as he was concerned, given the dire circumstances he was in – he had slept deeply, peacefully and without dreaming.

He waited, lying as calm as an infant, and ten, maybe fifteen minutes later was still lying, but wide awake now. It was then that Peter realised something else and it amazed him because it seemed completely illogical. The suicidal depression that had weighed down on him so much lately had disappeared, lifted completely, now that he was being held in bondage. How on earth could one explain that? He didn't feel happy as such in his current predicament, just slightly odd, detached somehow. He didn't feel anything really, apart from a bit hungry and rather in need of a piss.

Peter heard the sound of a key being turned in the lock and sat up in his chains. The door opened and the leather-hooded woman walked into the room once more. Then it hit him again, that blast of blinding white light. He gasped sharply and brought both manacled wrists up to try and shelter his eyes against the light as best he could.

He was just able to make out the woman's head, shadowy against the dazzling light, two dark eyes behind slits in the black hood, and then the rest of her cat-suited body as she moved sinuously towards him, her high-heeled boots clicking against the floor. She was carrying something now, had a tray balanced between her leather-gloved hands, and she set it down beside him. There was a glass of water on it and a plate on which there was a sandwich made of a slice of bread cut in two.

'Eat,' said the woman curtly from behind the hood. 'Drink.' And Peter did, taking one large bite and then another of the sandwich, ham and cheese, before holding the glass of water to his mouth and gulping half of it down.

'OK?' she asked.

'More than OK,' Peter said. 'Thank you very much, Madame.' He took another couple of bites out of his sandwich and a further gulp of water.

There was silence for a short while as Peter finished off the sandwich and the water, putting the glass back on the tray. Then the woman put the tray on the floor and reached under the bondage table, bringing out a plastic bucket. 'You probably need to take a piss,' she said and handed him the plastic container. The woman evidently wasn't French, Peter thought as he manoeuvred himself round in his chains to the side of the bondage table and began emptying his bladder into the bucket. She was presumably an American from the sound of her accent, although the accent was not very pronounced.

When Peter had finished urinating, the woman took the bucket from him, putting it back under the bondage table. 'There are a few things I have to tell you,' she said.

Peter sat back up on the bondage table, his chains rattling as he moved. 'What do you have to say to me, Madame?' he said, careful to keep his tone respectful. Should he be calling her something other than Madame, he wondered, given her likely nationality. Ma'am maybe, but no, that wouldn't do.

'What I have to say to you is this,' said the woman. 'First, while your manacles will be removed soon, don't get your hopes up – we have absolutely no intention of releasing you. Please do not even think of trying to escape, it would be pointless. We have thought of everything, believe me, and I do mean *everything*.'

'I will not try to escape, Madame,' Peter assured her, thinking: who exactly did she mean by *we*? There was her and the man in the hood, obviously; anyone else? Were they acting alone or part of a gang of some kind?

'I am pleased to receive your assurance,' she said. 'I hope you are a man of your word.'

'I am, Madame,' he said. 'But where am I and what is this all about?'

'All will become clear in the fullness of time,' she replied unhelpfully.

'What about Christine?' Peter said. 'What have you done with her?'

'I am not going to tell you,' she replied. 'All you need to know is that she continues to be safe and unharmed.'

'I am very relieved to hear it, Madame.'

'There is something else you need to be completely clear about,' she said.

'What is that, Madame?'

'I expect you always to do as you are told when you are with me,' she said. 'If you disobey me, or try any funny business, if you attempt to escape, or try to trick me in some way, your precious Christine will be killed. Is

114

that absolutely clear?'

Peter breathed in hard, finding it very difficult to speak.

'That's concentrated your mind, hasn't it,' the woman said, her tone sharp. 'Now, answer my question.'

'Yes, Madame,' he replied unsteadily. He breathed hard again 'I give you my promise that I will always do as you instruct.' His voice quavered with every word he spoke.

'I'm glad we understand each other,' she said. 'If you behave well and always do as you are told I can assure you that your wife will be treated well. If you do not ... I won't spell it out to you again ...you know what will happen.'

'Yes, Madame,' Peter replied, trembling noticeably.

'Oh, and one other thing,' she added.

'What is that, Mada ...?'

She touched his lips with two fingers of a leather-gloved hand to stop him saying any more.

'You are not to call me Madame,' she said. 'I am not, after all, French.'

'Right.'

'You are to call me *Mistress*.'

She then retrieved the tray and picked up the bucket by its handle and walked away from him. She left the room in silence, returning momentarily to switch off the harsh spotlight. Peter lay back down and stared into the dark. This mysterious woman, whoever she was, may have given him a little food to eat but she had left him with a lot more food for thought, some of it as unpalatable as could be imagined.

Peter remained motionless in darkness so black after that harsh white light that it was almost tangible, and he felt the pressure of each passing moment as if it was weighted with lead. Silence surrounded him and he had nothing to listen to but the pounding in his own chest.

One thought occurred to him: the woman was encased from head to toe in tight black leather and was obviously comfortable in her garb. By contrast, apart from his shackles he was stark naked and was neither too hot nor too cold. So, presumably this place was air conditioned. No shit, Sherlock, Peter said to himself. Where did that brilliant deduction get him? He still hadn't the faintest clue where he was.

What he did know was that the woman obviously meant business, and that it would be utter folly to cross her because it would be putting Christine's life at risk. Peter felt a rising anxiety as he thought about the unequivocal nature of what she'd said. He felt something else rising as well as he repeated inside his head her parting words to him: *You are to call me Mistress*.

Each time Peter said those words to himself it generated in him a little spasm of lust, and then a bigger spasm and a bigger one still. His cock swelled and swelled until the temptation to touch himself became too strong to resist.

Peter's heart pounded as he brought his fingers to his hard cock and gripped it tightly. He began to masturbate and as he did so he felt an indefinable yearning deep within himself start to be released. He let his imagination loose as never before, allowing it to travel into sadomasochistic territory that he'd always regarded as completely out of bounds in the past, strictly taboo.

Soon he was lost in fantasies about that mysterious leather-clad woman, that *dominatrix,* and what she might do to him. As he beat off he imagined her beating him. And all the while her instruction, *You are to call me Mistress*, played over and over in his mind like an unstoppable tape loop.

Peter was just approaching the point of no return, his manacled wrist moving with increasing urgency, when he was stopped in his tracks. The door burst open with a heavy crash and he saw the woman silhouetted in a rectangle of light. She switched on a torch and shone it in his direction before looking at him through the eye holes of her leather hood and shaking her head.

'There is one *other* thing I have to tell you,' she said, a hard edge to her voice. 'You are not permitted to masturbate when you are left on your own – under any circumstances. Is that perfectly clear?'

'Yes, Mistress,' he said, panting. He moved his hand away from his pulsing cock. The door closed again and he heard it being locked. Jesus, he wanted to come, was *desperate* to come. Just a little more friction from his hand would do it, just the merest touch. But he daren't, he daren't.

Chapter Seventeen

CHRISTINE AND SIMON WERE continuing to get along famously together as she absorbed like blotting paper everything he had to teach her about the art of erotic domination. Christine was proving to be a real star pupil. She was a very conscientious one too, believing that practice made perfect. And so it did …

It was early evening and the sun had at least another couple of hours before descending into night, not that Christine and Simon noticed. They were in another world: the world of BDSM. They were standing together in the living room, both of them completely naked.

'I intend to discipline you in the bedroom very shortly,' Christine said with a seductive smile. 'Would you like me to do that?'

Has Pinocchio got wooden balls, Simon thought, returning her smile. 'Yes, Mistress,' he said.

'Then follow me.' She promptly led him upstairs, his gaze transfixed by the curve of her backside and her swaying hips. As Simon followed Christine up the stairs, his sense of sexual anticipation grew with every step he took.

They continued down the corridor and went into the bedroom. 'Let's get one thing clear before we start,' Christine said firmly. 'You are not to climax unless I give you my permission. Understood, slave?'

'Yes, Mistress.' Simon couldn't help but think of Mistress Claudia's own standing instruction to him on this subject. Claudia was red hot on his exercising orgasm control, as he'd mentioned once to Christine in passing. One mention had clearly been enough. She really was a very quick student, he said to himself for the umpteenth time since meeting her, a very quick student indeed.

Christine then pulled his face to hers and kissed him hard on the mouth. She even kissed like a dominatrix, Simon thought. He felt her tongue probe between his lips aggressively. As she kissed him, gorging herself on his mouth, she pressed her shapely nude body against his, which aroused him even more.

She then broke the clinch and led him over to the wall opposite the bedroom window, its blinds partly drawn to keep out the evening sun. She told him to face the wall with his legs apart and arms outstretched. He leaned up against the wall, putting his wrists over his head and spreading them and also parting his legs. He tried to keep his breathing steady and waited for Christine to begin disciplining him. He did not have long to wait.

Simon gasped as the red-hot strike from the flogger Christine was now wielding landed across the middle of his backside. He gave another gasp of pain as her next stroke planted a second line of fire across his rear.

Christine continued to whip Simon hard, each searing stroke producing a sharp, fiery sting, and his backside rapidly reddened. He moaned and gasped at the pain and his flesh quivered constantly as she increased the momentum of his beating. The increasing vigour, accuracy and regularity of Christine's carefully aimed blows made Simon writhe and moan. His moans grew louder and in time with the swooping impact of the whip with which she was disciplining him with such innate skill.

Christine was proving to have a real gift for inflicting pain, Simon had found – the best kind of pain, that is. What she was doing to him with the whip hurt very badly, yes, a red heat that seemed to be burning into his skin, sinking deeper and deeper all the time. But Simon could also feel its heat spreading to his cock which had become fiercely erect. Christine kept on whipping him and every strike tingled deliciously through his genitals. His backside was now as red as an angry sunset and he was panting and shivering with both pain and pleasure.

One might have expected Christine to have paused at around this point to give Simon a little respite, a well-earned breather. But she didn't and she was correct to keep going remorselessly on. Simon had been right; she was a natural-born domina. It was like she'd been a domme for years, all her adult life. She kept on beating him until his pleasure-pain turned to a sensation of purest pleasure that flowed through his body. Blood was flushing into his pulsing cock that felt as if it might erupt into orgasm at any moment. He willed himself not to climax …And then – just before it was too late – she *did* pause.

Christine seemed to Simon to have a sixth sense that told her to the second how far she could take a slave. It was a facility that she shared with Claudia. She'd been the same as Christine when she'd first started, he remembered: a complete natural. Claudia and Christine really were two of a kind, dommes *par excellence*.

'Get onto the bed and lie flat on your back,' Christine then told Simon and he immediately obeyed, his rock-hard cock waving in the air obscenely. Christine was breathing hard with lust and felt indescribably turned on.

She knew that she could not wait much longer as she felt her blood boil and a frenzied excitement building within her.

Climbing on to the bed, Christine straddled Simon's upturned face and sat over his mouth. He began to lick her pussy and she moaned out her pleasure. He continued as he had begun, his tongue on her clitoris insistent as she quivered with passion.

Christine then leant forward and took Simon's hot shaft into her mouth, rolling her tongue up and down its length as he flicked his over her clit. They sixty-nined each other like this in a state of ever-mounting passion. Desire sang through them as they sucked and licked deliriously and it was not long before Christine climaxed. Her orgasm was long and violent and she took Simon's pulsing shaft from her mouth as she shuddered with ecstasy.

'You have my permission to come,' she gasped before engulfing his erection with her mouth once more. Simon groaned painfully and with massive relief, spurted out thick gobs of creamy cum right into the back of Christine's throat. She swallowed down every last drop of his delicious cum as her own climax continued to rage.

When her orgasm finally, steadily faded Christine pulled away from Simon and climbed off the bed.

'Thank you, Mistress,' he said, looking up at her in dazed admiration. 'That was wonderful.'

'I really can't understand why you're thanking *me*,' Christine replied, smiling mischievously. 'After all, I am merely your humble pupil. That *is* the case, isn't it?'

'Yes, Mistress.' Simon smiled back at her, his pale blue eyes twinkling. 'And I'm Attila the Hun.'

Chapter Eighteen

THE DOMINATRIX IN THE leather hood was a complete mystery to Peter, a very frightening one, it's true, but an increasingly exciting one as well. She was a mystery to Christine also come to that, because most of their conversation the evening they'd met had been about Christine's own intensely pressing problem. Yet Claudia wasn't such an enigma really. One thing she was, without doubt, was living proof that given intelligence, determination and more than a modicum of good luck a person can triumph over the most unfortunate of starts in life. She was also proof positive of the wisdom of not following the herd, of what can be achieved in life by daring to be different.

Born in New Hampshire into relative affluence, Claudia had been the only child of doting parents. But tragedy had been just around the corner. She had been barely five years old when her father had died of a heart attack, and only a year older when her mother had been killed in a car crash. Both lots of grandparents had died some years earlier and so Claudia was sent to live with her father's sister and her husband.

Her step-parents hadn't had any children of their own and, although they were not unkind, Claudia always felt as if she was in the way as part of their household. She overcompensated for this and for her general sense of aloneness by working very hard at her academic studies at junior high, high school and beyond with the result that she ended up with an extremely good University degree.

A mentally stimulating if rather lonely life in academia could well have been Claudia's destiny if she hadn't had two major advantages going for her. The first was an amazing facility for figures that she chose to take advantage of not in the groves of academe but in the world of commerce, and which she translated into an exceptionally successful career as a stockbroker. Claudia gained a reputation in that field for being clever, imaginative and bold. She was a calculated risk taker of the first order, one whose risks invariably paid off – and it made her a mint in the process.

Claudia's second advantage was her physical beauty, which she had inherited from her French-born mother and which was utterly radiant; she *glowed*. Claudia had never known a man who could resist her attention. And she had a similar effect on many women too. Yet nobody could pin her down either, male or female. She was the ultimate loner and was convinced that she'd continue to have casual affairs, sure, because she was an extremely sexual person, but that she would never fall in love.

Then Simon had entered her life. He was a corporate executive and God knows she'd met enough of those in the course of her work. But he was the sexiest one she'd ever come across by a long way. It wasn't just strong sexual attraction Claudia felt for Simon, though. She fell head over heels in love with him as well. At first she'd been taken aback that she could be vulnerable to such a powerful emotion, thought she'd closed all that off. But vulnerable was what she was. Claudia found that she couldn't get Simon out of her mind. All the time, whatever she was doing, she kept seeing his handsome, kindly face. The image of him never left her mind's eye.

Having previously reconciled herself to a life essentially on her own, Claudia found herself reborn through this unexpected passion. As for the sex between them, it was out of this world … at the start. Which is not to say that it deteriorated as such after that. Although after a few years it's true to say that everything did get a bit familiar and comfortable, started to feel a little tame somehow.

Then Claudia got it into her head that she'd like to give Simon a really good spanking, and that had been her – *their* – Eureka moment. They never looked back from that time onwards as they got ever more heavily into sadomasochism, with Claudia becoming increasingly dominant in their relationship and Simon increasingly submissive. They also developed more and more of a leather fetish. But it was the close friendship they made with the Femdom couple, Mistress Mandy and slave Mark, that proved to be the turning point for them. They looked at the way Mandy and Mark lived and they liked very much what they saw. Claudia and Simon began to feel strongly that they should go down the same route with their relationship when the time was right.

Theirs was a very happy, if increasingly unconventional, marriage. And it was an extremely prosperous one too. By the time they got to their mid-thirties they'd made more than enough money between them to leave America and 'retire' to the South of France, to the wonderful home they'd bought in Dauge. They'd furnished it in the grand style befitting such a grand residence. And then they'd got to work on its huge basement …

Claudia still felt the same way about Simon after all this time, loved him immensely. But, of course, the couple's wholehearted adoption of an extreme Femdom lifestyle shortly after moving to Dauge – and converting that basement into fully equipped dungeon quarters for Simon – meant that their relationship was radically different nowadays to the way it had been at the start, to say the very least of it.

Not that she was enjoying *any* sort of relationship with Simon at the moment, Claudia reminded herself. It was Christine who had that undoubted privilege. She herself was in the process of breaking in a new slave and it was time for her to show her face, literally.

Peter had been left in the dark with a raging hard-on, *this* close to climaxing, and strict instructions not to do anything about it. That had been something like half an hour ago by his anything but exact reckoning and his erection had only just subsided. He sat up when he heard the door being unlocked, and he automatically shielded his eyes against the burst of white light from that fearsome spotlight that he assumed would follow almost immediately afterwards. Instead Claudia simply turned the overhead lights on and the large room he was in was at once bathed in a pale radiance.

The objects in the room became visible in the soft light but it was not to them that Peter's eyes were drawn at first but to the beautiful woman striding towards him. So, this was what his mystery dominatrix looked like without her leather hood. He'd wondered for a while if she'd ever take the damn thing off. Well, she had now and all he could think was that it had been well worth waiting for. He was struck immediately by the perfect symmetry of her features and how lovely looking she was. Her beautiful face was framed by short dark hair and she had almond-shaped eyes that looked almost black, although he could discern a bluish tinge. Her cheekbones were prominent, her nose was slender and her wide fleshy mouth was extremely sensuous.

Peter's gaze then wandered up and down the woman's body and what he saw made him let out an involuntary groan of desire, he simply couldn't help himself. She was wearing leather boots with very high heels and her shapely form was perfectly outlined by the extremely tight leather cat-suit she had on, which clung to her body like a second skin. Every curve and swell of her figure, from the contours of her beautiful breasts and erect nipples to the slit of her sex, was delineated and defined by the black leather.

There were those same leather gloves, too. She was evidently still in the outfit, less the hood, she'd been wearing before, which he'd only barely been able to make out under the violent assault of that spotlight. Now he could make it out – and make her out too and …Wow!

Peter knew that he had grown erect again at the sight of the woman and as she strode ever closer towards him, swinging her hips as she did, he suddenly felt absurdly embarrassed by his tumescence. He looked away from her and wrapped his manacled wrists around himself, hugging his own body, trying to disguise his erection.

When Claudia arrived by his side she rested her hand firmly under his chin and pulled his face in her direction. 'It is time for your shackles to come off,' she said, her dark luminous eyes staring right at him.

She leant forward and unlocked his steel manacles, first the wrists and then the ankles and he breathed a sigh of relief to be free of them and the chains to which they were attached. Peter rubbed his wrists and ankles that had been locked so tightly for such a long time. But for how long? He simply had no idea.

'Get up,' Claudia said.

'Yes, Mistress,' he replied and got unsteadily to his feet.

'You all right?' she said, ostentatiously ignoring his pronounced erection. 'You're not going to fall over or anything?'

'I'm all right thank you, Mistress.'

'I'm glad.' She was smiling as she spoke, just a slight touch at the corner of her mouth. Peter liked that smile. It seemed strangely sympathetic and that surprised him. In his fevered imagination he'd assumed that this mysterious woman would have had a cruel smile.

She then ran a finger along the musculature of his arm for a few moments. Her touch was electrifying and he felt his breathing quicken. 'Take a look round your new home, why don't you,' she said. 'I'm going to sit down.'

Claudia sat in the grandiose high-backed chair, the throne Peter had seen her use once before. She scrutinized his every movement as he wandered around the spacious, windowless room, his bare feet smacking against its shiny black marble floor. She noted with an amused smile the way his eyes widened and his erection throbbed at the sights that befell him. For the room – the walls, ceiling and floor of which were all black – was decked out beautifully with the highest quality dungeon equipment that money could buy. It included a wall-mounted St Andrews cross and a suspension machine. There was a wooden spreader bar, with leather manacle attachments at either end, which hung from the ceiling by chains, and another spreader bar of metal, with similar leather manacle attachments, also hanging by chains. There was also a large metal-framed cage, and two multi-strapped torture chairs, one vertical and the other horizontal.

There was an open cabinet of dark wood fitted against

the length of one wall upon which hung a large collection of disciplinary instruments. They ranged from simple straps to tawses, crops, whips, paddles, canes, gags, chains, handcuffs and a variety of clamps and weights. There were also several strap-on dildos and dildo gags, butt plugs and vibrators and a variety of lubricants.

'What do you think?' Claudia asked and he turned away from the cabinet to look at her.

'I don't know what to say, Mistress,' Peter replied. But he didn't need to say anything; his throbbing erection said it all. Here was the man who'd insisted to his wife that he was frightened of pain. That might well be true, almost certainly *was* true, Claudia thought. But the idea of it obviously turned him on considerably as well, that couldn't be clearer.

'This dungeon is fully fitted in other ways too,' she said, gesturing towards a door. 'Take a glance in there.' Peter did and was surprised once more when he found a large kitchen-dining room, all spick and span and full of state-of-the art kitchen equipment.

'I'm impressed, Mistress,' Peter said, popping his head out of the door.

'Have a quick look in there now,' she said, pointing to another door. Peter found behind it a luxurious bathroom, all gleaming marble and chrome. It contained a large bath, a shower stall, a big full-length mirror, a WC, a bidet, a bathroom cabinet, and a wash hand basin on which there was a cake of soap, a new toothbrush and an unopened tube of toothpaste. A further inspection revealed that there were a variety of other toiletries in the room, including deodorant, shaving foam and a packet of safety razors, as well as a number of clean white towels. It was all very neat and tidy, like the kitchen-diner.

'What do you think of your gilded cage?' Claudia

asked when he emerged from the bathroom. 'You've seen it all now.'

'I'm lost for words, Mistress,' Peter said, thinking: a person could make this place his home, for heaven's sake. He found the idea of that perversely thrilling.

'Do you know what I want you to do right now, Peter?' she said, staring unblinking into the deep blue of his eyes.

'No, Mistress.'

'I want you to perform your ablutions,' she said. 'You know, all the usual stuff – clean your teeth, shave, shower, blah, blah.'

'Yes, Mistress.'

'Wash every part of yourself thoroughly,' she added. 'And I do mean every part of you.'

'Yes, Mistress,' Peter replied, continuing to look back into her extraordinary dark eyes. Those eyes seemed to be drawing him more and more into their orbit with every passing second.

'Do you know why I want you squeaky clean?' she asked, her eyes still drawing him to her, seeming to see right through to the very heart of him.

'No, Mistress,' he said in a croak. It was true, he didn't know why she wanted him nice and clean but he had a damned good idea.

'I want to have sex with you,' she said matter-of-factly.

'… Mistress …' he gulped. He could barely speak. An intense feeling of desire flooded through him.

'Oh, and Peter,' she added.

'Yes, Mistress.'

'You know I said I wanted you to wash every part of yourself?'

'Yes, Mistress.'

'That includes giving yourself a thorough enema. Do you know how to do that?'

'Yes, Mistress.'

'You'll find all the kit in the bathroom cabinet.'

'Why do you want me to have an enema, Mistress?' Peter asked, his mouth parting company for a moment from his brain. *You idiot, why do you think she does?* He immediately knew the answer ... and the dominatrix confirmed it for him.

'Because I'm going to fuck you in the arse,' Claudia said. She continued to look him dead in the eye, her gaze betraying no feeling at all. 'Have you ever been fucked in the arse before, Peter?'

'No, Mistress,' he croaked.

'That's going to change,' she said. 'I'm going to pop your cherry, and do you know what?'

'What, Mistress?'

'There's nothing you can do about it, is there?'

'No, Mistress,' Peter said, feeling a thrill of fear deep inside him.

'You're going to become Mistress Claudia's bitch, aren't you?'

'Yes, Mistress.' So, that was her name, he thought, Claudia.

'You want that, don't you,' she said continuing to look into his eyes, her gaze penetrating through him now like a laser beam. 'You want to be Mistress Claudia's bitch.'

'Yes, Mistress,' he said quietly. What else was he supposed to say for Christ's sake?

Peter could feel sweat gathering at his brow and his heart was beginning to beat like a drum but he strove to betray nothing of the fear that gripped him.

Of course he could do nothing to hide the *excitement* that gripped him. His cock was now hugely erect.

'Get on with it then,' Claudia said briskly. 'Make yourself ready for me.'

'Yes, Mistress,' he replied and hurried towards the bathroom.

Claudia sat in silence for a moment and then emitted a dry laugh. Everything was going exactly according to plan. She then got up and strode towards the big open cabinet to pick out a strap-on dildo and a lubricant suitable for buggery.

Peter padded nervously into the bathroom where he turned on the shower, filling the room with humid warmth. The heat slid over him and everything around him turned to fog. When he came out of that fog, he knew what was going to happen. She'd made it very clear indeed. He was going to become Mistress Claudia's bitch.

Chapter Nineteen

CHRISTINE'S TRAINING HAD NOW effectively come to an end. So she and Simon did the logical thing and carried on in a Mistress/slave relationship as they waited patiently to hear word from Claudia. She'd be in touch once she was done and not before, she'd told them unambiguously.

Christine was brilliant in her new role of dominatrix, Simon thought. It fitted her like a glove. She impressed him in so many ways, large and also small. Indeed it was those ostensibly minor flourishes that made all the difference, in his opinion. He was impressed, for instance, with the way Christine always kept nipple clamps and several whips and canes to hand so that she could discipline him whenever she felt so inclined. When she wanted to be pleasured she would often instruct Simon to crawl over to where she was seated and lick her pussy. That impressed him too. He liked the way she just used him for her own pleasure like this whenever the whim took her. She really was, he thought, one hell of a domme.

Christine found that she loved being a dominatrix, loved the scope it gave her to use her erotic imagination in all sorts of interestingly sadistic ways. And she found *such* exquisite ways to discipline Simon. She liked to attach coloured pegs to his scrotum and metal clamps to his nipples. The acute pain that this caused him was made even worse by the weights that Christine would go on to hang from his nipple clamps. She would then tell him to get on to all fours before proceeding to cane his backside, stroke after painful stroke, until he begged in desperation for mercy.

Frequently Christine would lead Simon upstairs into the bedroom, there to position him face down on the bed and in bondage. He would be blindfolded and gagged, his nipples and scrotum clamped, and his wrists and ankles strapped to the four corners of the bed. She usually left him like this for a long time – sometimes a very long time indeed – administering the lash to him whenever she felt like it. And, she discovered, she tended to feel like it an awful lot.

Simon worshipped Mistress Claudia but that did not stop the deeply masochistic slave from revelling in his secondment to his new friend Christine. He was able to thoroughly enjoy the fruits of his labours as he served hand and foot the superb dominatrix he had helped to create ... well, *facilitate* anyway. He spent much of his time, when not in bondage, kneeling at Christine's feet, serene, content and sexually excited, wondering what wonderful new depravity she would force upon him next...

The living room was filled with cool night air ... and mounting erotic tension. Christine was naked and Simon almost so, wearing only his slave's collar. She was seated on the black leather armchair while he was on his hands and knees before her. Christine had a light flogger in her hand and was idly whipping Simon's back and rear with it – a mere *bagatelle* – while contemplating what genuine torments to inflict upon him once she got serious. Her sexual excitement was both controlled and enhanced by the need for her to take a disciplined approach. Simon was also in an advanced state of erotic anticipation as he contemplated the punishment to come. His breathing was shallow and his erect cock throbbed as it oozed pre-cum in a steady stream onto the marble floor beneath him.

Eventually Christine stood up, instructing Simon to remain positioned as he was until told to do otherwise. 'You may masturbate,' she told him as she made to go up to the bedroom in order to prepare for his further discipline and delight. Simon slid a hand around his cock and began stroking it rhythmically, his excitement steadily growing as he waited for the summons from Christine.

When Christine was ready she stood at the open door to the bedroom and called down to Simon to come to her on his knees. He obeyed immediately, crawling up the stairs and along the upstairs corridor before kneeling inside the bedroom at her feet.

Christine picked up a thick leather tawse, feeling its weight and suppleness. She then began to beat Simon on the backside hard, each of her strikes a flash of burning pain. While she was doing this he covered her feet with a shower of kisses. Simon *loved* foot worship, had a real thing about it. And Christine's feet were beautiful, as lovely in his view as Claudia's – and that was saying something.

Christine continued beating Simon's rear with the tawse, the leather snapping hard each time, and didn't stop till his flesh blazed like a red-hot furnace. She then told him to crawl across the room to the bed and lie on it on his stomach. She used black bondage tape to blindfold him and to bind his wrists behind his back and his ankles together. She recommenced beating his backside remorselessly with the tawse, strike after agonizing strike, until his flesh was a glowing, fiery red again.

Eventually Christine removed the bondage tape that she'd used to blindfold and to bind Simon. She told him to get off the bed and to stand and masturbate to orgasm while she beat him yet again, this time with a fibreglass cane. She administered a severe beating to his backside with this cruel implement, causing a fierce red agony to burn into his body, while he masturbated feverishly, stroking himself more and more quickly. Christine increased the vigour and severity of her carefully aimed blows until Simon, emitting an excruciating cry of pain, climaxed violently, spurting out great ropes of pearly cum into the air. Christine ceased beating him then and used her fingers, fast and furious, to bring herself to her own shuddering climax.

She climbed on to the bed after that, motioned to Simon to join her and the couple lay in each other's arms for a long while, kissing and caressing languorously. It had been another memorable BDSM session – although one during which Simon had taught Christine precisely nothing.

Christine liked Simon even more now than when they'd first got to know one another. She could imagine that if their lives had been different she could really have fallen for him. But their lives weren't different. Simon was a lovely man and she liked him a lot but he wasn't Peter.

She wondered sometimes if she actually liked Peter at all, the man he'd become at any rate. It didn't matter in the final analysis because she loved him. She wondered how he was faring in Claudia's dungeon. She prayed with all her heart that Claudia's proposed 'cure' for what ailed him with such potential lethality would actually work.

She strongly suspected that, if it was to do so, it would involve him having to swallow some bitter medicine, some bitter medicine indeed.

Chapter Twenty

CLAUDIA FOLLOWED PETER INTO the bathroom once she'd had her depraved way with him. The first thing he did when he got there was to brush his teeth and gargle like mad. This made her smile and let out a hard little laugh. Under the circumstances, when Claudia considered what she'd made him do after she'd finished buggering him, she could understand why he was doing that. He then squatted down and washed his genitals and anus in the bidet. Claudia waited until he'd finished and then announced with her customary coolness, 'I like any slave of mine to be completely free of body hair.' So, he wasn't just her bitch, Peter thought with a shiver of excitement, he was her slave too. 'I'm going to leave you alone for a while,' she continued. 'When I return to the dungeon I will give you a thorough inspection and will expect your body to be completely clean shaven.' With that Claudia turned briskly away from him and opened the door of the bathroom with a flick of the wrist.

'Yes, Mistress,' Peter said to her departing form. He listened to the sound of her retreating footsteps, her stiletto-heeled boots echoing on the marble floor, and heard the opening and shutting of the door to the dungeon and the sound of the key turning in the lock. Then all was stillness and silence once more.

Peter took hold of a disposable razor and a can of

shaving foam and stepped into the shower, which he switched on. He shook the can a few times, sprayed foam on the palm of one hand, then used the other hand to smooth it onto his chest. He'd shaved his face and neck before, so he thought he'd carry on down his body. He shaved his chest and armpits and then his pubic region and anus followed by the rest of him. Peter was not exactly hirsute, so it didn't take long but he was meticulous nonetheless.

He showered off the remains of the body hair that he'd removed with the razor, towelled himself dry and opened the bathroom door for a short while to allow the full length mirror in there to demist. He checked the results of his efforts very carefully, with the assistance of the big mirror. Mistress Claudia should be satisfied, he thought. His body was now completely smooth.

Then Peter stared at the reflection of his face in the glass. He saw the face of the man looking back at him in the mirror become tense with remembrance of the all too recent past.

God Almighty, he said to himself, he had allowed this Claudia woman to sodomize him …and more. He hadn't objected at all, hadn't put up any resistance whatsoever. What sort of man behaves like that? A man who's trying to save his wife's life, he answered himself, because argument, struggle, resistance of any kind had been ruled out of court by Claudia's terrifying ultimatum.

He was a positive hero, then; was that what he was? No, he was hardly that. What he was, Peter decided, was a man whose every action was now being determined by this one person. He truly was helpless. He'd had no option whatsoever but to let Claudia do what she had done to him.

So, he asked himself, how had the experience left him

feeling? Honestly? *Yes, honestly, Peter.* He felt ashamed, humiliated, certainly, but in a deliciously sexual way, that was the plain unvarnished truth of the matter. He was growing erect all over again just thinking about it. He felt sexually excited in spite of himself, there was no avoiding that fact. The evidence was standing there in front of him in the full-length mirror. And why was that? Why had he been, was being now, so excited by what Claudia had done to him. It was precisely *because* it was all so humiliating and shameful, that was why.

What did that say about him, about the kind of man he *really* was? Enough already, Peter said to himself. He began humming, a noisy tuneless sound, to try to obliterate the uncomfortable thoughts that were nagging at his mind. He didn't want to agonize any more about the implications of what had happened to him. He just wanted to fix his mind on remembering the experience itself, which, he had to be perfectly honest with himself again, he had found to have been nothing short of exquisite.

His hard cock pulsed as he stared into the mirror and started to relive it all, luxuriating in the wave of desire that engulfed him. Peter would have liked so much to masturbate but he'd had his instructions. His eyes clouded over and those recent images came flooding back into his mind …

When he had emerged from the bathroom, his heart pounding in his chest and his cock powerfully erect, it had been to find that Claudia had buckled on a strap-on dildo harness. She tightened the straps of the harness, testing the black phallus that was jutting out from her leather-clad pubis, and went on to heavily lubricate it. She ordered him to lean over the bondage table, and then positioned herself behind him.

'Open up your arsehole for me,' she demanded and Peter obediently reached back with both arms and held the cheeks of his backside apart, presenting the pink rosebud opening of his anus to her.

He braced for the pain he felt sure was coming but Claudia was extremely skilful. She gently worked the thickness of the dildo in and out of the opening of his anal hole a few times, pushing it in a little further with each thrust and stretching his reluctant sphincter. He suddenly felt the dildo spasm into him until his anal ring was right against its base. It felt *so* good.

Peter put his hands back in front of him and Claudia began to fuck him in the arse. As she moved inside him with the dildo, her breath hot against his neck, her strokes were at first slow and powerful and then fast and thrusting. Her leather-covered breasts brushed his shoulders as she moved in and out with increasing vigour until she was riding him really hard. His anal muscles squeezed and released deliciously, yes that was definitely the word, *deliciously*, around the dildo she was pounding into him. Her rhythm was strong, each thrust going deeper into his anus, filling him, penetrating him until he was moaning and shuddering deliriously.

'Come for me now, bitch,' Claudia said eventually and it was those words that triggered Peter's orgasm. It was amazing: he hadn't laid a finger on his cock and nor had she. But he came on her command, just like that. And what an orgasm it was, the most intense he'd ever experienced. He began to tremble uncontrollably and then yielded to the ecstasy of release. He called out a wordless explosion of desire as his cock erupted, sending one thick spurt after another of ejaculate splashing onto the leather surface beneath him. Claudia stopped fucking Peter then and stayed locked together with him for a moment before she withdrew the dildo from his gaping anal hole.

'Good bitch,' she said, stroking his shoulders. And he found – here was the insane thing – that he was glad, no *delighted*, that he'd pleased his Mistress, had received her approbation. He was also grateful to her that she had allowed him his ecstatic release by ordering him to climax.

'Thank you, Mistress,' Peter said, his voice unsteady.

'It was my pleasure,' Claudia said. 'Now lick all that cum up from the bondage table, then swallow it, every last drop.'

And that's what he'd done, God help him, that's exactly what he'd done. Like the good, obedient bitch he was, he'd licked up all his own cum greedily, swallowing it down and wallowing in his own degradation. It had all been so *deliciously* humiliating.

Chapter Twenty-one

CLAUDIA COMPLETED HER INSPECTION of Peter's freshly shaved body and deemed it satisfactory with a brusque, 'That's fine.' When she said what she said next he felt a powerful electric sensation, a combination of fear and desire, start to vibrate within him. 'I am going to demonstrate the pleasures of pain to you now,' she announced. 'How do you feel about that?'

'Frightened, Mistress,' Peter replied, swallowing hard.

Amusement flickered in Claudia's dark eyes. 'Why the erection then?' she asked.

'Because you look like that, Mistress,' he said, eyeing her up and down and shooting her a small smile.

And his reply was at least partly true because Claudia was now as naked as he was, and she had the most glorious body, with firm breasts tipped with erect nipples, shapely legs and a prominent, hairless mound.

'You are sexually excited only by the sight of my nudity,' Claudia said, raising a quizzical eyebrow. 'Is that what you're saying to me?'

'No, Mistress,' he replied. 'Everything about you excites me.'

And his reply was entirely true this time. The more time Peter spent with Claudia, the more time he spent *thinking* about Claudia, the more exciting he found her. There was a powerful aura of sadistic sensuality that emanated from her. She communicated it most of all with those amazing midnight blue eyes of hers that seemed to glitter with the promise of dark exquisite torments. He was mesmerized by those eyes.

Claudia seated herself on her throne. 'Do you know what I want you to do before I discipline you?' she asked.

'No, Mistress.'

'I want you to worship my feet.' She gestured that he should kneel before her. 'Make a thorough job of it, concentrating on my toes.'

Peter obeyed, licking each toe individually, and between each toe of first one and then the other of her beautiful bare feet.

'Extremely pleasurable,' commented Claudia. 'You have a real gift for foot worship.'

'Thank you, Mistress,' Peter replied before returning to his wholehearted worship of her feet. It was wonderfully demeaning; he loved it. Who would ever have thought he could feel this way about degrading himself in such a grovelling manner, Peter said to himself. But that was exactly how he *did* feel, there was no getting away from it.

'Full marks, slave,' Claudia said after a while, indicating that he should stop.

'Thank you, Mistress.' He'd pleased her. Peter liked that. She'd called him her slave again. He liked that too. He rolled the word around in his head, *slave*. She was his *Mistress* and he was her *slave*. His erection throbbed.

Claudia rose from her throne. 'Stand up,' she ordered. 'And be quick about it.'

Claudia led Peter by his erect cock to the area of the dungeon where the metal spreader bar with leather manacle attachments at either end hung by chains from the high ceiling. She placed another identical spreader bar on the ground beneath it and then manacled Peter's wrists and ankles to the ends of the bars so that he was standing in a spread-eagled position. 'You look too comfortable there,' she told him. 'I need to put that right.' She attached clover clamps to his nipples and a ball stretcher to his scrotum, causing him to cry out in pain.

'We mustn't have you making a noise like that,' Claudia said and promptly gagged Peter with a ball gag. 'Also, slave,' she added as she picked up a blindfold, 'I think I'll keep you in the dark from now on.' She carefully adjusted the blindfold over Peter's eyes to make sure that he could not see even the tiniest amount of light.

'Let's make some use of this riding crop,' she said as she picked up the implement. 'That hard cock looks too inviting to resist.' Using the leather tip of the crop, Claudia beat his penis, concentrating her attentions particularly on its swollen head. The pain was bearable at first, her beating initially quite restrained, but the severity of her blows rapidly escalated. The resultant pain was starting to become unendurable when, all of a sudden, she stopped.

'I'm going to leave you now,' Claudia said. 'If you need anything, just shout. Oh, you can't, of course, can you,' she added mockingly. 'Bye now.'

And with that she was gone, the door to the dungeon crashing shut behind her. Peter was left in the darkness for a long time – how long he had no idea but it seemed like an eternity – a blissful eternity. The silence was as complete as the darkness before his eyes, which he found that he didn't mind at all, quite the contrary. What had happened to that fear of the dark of his that had returned with such a vengeance when he'd first discovered that he was incarcerated and in chains? What had become of his fear of pain? Both seemed to have been subsumed into an overwhelming sensation of sexual arousal … and peace. It was really strange, surreal, almost *spiritual*.

For what length of time so far Claudia had left him alone attached to the spreader bars Peter had no way of knowing. However he did know that the pain from the nipple clamps and the ball stretcher was starting to become intense. Trying his best to ignore it, he drifted into an endorphin-induced trance. This was broken by the sound of the dungeon door banging open as Claudia returned.

'There you are, slave,' she mocked. 'Still hanging around, I see!'

Claudia released Peter from the spreader bars but left his blindfold, gag, nipple clamps and ball stretcher in place. She led him carefully by the arm to the other side of the dungeon, telling him she was going to strap him to the wall-mounted cross. She stood him with his face to the St. Andrews cross and strapped his wrists and ankles to the equipment.

'Let's warm your arse up,' Claudia announced next. She did this very effectively indeed, vigorously spanking Peter's rear with her hand, and then a paddle – a wooden one, she told him – and then switching to a leather strap. She beat him at length and with ever-increasing ferocity, making him jump and shudder constantly in his bonds. And then she stopped suddenly.

'Your arse is extremely red now, slave,' she said. 'Is it very sore?' Peter nodded his head in response. Sore wasn't the word. Christ, it hurt.

'What a shame,' Claudia said in a tone of patently bogus concern. 'In that case, you won't appreciate this.' She rubbed a spiked leather mitt over his punished rear and he squirmed in pain. 'And if you didn't appreciate that,' she continued, 'you certainly won't like this.' The feel of an even more painful instrument of correction – a multi-spiked stimulator – replaced the spiked mitt.

When Peter began to think he could take no more of this latest cruel punishment, Claudia stopped and released his arms and legs. But this was only so that she could turn him around and re-attach him to the cross.

'I see that your cock is still nice and hard, slave,' she told him. And it was – very hard; that was the inexplicable thing to Peter. Claudia went on, 'It's almost begging to be tortured some more.' The dominatrix returned to using the riding crop. She beat the head of Peter's shaft with the leather tip of the crop with ever increasing vigour until the pain was extreme, until he was certain that he could stand no more. And then, mercifully, she stopped.

Claudia removed his ball stretcher but not the nipple clamps nor the blindfold and gag. She detached Peter from the cross and, taking him by one of his trembling hands, walked him over to the leather-covered bondage table.

'Stand still,' she demanded. 'I'm now going to attach six red pegs to your scrotum.'

That's going to hurt like fuck, Peter thought. He wasn't wrong. The pain was excruciating.

'Now I want you to lie on the bondage table on your front with your arms and legs outstretched and spread wide,' Claudia said. She helped him to get onto the table and when he was in position she locked the chained manacles to his wrists and ankles. Peter then heard a winching sound and felt the four slack chains attached to his manacles tighten until he was held firmly in place in a spread eagled position.

'Your arse is as red as can be,' she told him. 'It sets off

those pegs attached to your scrotum very nicely. But I can do better than that. I want to see some painful welts on your body and I've got just the whips to do it.' Claudia started by flaying Peter's back and rear with a cat-o'-nine tails, each of her blows a sharp explosion of pain that made him buck hopelessly against his bonds. She followed this with a braided leather flogger that stung even more painfully than the cat. Peter was in a state of agony now that was so acute that it had transformed itself into a kind of ecstasy, his system by this stage thoroughly awash with endorphins.

Next he heard the sound of a match being struck followed by the distinctive smell of burning wax. 'It's time for some wax torture,' Claudia said. 'I'm now holding six lighted black candles. Guess what I'm about to do with them...'

The sharp stinging pain that Peter experienced when the hot wax was splattered onto his by now severely punished back and rear was acute. His body jerked sharply in his bonds in reaction to the intense pain ... which was also, mystifyingly, intense pleasure as well. How could that be, though?

'What a lovely inviting anus you have, slave,' Claudia said next. 'It's all open and pulsing there just begging to be entered again. Now where's my favourite lube? Ah, there it is, right next to that impressively large black butt plug.'

Peter tried to relax his sphincter as he waited for what he knew must be coming next. He felt Claudia rub the head of the big anal plug gently against the tight ring of muscle. Then she eased it further in until he could feel it inside him, and it fucking *hurt,* yet it was wonderful too. She wriggled it gently and a pulse of desire spread through him. Peter began to tighten and relax his anus to accommodate the large intruder. The butt plug was stretching him now, filling him. It was ecstatically painful.

'What a pretty sight you make, slave,' said Claudia, 'squirming there, your back and rear all red and covered in welts set off nicely by black candle wax, your scrotum a mass of red pegs, and your anus throbbing invitingly round that big black butt plug. You're a vision in black and red and I'm going to sit and enjoy the view in a moment, but first ...'

Peter heard the buzzing sound of what he assumed to be a vibrator. His assumption was confirmed when Claudia told him that was what it was. She held it to the base of the butt plug, causing it to vibrate in his anus excitingly. His sphincter contracted suddenly and he felt a pulsing throb deep in his anus and the sensation of his cock spurting pre-cum.

Claudia said, 'Now, I shall take a seat on my throne and just admire the view.' Peter heard her pleasuring herself – the noise of the vibrator again, the sounds of her increasingly heavy breathing and her moans of delight as she brought herself to a noisy climax.

'Thank you, slave,' Claudia purred, switching off the vibrator. 'You've just given me a wonderful orgasm and you didn't even have to move a muscle – well, apart from all that squirming around you were doing. I don't know,' she added in a tone of phony bewilderment, 'anyone would think you were in *pain* or something.'

'Anyway, let's turn you over now,' she continued, unlocking and releasing the four chained manacles that held his wrists and ankles. 'We'll give that punished rear of yours a break – for a bit anyhow – although we'll leave the butt plug in place. I can see you're enjoying it.' Peter turned onto his back and, on Claudia's instruction, adopted a spread-eagled position so that she could manacle his wrists and ankles again.

'Mmmm, what a gorgeous, hard cock and, my word, what a lot of pre-cum,' Claudia remarked appreciatively, standing by the side of the bondage table. 'But those pegs on your scrotum must be very painful by now, would I be right?' Peter nodded his blindfolded head in agreement, mumbling something incomprehensible into his ball gag that was meant to be, 'Yes, Mistress.'

'I see that you are agreeing with me that the pegs are very painful,' Claudia said. 'So, you wouldn't want me doing this.' She flicked the pegs several times, causing him to shudder with pain. 'Likewise, those nipple clamps,' she continued. 'You've had them on an *awfully* long time. When I remove them, I'm afraid it's going to hurt like hell.' With that, she removed them – the pain was extreme, two lightening flashes of agony, as the blood rushed to the formerly constricted flesh of his nipples.

'It would, therefore be exceptionally cruel of me, would it not,' Claudia went on ominously, 'to squeeze those punished nipples of yours really, *really* hard – So, I'll do just that.' The ball gag stifled Peter's agonized cries as he wrestled desperately with sharp spasms of burning pain that felt perversely almost, what was the word, *orgasmic*; it was incredible.

'You know, slave,' Claudia said blandly, 'I'm sure you were trying to tell me something there but your ball gag prevented you. I think I'd better remove it.'

'That was definitely worth doing,' she commented after she had unbuckled the gag. 'I can see your delightfully sensuous mouth again, which I'm now going to kiss, I can't resist it.' He parted his lips to meet her kiss. Her lips were warm. She kissed him violently,

149

forcing her wet tongue over his.

When she finally removed her lips from his own, all Peter could say was, 'Thank you very much indeed, Mistress.'

'What for, slave, the kiss?'

'For that and for everything, Mistress,' Peter said with great feeling. 'Thank you for … for showing me who I really am, forcing me to accept it.'

Claudia unlocked his chained manacles, freeing him from the bondage table but left him blindfolded and his scrotum pegged, his anus plugged.

'Kneel down, slave,' she ordered, holding onto his shoulders. 'Worship my breasts and tell me again how grateful you are to me for bringing you a measure of self-awareness at long last.'

'I'm so very grateful, Mistress,' Peter said, kissing and licking her beautiful breasts, 'just as grateful as I can be.'

'I'm glad to hear you say it,' Claudia said. 'Now let's throw some further light on the situation.' She started to remove his blindfold. 'You've been in the dark long enough.'

At last Peter could see. And what he could see as he looked up was Claudia standing naked above him, her dark eyes aglow, their pupils wide. She looked like a Goddess to him at that moment, *was* a Goddess.

'I have one last instruction for you on this occasion,' Claudia stated, gesturing to him that he should get up from his knees. 'I want you to masturbate as hard as you can and bring yourself off while I give you a final beating. I'm going to use this rattan cane and I will be beating your arse extra hard with it. When I get to the tenth stripe you are to climax. But, be clear, you can *only* do that when I give the word. Understood?'

'Yes, Mistress,' Peter replied, panting. Then he took

his erection into his hand and closed his fingers around it. He began masturbating energetically, the six red pegs that were still attached to his scrotum clattering together in cacophonous rhythm with his feverish strokes. The butt plug was still stretching his anus beautifully, adding still further to his intense sexual excitement.

'That's right, pull on your cock really hard,' Claudia said to him, before adding, 'Tell me, my oh so grateful slave, how close do you feel you are to coming?'

'Incredibly close, Mistress,' Peter replied desperately as he felt his cock flex and pulse against his pounding fist, felt his anus spasm around the giant butt plug.

'You know you mustn't climax until I say so?' Claudia said.

'Yes, Mistress,' Peter gasped.

'Then it's fair to say, isn't it, that'

Swish!

'you'

Swish!

'wouldn't'

Swish!

'appreciate'

Swish!

'me'

Swish!

'dragging'

Swish!

'this'

Swish!

'out,'

Swish!

'would'

Swish!

'you?'

Swish!

'No, Mistress,' Peter replied frantically, his backside feeling as if it was on fire and his cock about to explode at any moment.

'Ten stripes of the cane duly delivered to my grateful slave,' Claudia announced, speaking with slow deliberation so as to prolong his agony for as long as she possibly could. 'That means we have now arrived at that time, slave, when you are permitted to climax.'

And he did, God how he did. He was so grateful he just gushed and gushed and gushed.

Chapter Twenty-two

SPOOL FORWARD A DAY and Claudia was back in the dungeon with Peter again and was as naked as he was once more. Peter was standing before her, his cock rigidly erect. 'Let me ask you a few questions before I start disciplining you again,' Claudia said and stepped closer, her proximity making his erection twitch. 'I want to establish precisely where I am with you now.'

'Yes, Mistress.'

'First,' she said. 'Are you afraid of the dark?'

'I used to be, Mistress,' Peter said. 'But I'm not any more.'

'Do you like to be in control sexually, would you say?'

'I used to think so, Mistress,' he replied. 'But I don't think I ever did really. I was just kidding myself.'

'Did you like it when I fucked your virgin arsehole?'

'Yes, Mistress.' He felt his anal sphincter tighten a little as the thrilling recollection of his deflowering flashed back into his mind once more.

'Did you like it when I worked that great big butt plug up your arse?'

'Yes, Mistress.'

'Do you like to be disciplined?' Claudia said. 'Do you accept that you are a sexual masochist?'

'Yes, Mistress,' he said. 'I accept it completely.'

'Do you like it when I dominate you, tell you exactly

what to do?'

'Yes, Mistress.' Peter said quietly. Like when she'd told him to climax when she was sodomizing him and he had done, instantly. Like afterwards when she'd told him to lick up and swallow the copious amounts of cum he'd ejaculated, and he had, every single drop. Like when she'd told him to climax after the tenth strike of the rattan cane and he had done, exactly at the point she'd told him to. 'I do like it when you dominate me.'

Claudia saw his face redden. He didn't just like it, she thought, he loved it, *adored* it: being powerless and under her complete control.

'Would you like Christine to dominate you if she was here?'

'Yes, Mistress,' Peter said, breathing heavily. His shaft was steely-hard now.

'Would you like her to *discipline* you?'

He gave a hesitant look. 'Yes, Mistress,' he said in a whisper.

'Speak up.'

'Yes, Mistress.' His lips trembled and there was a break in his voice as he spoke. 'I think I've always wanted that deep down.'

Claudia noticed the tension leave his face as soon as he'd made his admission, as if a huge burden had been lifted from his mind.

'Would you like Christine to discipline you *severely*?'

'Yes, Mistress,' he gulped.

'Christine isn't here, is she,' Claudia said, giving him a radar-like gaze. 'Do you want me to discipline you instead? Do you want me to discipline you *severely*?'

'Yes, Mistress,' he replied, his eyes shining. 'I want that very much.'

'Then it shall be so,' she said. 'I can guarantee that you

will find what I do to you very painful indeed – but even more exciting.'

'… Mistress …' Peter was barely able to utter. Already the anticipation and the shame and the fear were combining in a heady cocktail, making his breath quicken and his erection throb.

'Finally, I want to make it clear that you are not permitted to climax unless I give you permission. Do you understand?'

'Yes, Mistress.'

'Good. Now go over there.' Claudia motioned in the direction of the wooden spreader bar attached to chains hanging from the dark ceiling.

'Yes, Mistress,' Peter said and moved into position.

'Raise your arms above your head,' she demanded before placing his wrists in the leather manacles on either end of the spreader bar and buckling them tightly.

Next Claudia moved behind Peter and told him to bend forward as far as his bonds would allow. 'Time for a very special spanking,' she said, slipping on a spiked leather glove. Peter saw this out of the corner of his eye and waited in trepidation for his 'very special' spanking to start. And waited and waited … and waited some more, his breathing quickening all the time. But Claudia took her own good time as she gazed approvingly at his curved cheeks, all bare and vulnerable.

She began to stroke his rear tantalizingly – and frighteningly – with her spike-gloved hand, teasing and tormenting him. She carried on doing this unmercifully, before at last raising her hand high and bringing it down with a smack so hard and sharply painful that it made Peter squeal. She raised it again and brought it down a second time as swiftly and as hard as the first time and then kept on spanking him. Each of her smacks with that spiked glove brought sharp stabs of fire that steadily accumulated, becoming an angry red heat that spread through his backside and leaked through his body, linking with the pulsing stiffness of his erection.

Next Claudia took off the spiked glove and switched to disciplining Peter with a heavy leather flogger. It hurt even more, that flogger, each strike a white flash of pure pain that caused Peter to jump and shudder and cry out in his bonds as she used the cruel implement on his already punished rear. The flogger landed on each occasion with a sharp resonating sound and he felt its harsh sting time and time again as she swung it through the air faster and faster.

The cheeks of Peter's backside began to smart with a fire that made him jump and tense and squirm against his restraints as the full effect of the flogging spread through his body. By the time she stopped, his rear was heavily marked with vivid stripes and he was in excruciating pain that also perversely felt like the most exquisite pleasure.

Claudia then shifted position, standing in front of Peter, and also changed disciplinary implements, picking up a small leather whip. She told him to stop bending forward and to stand upright instead. She began to whip his chest, every blow stinging and sharp, before switching to his genitals, concentrating her blows on his helplessly exposed cockhead. This caused Peter to cry out in pain over and over, his agonized cries echoing round the dungeon. But the pain, intense as it was, did nothing to diminish his sexual excitement. In fact it had the very opposite effect. He felt on fire with lust.

Then Claudia moved behind Peter again, told him to bend forward as before, and reverted to the heavy leather flogger. She flogged his backside once more, every skilfully aimed lash striking his rear in a regular rhythm and each time bringing that white flash of sensation again. His flesh quivered constantly as she increased the momentum of the beating, showering him with blows. She did not stop until his naked body was covered in lacerations and the pain, correction, the *pleasure-pain* that soared through him had become well nigh overwhelming.

'Now for a change of pace,' Claudia told Peter, who couldn't stop himself from trembling. She detached him from the wooden spreader bar, motioning him to get on to his knees. 'I want you to lick my arsehole, like a good slave,' Claudia ordered, turning around and bending forward slightly. Peter complied straight away *like a good slave*, planting a kiss between the cheeks of her backside, touching his lips to her anus. He pushed his tongue into her, pushing against the rim of muscles and going into her body. He darted his tongue as far up her anus as it would go, probing and prodding hard into her hole.

Claudia squeezed her anal muscles around Peter's tongue and at the same time brought her fingers to her sex, which was gleaming with silver wetness. She stroked her clit before pressing two fingers directly into her pussy, sliding between the tumescent labia and penetrating hard and fast.

Peter's cock swelled even further and a stream of pre-cum began to seep from its slit as he listened to the wet sound of Claudia's agile fingers working in and out of her sex. He brought his hands up to spread her buttocks further so that his busy tongue could cut a path even deeper inside her. Peter licked Claudia's anus ever more vigorously *like a good slave*, his pace growing faster in time with her masturbating fingers, until a shuddering moan escaped her and she climaxed again.

Claudia allowed herself a few moments to compose herself, and then led Peter over to the horizontal torture chair. She buckled his wrists behind his head, his knees right up and his legs wide apart.

'Very nice,' Claudia purred, admiring Peter's hard shaft, which was jutting into the air, and his exposed anus which was pulsating.

'Thank you, Mistress,' he gasped.

Claudia harnessed on the same strap-on dildo with which she'd sodomized Peter before, and again coated it liberally with lubricant. She let him watch her doing this before she wrapped a black leather blindfold round his face, buckling it tight.

'Do you know what I want from you now, slave?' she said, whispering hotly in his ear.

'No, Mistress.'

'I want you to be Mistress Claudia's bitch again.'

She eased the dildo into Peter's anus and he let out a groan, his cock spitting out a throb of pre-cum as his sphincter tightened and relaxed around the cock-shaped intruder. Claudia began to fuck him hard and, as she built up ever greater momentum, also started pulling on his shaft again, her hand moving with a swift, urgent rhythm.

As she continued to bugger Peter furiously she worked her hand up and down his hard cock with equal fervour. Her fingers became increasingly smeared with pre-cum until they were covered with copious amounts of the fluid. Peter felt on the verge of climaxing. But he mustn't, he mustn't. *He must be a good bitch, a good slave.* Then Claudia stopped both buggering and masturbating him – and not a moment too soon as far as he was concerned.

'Lick my fingers clean,' she told him, pressing them to his lips. Peter opened his mouth and closed his lips around Claudia's fingers, sucking feverishly while desperately willing his impending orgasm to abate. And he succeeded ... just.

Claudia removed the strap-on dildo from his open anal hole and took off the harness. She took hold of the small whip again and began to strike him furiously between the legs, aiming her blows first at the insides of his thighs and between the anus, and then at his genitals, concentrating on his now painfully engorged cock. Each blow to his aching shaft made Peter shiver with pain and desire. His whole body now ached with extreme pain that burned like a fire into his flesh and yet he'd never known such sexual excitement in his entire life.

Being blindfolded, not able to see even the tiniest sliver of light, seemed to make the experience more intense, more delirious somehow. It meant that he was even more at the mercy of Mistress Claudia, the magnificent cruel dominatrix who was playing his body like a Stradivarius. A swelling sensation of pre-orgasmic pleasure flooded through him. But Peter did resist it, he really did, as he was all too aware that he must not climax until she gave him her permission.

So, what did Claudia, this paragon of dominance and depravity, do to 'help' Peter? She started to masturbate him again, that's what she did, her hand moving up and down the length of his stiffness quicker and quicker. Jesus, I hope she stops soon, thought Peter frantically, getting closer and closer to boiling point. Every nerve in his body told him he was going to ejaculate at any moment, despite the fact that he was doing his very utmost, straining every sinew, to hold himself in check. Then she stopped, praise the Lord, then she stopped … But only because she had an even more excruciating torment in mind for him.

Claudia leant forward so that she could suck Peter's cock, rounding her lips and closing them around his hardness, taking it into her mouth, pressing against the wet head of his shaft with her tongue. Her lips kissed and rubbed against it so that it strained against her mouth. She positioned herself further forward so that she could pull more of his length into her mouth. The up-and-down movement of her head went ever faster as she sucked his cock harder and harder.

Peter writhed in his bonds with agony and sensation, ached with pain and lust. His nerves were on fire, the heat of desire swept through his body, and blood coursed in his aching cock as it pulsed with the tremor of the gigantic orgasm he was trying so desperately to hold at bay.

Claudia must surely give permission for him to come any moment now, Peter told himself desperately. He must hold out until then, he must hold out, he must … but he couldn't any more, couldn't hold out any longer against this most relentless, most voracious dominatrix. Try as he might, Peter simply couldn't hold on to his ever-mounting erotic rise even a second longer, it had become volcanic, and he climaxed convulsively. Arching up and writhing helplessly in his bondage, he pumped out great surging waves of cum into Claudia's hot wet mouth.

Chapter Twenty-three

CLAUDIA MOVED HER LIPS from Peter's cock and he was conscious of her levering herself upright again. Peter thought that she'd be bound to understand that he'd done his absolute level best not to climax, given it everything he'd got. But as soon as she unbuckled and removed his blindfold and he could see the expression on her face he realised he couldn't have been more wrong. Claudia's face was now so sharp and vicious in appearance that it caused fear to cook inside him. She spat his ejaculate into her right hand.

'You have disobeyed my direct instruction to you, which was *not* to climax unless I gave my consent,' Claudia said angrily, her dark eyes blazing. 'That can't be tolerated.' With that, she hauled back her cum-filled hand and slammed it hard against Peter's face. He couldn't prevent himself from letting out a cry at the hot slash of pain that accompanied her blow and the impact immediately painted wet red images of her fingers on his cheek. Before he could recover from the shock of the whiplash impact of that hard blow against his cheek, she slapped him just as hard again.

'I'm sorry, Mistress,' Peter said, his face smarting painfully. 'I'm really sorry. I did my very best, I honestly did. You see, I …'

'An apology won't cut it with me, you miserable cunt,'

Claudia interrupted harshly, anger blazing even more furiously in her eyes. 'You have pissed me off, pissed me off mightily.'

'I don't know what else to say, Mistress.' Peter could feel beads of perspiration on his upper lip. Claudia was being so unfair, so incredibly unfair, but where in God's name was she going with this?

There was a long silence, heavy with the most unbearable tension.

Then Claudia snorted in disgust. 'You're a real piece of work, Peter, you know that?' she said, grabbing him by the hair and twisting his head back. 'Remind me what I told you would happen if you ever disobeyed me.'

'You said that Christine would be ki–' His tongue just froze. He couldn't get the word out and he felt his stomach turn.

'Killed, that's right,' Claudia said, finishing Peter's sentence for him and fixing him with a harsh, psychotic gaze. 'Well, that's what's going to happen now.'

Peter gasped in horror. 'You can't be serious,' he said, his mind reeling.

'Oh can't I?' she said, looking menacingly into his horrified face, her eyes boring into his like a laser beam.

Peter could feel a colossal sense of panic welling up within him, mingling with utter terror. 'No, Mistress, please, I beg of you,' he cried. 'This isn't right, isn't right at all.' Tears began to sting at his eyes, and sobs to choke his words.

'It isn't right, you say,' Claudia snapped. 'No, it isn't at all right that you should have gambled with Christine's life for the sake of your own sexual gratification.'

'It wasn't like that, Mistress,' Peter said, choking back on the sobs that were now filling his chest. 'It wasn't like that at all.'

'It was *exactly* like that.' Claudia looked at him with disdain. 'I don't believe you gave your wife a moment's thought, not one single moment, when you were trying to prevent yourself from coming. I'm dead right, aren't I?'

'I admit it, Mistress. But ...'

'I rest my case,' Claudia rasped. 'Now the price must be paid.'

'No, Mistress, no ...' Sobs wracked Peter's body, coming from deep within him. 'Please forgive me.'

But Claudia kept the same unforgiving look on her face. 'Stop your snivelling!' she ordered and he swallowed back another sob, coughing.

'Can I say just one thing, Mistress?'

'What's that, motherfucker?'

'Kill me, if you're going to kill anyone,' he said, his voice pleading. 'I'm the guilty one. But don't kill Christine, I beg you.'

'You'd like that, wouldn't you?' Claudia said contemptuously. 'You'd like to end it all.'

'No, I wouldn't, Mistress,' Peter said. His hands were trembling without control in their bonds. 'I had been feeling like that recently, I admit. I'd kind of boxed myself into a corner and couldn't see any other way out. Anyway the thing is I don't feel like that at all any more. I want to live, I want to live so very much. But if you kill Christine my life won't be worth living. She is the whole world to me.'

'You are asking me to kill you?'

'Yes, Mistress.' His heart was beating wildly.

'Then I shall,' Claudia said. She stared at Peter for a long moment with such a pitiless look on her face that it made his blood run cold. Then she turned and walked briskly out of the dungeon, zapping the lights off as she went. The door shut decisively behind her and then he heard her lock it.

Peter lay strapped to the horizontal torture chair in total darkness. He bit down on his lower lip to keep the tears at bay, to stop them from capturing his whole body.

'But I don't want to die any more,' he said pathetically into the silence of the dark room, his body quaking in its bondage. 'I want to be with Christine, that's all I want.'

And then the tears and sobs returned with their fullest force. They wracked Peter's whole being, flooding him with misery, as he surrendered to the utter meaninglessness of his life. He let every one of his shortcomings find expression in sob after wracking sob. He cried and cried and cried until, exhausted, he finally fell quiet.

All was silence at last in that dark dungeon. But it was the awful deathly silence of despair. It surrounded Peter, filling the air around him. He knew that he was very close to the destination to which like a blind fool he'd been willing himself of late: his own death. The desperate irony of his situation, he realised, the appalling tragedy of it, was that he was now indeed a changed man. That was the most gut-wrenching part of it. He'd become the man he'd always been deep down; become his true self. And it was too late, wasn't it, too fucking late.

Chapter Twenty-four

PETER LAY IN THE blackness, strapped to the horizontal torture chair. He listened to the pounding in his chest as the time he dreaded to the very depth of his being drew inexorably closer. His body tensed in terror and broke instantly into a cold, heavy sweat when he heard the door to the dungeon being unlocked. He could feel the sweat drenching him, feel the tooth-chattering chill of it penetrate his whole body. Here it comes, Peter thought with a petrified shiver, here *she* comes. The door was opened, the lights flicked on and there indeed was she. There was Claudia in all her nakedness, her presence filling the room.

She closed the door once more and he watched her body as she strode towards him, her breasts lightly quivering, her thighs rubbing gently together. She looked so radiantly, ravishingly beautiful, Peter thought; had such an incredibly charismatic personality, this domme of all dommes, this woman he'd come to think of as nothing less than a Goddess. And yet she was clearly deranged beyond all reason, pathologically mad.

But hope springs eternal even in the direst, the most desperate of circumstances and Peter hoped against hope that, demented as she undoubtedly was, Claudia would somehow have changed her mind. Time stood still for one agonizing moment before he found the courage to look directly at her face and the cruel truth became clear to him straight away. For it only took one look at Claudia's stony expression for Peter to know she hadn't changed her mind at all. He experienced a sudden ache in his chest as if his life was being squeezed from him right there and then.

Peter felt frightened beyond words as Claudia reached toward him and he flinched at her touch. She began to unbuckle the leather straps that were securing him to the torture chair.

She said nothing as she continued with her task, only breaking her silence when she'd released all the straps. 'It is time,' she said, her voice cool and remote.

'Please, Mistress,' he said piteously, his voice cracking as he spoke. 'Please don't do this dreadful thing. Please change your mind.'

'Nothing doing,' Claudia said, gazing at him with all the warmth of a rattlesnake.

'But, please …'

'I said nothing doing,' she repeated in a tone of irritation, her lip curling. 'Now, go and sit on the edge of the bondage table without delay.'

Peter obeyed her instantly. Surely she won't go through with it, he shrieked to himself, surely she won't. He could feel his heart pounding hard against the inside of his chest as if it was fighting for all it was worth to be free.

'Don't worry,' Claudia said, standing before him and holding her arms around herself. 'It won't hurt a bit.'

Don't worry, she says! Jesus Christ, she's about to kill me! 'But I don't want to die,' Peter cried in desperation, shaking his head rapidly. 'I want so much to live.'

Claudia did not respond to this entreaty in words but her face said it all: she didn't give a shit what he did or didn't want.

'Oh please, please have mercy on me, Mistress,' Peter wailed in anguish. 'I'll do anything you demand but please don't kill me.'

'Shut up!' Claudia ordered angrily. 'You are trying my patience. Just keep quiet and prepare to meet your maker. Unless you've changed your mind, of course,' she added with an unpleasant smirk, 'and you want Christine to die in your place.'

'No, Mistress,' Peter said, his voice suddenly subdued. 'I definitely don't want that.'

'Good, we're all settled then,' Claudia said briskly. 'On to the last stage,' she added and began to stride away from him in the direction of the dungeon door.

Peter looked down and wept in silence, his shoulders shaking. He listened to the little slapping sounds Claudia's bare feet made against the shining black marble floor as she made her way to the dungeon door. He heard her open the door, then in what seemed like no time at all she was standing over him again with three red pills in one hand and a glass of water in the other.

'Swallow the pills,' she said, holding them out to him along with the water. 'Do it quickly, get it over with.'

Peter did as she had told him, placing all three of the red pills on his tongue at the same time and then washing them down with the water in one gulp.

'It's done,' Claudia said quietly, taking the glass from his hand and putting it on the floor by the side of the wall.

Peter hunched forward, clasped his arms between his thighs and began sobbing bitter tears, he couldn't stop. The tears dropped from his closed eyes, falling to the dungeon floor like rain.

'Lie down on the bondage table now, Peter,' Claudia said when he seemed all cried-out. He nodded miserably and let out a short whimper as he lay down on his back.

'Please don't harm Christine, Mistress,' he said, his voice plaintive, beseeching. 'I beg you, please don't harm her.'

'Look at me, Peter,' Claudia said, sitting down by his side. 'You have my word that no harm will come to her.'

'Thank you, Mistress,' he said softly. 'Thank you for that.'

'And no harm will come to you either,' she said and her dark eyes remained fixed on him.

'But I don't understand,' Peter said, or rather tried to say. His tongue was suddenly so heavy that it got in the way of the words.

'You're not going to die,' Claudia said, at least that's what Peter thought he heard her say but her voice sounded off in the distance somewhere. He felt incredibly drowsy and his eyes were closing. He had to stay awake, though, had to. This couldn't be more important and there was something he felt it was important, no *essential* that he make clear.

'I worship Christine,' he said, forcing his eyes open and the words through his throat with a huge effort. 'I want to live for her, dedicate myself to her.' He tried to sit up but found that he could barely move at all.

'I know you do,' Claudia said with a wry half smile. 'That's what this whole elaborate charade has been getting to.' She leaned forward and placed a hand gently on his arm. 'Christine is your true Mistress. I'm sure you see that now.'

Peter did too, saw it with the utmost clarity, and wanted to say so but the words wouldn't come and his eyes rolled back once more. He forced them open again and tried to speak but the words became jumbled on the way out of his mouth.

He made a monumental effort and tried yet again, only

to find that his tongue had become way too heavy for his mouth and he was only able to manage a mumbled exhalation, a whispered sigh that meant nothing.

All he could do now was to try as hard as he could to keep his eyes open and say her name inside his head: Christine. Christine. Christine. Christine. Chris … And then that was it. His eyes closed shut for the last time and unconsciousness rolled over him like a black shroud.

Peter's eyes remained closed, his breathing barely audible, almost not there at all. But he was slowly beginning to wake up from his heavily sedated slumber and he felt as if a very long time indeed had passed in that deep dead sleep. Peter drifted half asleep again, his foggy memory of what had happened to him just beyond reach. He couldn't remember anything precisely because he wasn't yet with it but he knew what he could feel, which was a profound sensation of well-being and tranquillity …

And it showed on his face. Peter looked so tranquil, Christine thought as she snuggled her naked body against his in their bed, in the grey light of dawn. She stroked a loose shock of his hair that was hanging boyishly on his forehead. In the past few years Peter had never looked truly at peace even in sleep. Now all the tension, all the anxiety had left his face and he looked utterly content, his expression so much softer than she'd ever seen it before. What a massive relief it was to have him back safe in her arms. Oh thank you, thank you, Claudia, Christine sang inside. Thank you so very much for coming into my life at exactly the right time, that Peter might be saved, that he might be reborn.

Christine reached to grasp her husband's hand and this stirred him to wakefulness at last. 'Hello, Peter,' she said … and it was such a joy for him to hear her voice that his heart felt like bursting.

Hello, Mistress, he thought.

'Hello, Mistress,' he said, blinking open his eyes and turning his face to look into hers. 'Hello, my beloved Mistress.'

Chapter Twenty-five

IT WAS THE MOST idyllic of days, full of sparkling sunlight and warm confiding breezes. The sky was cloudless and flowers filled the air with their intoxicating fragrance. Christine lounged naked by the villa's swimming pool, its rippled surface reflecting the brilliance of the sun, and gazed idly at Peter splashing about in the water. She sighed as she watched him lever himself athletically out of the end of the pool and walk towards her with an elegant stride, water trickling down his glistening, nude body.

The wonderfully relaxed look on his handsome face, the sparkle in his blue eyes, his lithe and limber physique, his smooth dark skin, the way his big attractively shaped cock and nice firm balls swayed as he walked; he looked absolutely fantastic. Gazing at him made Christine wet between the thighs. She ran a finger briefly and lightly over the smoothness of her mons and continued to admire the view. Her husband looked like a Greek God. Correction, he looked like a Greek *slave*.

'A penny for your thoughts, Mistress,' Peter said as he arrived at her side, picking up a towel.

'I was just thinking how great-looking you are.'

'Not compared to you, I'm not,' he said, beginning to towel himself dry. 'I don't come anywhere close.'

'Disagreeing with your Mistress, huh?' Christine said,

her eyes twinkling. 'I'll have to punish you for that tonight, won't I?'

Peter kept a straight face. 'Yes, Mistress,' he replied. Straight-faced he may have been but Christine noticed his cock start to swell. She stretched out and turned her face upward to the sun, a sensual smile playing across her lips. Christine was proposing to really put Peter through his paces tonight, which would be the last one of their vacation.

And what an amazing, what a *cathartic* vacation it had proved to be. The way it had turned out – all thanks to Christine's chance meeting with the remarkable Claudia – had been life-changing for the couple, life-*saving* in the case of Peter. The 'shock treatment' Claudia had devised for him had indeed achieved the effect she'd said it would. It had killed off once and for all the old unhappy Peter and brought to life the man he'd wanted to be all along deep inside his troubled soul.

Christine had been determined to give Claudia a parting gift, something that would go at least some way to reflect her immense gratitude to her for the miracle she'd worked on Peter. One thing Claudia definitely didn't need as a gift, Christine had reflected sardonically, was acting lessons! From what she'd heard from Peter, Claudia really was the consummate actress she'd claimed all the best dommes to be.

The gift Christine had decided on in the end had been magnificent: a choker of soft black leather and sparkling diamonds. Claudia had been reluctant to accept such a lavish present but Christine wouldn't take no for an answer. But it was far too pricey, Claudia had protested. 'What price a life?' had been Christine's unanswerable reply.

How do you top that? Claudia hadn't even thought

about trying to. Her parting gift to Christine had been a token one: a set of three hand-crafted disciplinary implements. Tokenistic though they were, they nevertheless meant a lot to Christine. She intended to use each of them in turn on Peter tonight as a prelude to doing something else with him, something very special – something they hadn't done even once in three whole years.

The night was calm and quiet, the noise of the waves on the Dauge shoreline tempered and discreet. A warm breeze softly rustled the branches of trees. These tranquil, sensuous sounds reached the ears of Christine and Peter who were in their bedroom but not in their bed. They were both naked, their skin gleaming in the soft light of the bedside lamp. Christine was on her feet and Peter was kneeling submissively before her.

'Stand up,' Christine said and once he'd done so she looked him in the face, her expression stern but her lustrous eyes glowing with desire. Peter gazed back at her with a look that was beyond adoring; it was nothing less than worshipful.

Christine took hold of the first of the three implements of discipline Claudia had given to her, which she proposed to use on Peter tonight. It was a hefty leather paddle.

'Turn and face the bed,' she ordered, gesturing with the paddle. 'Lean over it with your arms in front of you, hands resting on the bed and your back arched.' Peter obeyed and also spread his thighs so that his backside was spread wide. Christine looked at him from behind, the delicious sight of his splayed rear and the straining hollow of his hips. She could see the pink opening of his anus pulsing invitingly and below that his hard throbbing cock, drizzling a rivulet of pre-cum. All *very* arousing.

'I'm going to beat your arse two dozen times with this paddle,' Christine said. 'I want you to count off each strike. Is that clear, slave?'

'Yes, Mistress,' Peter answered through quivering lips.

Christine brought her arm down vigorously. Thwack! That first ferocious blow brought a blast of searing pain that nearly knocked the stuffing out of him. 'One, Mistress,' Peter gasped. Thwack! 'Two, Mistress,' he panted. Thwack! 'Three, Mistress.' Thwack! … And on and relentlessly on. Christine continued using the paddle on Peter's backside, beating him ever harder until by the twenty-fourth and final strike of the paddle he felt as if his rear was ablaze.

'And now the cane,' Christine announced, remaining behind Peter and picking up the thin length of smooth rattan. 'The caning I am about to give you will be particularly severe, understood?'

'Yes, Mistress,' Peter replied. His eyes were starting to brim with tears, pain and fear colliding in his punished body.

Christine bent the cane slightly and gave it a couple of strokes through the air and then Swish! Peter suffered acutely the sharp sting of the first stroke of the cane as she brought it down hard across the punished cheeks of his backside. Swish! The second stroke was even more painful and the third and fourth more painful still. For a long time the bedroom resounded with the swish and crack of rattan against flesh. Christine caned Peter's backside with remorselessly fierce strokes until it was criss-crossed with clear stripes and he was whimpering with pain.

'Now, lie on your back on the bed,' Christine demanded as she put the cane to one side and picked up disciplinary instrument number three. It was a small but vicious flogger made of braided leather. Her eyes shone with a sadistic glow that not only turned Peter on immensely but also really frightened him ... which turned him on even more. 'I am now going to take you to your limit – and beyond,' Christine said. 'The only time you will be allowed to utter a word is to beg for mercy and you *will* beg for mercy, slave, believe me.'

She started to beat Peter's cock with the small braided flogger, at first quite lightly and then with ever increasing ferocity, concentrating her attentions on its bulbous head. His cock was now rock hard and its head a furious purple in colour. On and on Christine thrashed his cock until the pain Peter was experiencing became so excruciating that he reached the end of his tether – he simply couldn't take any more. 'Mercy, Mistress, please, please,' he cried out in desperation.

Christine immediately stopped the beating, for a moment watching in awe as Peter writhed helplessly before her. She knew what a slave he was to her every command now – a deeply thrilling truth.

She put the vicious little flogger down and looked into Peter's glistening blue eyes. 'Fuck me now, slave,' she said, her pulse racing wildly in her breast. She lay down on the bed next to him and opened her legs wide. 'And you'd better fuck me hard.'

Peter plunged straight into her and she felt a shiver run through her whole body. He kissed her at the same time too, with the utmost passion. Christine savoured the slick, demanding feel of Peter's mouth and tongue and the throbbing hardness of his cock between the damp lips of her sex as the couple made love in a fury of unbridled passion.

The strokes of Peter's cock were fast and powerful as

he pounded deep into Christine's dripping wet pussy with a rhythm that made her delirious. She sighed and gasped as the pleasure escalated ever higher. The strokes of his cock became quicker still – frenzied, his balls banging hard against her quivering thighs, which were smeared with love juice.

Christine and Peter's excitement grew and grew in mighty waves until they climaxed together lavishly with a series of great shuddering tremors that seemed as if they would go on for ever. It was the longest, the most ecstatic, the most out-of-control orgasm either of them had ever experienced.

Afterwards the couple lay together panting for a long while and then remained in one another's arms, luxuriating in the afterglow. Christine pulled Peter a little closer to her and stroked his hair. 'How do you feel right now, slave?' she asked.

'Extremely happy, Mistress,' he replied.

'And how do you feel about going home tomorrow?'

'I'm extremely happy about that too, Mistress,' Peter said. 'To be honest, I can't wait.' And he meant what he said, magical though these last few days had been since he'd been reunited with Christine – magical though what they'd just done together had been.

Peter couldn't wait to go home for the simple reason that Christine had told him the type of life he could expect when he got there and he found the prospect of it deeply appealing. She'd said that once they were back in their house he would be her slave behind closed doors – where he'd be kept for most of the time, usually naked.

Christine had said that they would arrange for everything they owned – the house, the cars, whatever – to be signed over to her name alone in order to reinforce their new Mistress/slave relationship. She'd also emphasized that as her slave Peter would be disciplined constantly either in the house or in the dungeon into which she was going to have their basement converted.

Finally Christine had told Peter that she would continue to enjoy erotic encounters with strangers but that these would be entirely on *her* terms from now on, not his. Apart from anything else, he – not she – would be the 'bait' when it came to setting them up. Peter would be fully participating in such encounters too, Christine had stressed. There would be no more masturbating behind a one-way mirror for him. There would be no more one-way mirror, full stop.

Christine had made clear that Peter would have to do everything – *everything* – she told him to do when participating in these erotic encounters. Just think of the possibilities, she'd said. Just imagine all of the depraved and perverted things he would be required to do, all the sexual excesses that would be forced upon him. Peter was a new man now and this was going to be his new life. He couldn't help wondering where it was all going to lead. Thinking about it made him shiver with excitement.

Part Two

A NEW WOMAN

'A man is a poor creature compared to a woman.'

Honoré de Balzac

Chapter Twenty-six

ZAP!, THAT WAS THE name of the nightclub and it had been going strong for an hour or two the night Liz Thomson sashayed through its neon-lit entrance. The flame-haired beauty, a glossy black handbag slung loosely over her bare shoulder, was wearing nothing at all under her figure-hugging short red dress, which was a striking little number. Its cleavage finished barely an inch from her stiff nipples and its hem was not much further away from her shaven sex, leaving her long bare legs on full display from her shapely thighs down to the shiny black stiletto-heeled shoes she had on.

Liz descended the stairs to the club's dance area to find it packed to the rafters. It was heaving with glamorous hedonists moving their bodies sinuously to music that was much too loud for her taste. She could hardly hear herself think. But that was all right, Liz didn't want to think. She didn't want to dance either, come to that. What she wanted to do – and she wanted it badly – was to have sex. That was why she'd come here to this raunchy West London nightclub: to pick up a sexual partner for the night.

She started to scan the big darkened room and spotted a likely candidate almost immediately. He wasn't dancing but was sitting alone at the busy bar, crowded into a barstool. The man was dark-haired and handsome with a fine body, broadish shoulders on a slim frame. He was wearing tight black leather jeans and short boots of the same colour and had on a thin long-sleeved maroon top.

Liz wasted no time. She wedged her body next to his at the bar, lifting her already extremely short dress even further up at the thigh in the process. The deep red of the dress brought out the contrast of the porcelain whiteness of her skin. 'Hi, I'm Liz,' she said, leaning one elegant elbow on the bar's black lacquered surface and looking the man straight in the eyes.

'And I'm Peter,' he replied, directing his seductive, lop-sided grin at Liz.

'What are you drinking?' she said, reaching into her handbag.

'No, please, let me,' he said. 'I was just going to order for myself anyway.'

'But I insist.' Liz said, her green eyes piercing.

'Whatever you say,' Peter replied with a compliant shrug. 'A small scotch on the rocks please.'

Liz ordered the scotch for Peter and a vodka tonic for herself and when the drinks arrived the two of them clinked glasses, ice cubes rattling. They made small talk for a while and sipped at their glasses, which gleamed with rivulets of condensation. The noise from the dance floor was deafening and Liz swivelled on her barstool so as to talk with Peter better. This caused her knee to press against his leather-covered thigh and she felt a distinct frisson of desire, a twinge between her legs. Yes, he'd do very nicely for an uncomplicated roll in the hay tonight, she decided.

Conversation was virtually impossible because of the volume of the music, which seemed to be getting ever louder, and they had to lean very close to each other to have anything approaching a sensible conversation. They soon gave up. It was just too damn noisy. But did it matter? It certainly didn't to Liz. She wasn't here for the conversation after all. Nor was Peter, needless to say. 'Dance?' Liz said, shouting over the din.

'Sure,' Peter replied, his blue eyes gleaming, and he swallowed down the remains of his drink. He and Liz slid off their barstools and on to their feet. They made their way towards the packed dance floor to join the throng. Flashing lights illuminated the dancers as they moved their bodies with abandon to the pounding music that swept in waves through the club.

Liz and Peter began to dance, moving sensuously to the music. Sometimes they were pressed together, their bodies merged, their arms around one another's waists. Other times they pulled apart slightly, their arms out sideways, their hips thrusting to the rhythm of the music.

Not too long after they'd got on to the dance floor the DJ decided on a reduction of decibels and a change of pace. The next track he put on was a slow, sultry number. As they moved among the dancers, Liz allowed herself to press more insistently against Peter, pushing her crotch against his. Liz could feel the sexual tension building in her. Oh yes, this guy Peter would do very nicely indeed. She was seriously in need of a zipless fuck tonight, a steamy one-night stand, and he was definitely the man she wanted to have it with. Peter hit the spot, no doubt about it. He had her clit buzzing as if his cock was already thrusting away inside her.

As they continued to dance their slow sexy dance, Liz began to nuzzle Peter's neck. She also brought her hands down the thin fabric of his maroon top and over his leather-clad rear, pulling him more tightly against her. She could feel his taut abdomen, could feel his thick cock in his skin-tight leather jeans. It made her heart start pumping, made her go wet with desire. She was beginning to feel incredibly turned on.

She wasn't the only one. Peter was all sexed-up too. He was extremely taken by this beautiful young woman who'd just picked him up so boldly, so brazenly – who he'd *let* pick him up. She was the latest of a steady stream of pick-ups over the last six months. They had usually been lone women like her, sometimes couples, the occasional lone man. It all depended on what Christine demanded on the night. Peter never had any say in the matter, which was just the way he liked it. But this one showed distinct signs of being by far the sexiest of the lot.

Peter was seriously aroused by Liz. He was aroused by her oval green eyes that glittered with such seductiveness and by her full sensuous lips. He was aroused by her exquisite bone structure that gave her such a look of sensuality and strength and by the way her hair, which was so dark and red, framed her high-cheek-boned face and fell softly over her bare shoulders. He was aroused by the way her tantalizingly short dress moulded itself to the contours of her body, by her firm, round breasts revealed by its plunging cleavage, by the way her stiff nipples pressed hard against the constricting material of the dress. He was aroused by the curve of her backside, by the enticing length of her legs. He was aroused by the feel of her, the warmth of her body. From looking at her earlier Peter had been almost sure that Liz was wearing nothing underneath that killer red dress. Now that they were dancing so closely together, he was certain of it.

Liz was equally certain that Peter was wearing no underwear underneath his tight jeans. His upward pointing tumescence was delightfully evident beneath the soft leather. Would he make a move on her soon, she wondered. Then she thought, Why wait? And *she* made a move on him. Liz put a hand down to feel the outline of Peter's erection, which was thick and hard beneath his leather jeans. She began smoothing her palm over it, pressing it, teasing it.

'Fuck, you're hot,' Peter said in urgent response to what she was doing, his lips brushing hers as he spoke.

'So are you,' Liz replied. There was an ache between her legs and her pussy felt slippery. She was feeling *so* horny.

Their tongues were touching now, a light stimulation that only made the contrast of the heavy ache in Liz's groin more piercing. She *had* to have sex – rampant sex – with this dishy man and the sooner the better.

I might just as well cut to the chase, Liz thought. 'I want to have sex with you,' she said simply, her mouth still against his, her hand still caressing his leather covered erection.

Peter made no reply but instead brought his mouth fully to hers. They kissed deeply. She let him explore her mouth with his tongue, let him breathe her hot breath. Her heart was beating like crazy with excitement now. She could feel blood singing in her veins and her sex felt wetly aroused by the responsiveness of this handsome stranger's body.

Liz stopped kissing Peter, pulled away from him slightly. 'I said I want to have sex with you,' she repeated. She continued to stroke his hard-on persuasively, her hand slowly moving up and down over the leather that tightly covered it.

Peter still made no reply, just brought his lips to hers once more. They kissed again, even more passionately, and all the time her fingers continued to move slowly against the hardness of his cock.

He was a great kisser, a *superb* kisser. But why hadn't

he said anything in response to what she'd said – twice now, Liz wondered. This was all very straightforward surely. She wanted to have sex with him and he wanted to have sex with her, that was perfectly clear. She was aware of his sexual excitement. She could see it in his glittering blue eyes, in the response of his body and his warm lips on hers. She could feel it as he pressed his hardness against her stroking hand, letting her know just how intensely physical his desire for her was.

But if this handsome stud could wait so could she, Liz thought. Why not draw out the delicious sexual tension a little longer until the inevitable happened and he too said outright what it was that he wanted. Liz carried on kissing him passionately but took her fingers away from his hard-on. She held Peter with both hands and pulled him closer so that she could feel again the leather-clad outline of his backside with her fingers and grind her pulsing sex against his leather covered erection.

That was when Liz felt the tap on her shoulder and turned to see the other woman. 'I see you've met my husband,' the woman said, her voice heavily edged with sarcasm.

Liz groaned inwardly. It would have been as clear as day to the most casual of observers what she and Peter had been up to on that dance floor. This other woman – Peter's *wife* for Christ's sake – even if she'd only just this moment turned up, would have seen all she needed to see to draw the obvious conclusion. She hoped the woman wouldn't make an embarrassing scene. But whether she did or whether she didn't, one thing seemed certain to Liz at that moment. She could wave goodbye to her zipless fuck with Peter.

Chapter Twenty-seven

AFTER HER INITIAL REACTION, which had been a combination of shock, embarrassment and above all acute disappointment, Liz noticed two things more or less simultaneously. The first was that while the woman's tone had been predictably sarcastic when she'd tapped Liz on the shoulder and made her pronouncement, it was not matched by the expression she now saw on her face. That was both composed and perfectly agreeable. The other thing she noticed – and it quite took her breath away – was that the woman was very good-looking. No, scratch that. She was more than very good-looking, much more. She was stunningly beautiful. Liz looked her up and down in amazement.

She wondered why Peter would want to even glance at another woman let alone do what he'd been doing with her on the dance floor when he had a wife who looked as gorgeous as this. Liz thought the dark-haired woman she was looking at was an absolute knock-out: a vision of loveliness with her sculptured cheekbones, her straight nose, and big hypnotic blue-green eyes. There was a hint of darkness in her skin, too, which, along with her wickedly sensuous lips, added to her siren-like attractiveness. The woman had a luscious body as well, sumptuous and well-proportioned. It was displayed to great effect by the diaphanous black mini dress that she was wearing that cupped and undulated across the defined roundness of her magnificent breasts and thighs.

Liz wondered who in their right mind would dream of playing around when he was married to such a glorious-looking creature. Peter must be fucking mad! What had he been thinking in letting things go the way they'd gone on the dance floor with her? Why take such a risk?

'Let's go to the upstairs lounge,' the woman said. 'It's a lot quieter up there.'

How could she decline, Liz thought to herself, and she and Peter duly followed her off the dance floor and up the staircase. Liz noted the way the flimsy black dress rode up over the woman's shapely thighs that quivered and rubbed together provocatively as she strode up the stairs. Was she too going commando tonight, Liz wondered. She was willing to bet she was.

At the top of the stairs, the exit to the club was to the left and the lounge to the right. They progressed towards the lounge, which had dark walls and muted lighting and contained markedly fewer people than the crowded dance area below. When they'd got to the middle of the room the woman turned to Liz and said, 'You obviously find my husband sexually attractive.'

'I do,' Liz replied. 'But under the circumstances ...' Her voice trailed off. It was getting quite late now, a glance at the clock behind the bar confirmed; and she knew that she'd missed out on having sex with Peter or, realistically, anyone else that night. Lightning wasn't going to strike in the same place twice. She'd just have to go home and have a long luxurious wank while she fantasized about Peter ... and his stunning wife. Thinking about it, she couldn't wait. She could feel her sex moisten and pulse all over again.

'I'm Christine,' the woman said, interrupting Liz's

auto-erotic reverie.

'Pleased to meet you, I'm Liz' she replied, immediately berating herself for what she felt was her ridiculously formal response. This stunning Christine woman had just watched her dry-humping her husband on the dance floor and now she, Liz, was talking to her as if they were at a vicarage tea party or something, it was ludicrous. She really should get out of this club pronto, Liz thought. She should make her escape before she embarrassed herself further. 'I have to be going now,' she said.

'Do you really have to go?' Christine asked, looking genuinely disappointed.

'Yes, I've got an early start tomorrow morning,' she lied. 'I need to grab a taxi and get off home now.'

'That's a shame,' Christine said, glancing over at Peter and back at Liz. 'Are you sure we can't persuade you to stay a little longer?'

'No, I really must be going,' she insisted.

'That *is* disappointing,' Christine said, a mysterious smile on her face. Was she making fun of her, Liz wondered. But, no, she didn't think so.

Peter chipped in at this point. 'Are you sure you can't stay a little longer?' he said.

'Yes, are you sure?' Christine added.

Liz couldn't work out what the hell was going on here. Peter wasn't the slightest bit shame-faced in his wife's company and yet surely he should have been under the circumstances. Christine ought to be angry, furious even, at what she'd witnessed on the dance floor but the expression on her face didn't fit with any such emotion.

'I know what we can do,' Christine suggested. 'Let's all three of us go now – back to my place.' *My* place, Liz noticed, not *our* place. What *was* going on here? It was all very curious.

Peter chipped in again. 'Please say you will, Liz,' he pleaded, giving her that seductive crooked smile of his again. 'It isn't far from here.'

Liz found herself floundering in a sea of confusion. She really didn't know what to do. She felt a powerfully strong sexual attraction towards Peter, she couldn't deny that. She remembered how the feel of his leather-covered hard-on had been pure delight under her fingers. One thing should have led to another but instead everything had abruptly stopped. It felt like coitus interruptus. And she badly wanted the coitus.

But what about Peter's wife, the delectable Christine? The situation was weird to say the least, and Liz wasn't at all sure she wanted to get involved in whatever was going on between this highly unusual couple. Her head said, You know where the exit is. Walk away from this bizarre situation right now. But her loins told her something very different.

'Listen, Liz,' Christine said. 'I've got eyes in my head. I could see exactly what you two were doing when I arrived on the dance floor. And I have to say, hand on heart, that I honestly don't mind. More than that, I *approve.*'

'Really?' Liz could hardly believe what she was hearing. It beggared belief.

'Yes, really and I'll prove it,' Christine said. 'Kiss him again.' Not kiss again or let him kiss you again, Liz noticed. Kiss *him* again. Curiouser and curiouser.

So Liz did just that. She reached out, put her arms around Peter's neck and drew him to her body. She kissed him again full on the lips and with great passion. Her tongue slid in his mouth quick and tight. And as she kissed him she clung more closely to his body, feeling the heavy push of his leather-covered hard-on against her abdomen.

When she released Peter, his blue eyes were shining with desire. Behind him, Christine smiled at Liz. 'Back to my place?' she said, raising an enquiring eyebrow.

'Back to your place,' Liz replied, wondering what in God's name she was getting herself into.

Chapter Twenty-eight

WHEN THE THREE OF them had left the nightclub Christine indicated to Liz where her car was parked. It was a smart new silver Daimler, which Liz realised must have cost a bomb. Christine called this expensive vehicle *her* car and not *our* car, Liz noted. A pattern was emerging here but of what precisely, she asked herself bemusedly. Was Peter a kept man of some sort?

The night air was still moist from rain earlier in the evening, the street shining with long red and white reflected lights. Christine strode on ahead towards the vehicle and Peter fell into step beside Liz, taking her arm. 'Confused?' he said.

'You could say that,' Liz replied. 'And not a little uneasy.'

'Uneasy?'

'That's right,' Liz said. 'I don't understand what's going on with you two at all and – I can't help it – that makes me uneasy.'

'Everything will become clear soon,' Peter said, a cryptic reply that did nothing whatsoever to put her mind at rest. In fact it made her even more uneasy.

'I don't want to get hurt by all this,' Liz told him.

'I promise, you won't get hurt,' Peter said. Great, thought, Liz. I've just received a promise from a man I barely know that I won't get hurt by whatever it is I'm getting myself into here. That's OK then, no worries! But something else niggled at the edges of her mind. She thought she'd heard a slight inflection on the word 'you' when he'd given her that undertaking ('*You* won't get hurt'). Or had she imagined it? Yes, that was it, she decided. She'd imagined it.

'You said you've got an early start tomorrow,' Peter said. 'Have you got to go to work?'

'I lied,' admitted Liz, who didn't have any work to go to. Earlier in the year her aunt had died and she'd come into a modest inheritance, which was sufficient for her to live off for some time as long as she was reasonably careful. It had prompted Liz to give up her office job working for an insurance company, which while having the advantage of being only a brief commute from her flat had been mind-numbingly boring.

'So, you don't have to go to work tomorrow,' Peter said.

'No, not tomorrow – not at all actually at present,' Liz replied. 'I used to be a wage slave up to recently. Nowadays I'm nobody's slave.'

'I'll bet you're not,' Peter smiled.

At that point Christine stopped beside the Daimler, unlocked it and got into the driving seat. Peter held the rear door for Liz to get in and then slid on to the seat beside her.

'Why don't you carry on with Peter where you left off on the dance floor,' Christine suggested, twisting round in her seat to address Liz.

'Oh, I don't know …'

'OK, why don't you do what you were doing with him before that,' Christine said. 'Why don't you rub his cock through his leather jeans again?' So she'd seen that as well, Liz thought. She'd seen everything.

193

'Yes, why don't you,' Peter added. He took her hand and placed it on his crotch, smiling encouragingly.

Christine turned towards the road then, switched on the car's ignition and headlights and drove off. Liz sat motionless for a moment and then thought, The hell with it. She began to slide her fingers back and forth across Peter's swollen cock, feeling it flex within the thickness of his tight leather jeans.

'How about Peter doing some work here,' Christine called over her shoulder to Liz. 'Would you like him to finger-fuck you while you rub his hard-on through his leather jeans?'

'Well, yes but …'

'Do it, Peter,' Christine interrupted, and he immediately moved his hand towards Liz's sex.

Liz parted her thighs slightly as his fingers stroked the sensitive lips of her bald pussy, making her moan with desire. She moaned again as he started to finger the wetness that had once again begun to ooze inside her. And all the while she continued to use her hand to squeeze and caress his erection, which strained and throbbed excitingly against the tightness of his leather jeans.

Then Liz noticed that Christine was doing more than driving. She was watching them intermittently but very intently through the rear-view mirror. And that unnerved her. Actually it did more than unnerve her. It was enough to make her stop what she was doing to Peter and for her to make Peter stop what he was doing to her, which she did by pushing his hand away from her wet pussy. The fingers he removed glistened, sticky from masturbating her.

'Don't mind me,' Christine said reassuringly into the mirror, seeing what had happened.

'But I do mind,' Liz said.

'Why?' Christine asked, glancing quickly over her shoulder. 'I don't understand.'

'I guess it's a matter of "do as you would be done by",' Liz said.

'Meaning what exactly?'

'Meaning that if Peter were my husband,' Liz explained, 'I'd do the very opposite to what you're doing. I'd keep him away from other women.'

But she hadn't done that, had she, Liz said to herself as soon as the words had tumbled out of her mouth. She hadn't done that at all. She'd failed *spectacularly* to keep her own dishy husband away from other women.

She'd met him at a nightclub very like *Zap!*, Liz reminded herself, and she'd wanted him on the spot, like it had been with Peter tonight. He'd had sparkling blue eyes like his and thick shiny dark hair like his and a sexy smile like his and had been charming like him. He'd been outstandingly attractive like Peter too, but in a different, a more girly-boyish way. He'd been sharply and darkly pretty, strangely androgynous, an effect that was accentuated by his long-lashed eyes, his full lips and the fact that he wore his naturally wavy hair on the long side. He'd had a soft voice and soft little hands and feet too. By contrast he'd had a big cock – and he'd certainly known how to use it. Anyway, almost girlish though he was in many ways if not in *that* way, the long and short of it was that Liz had found him hugely attractive from the word go. The man – Sam Craven had been his name – had completely bowled her over, though later she didn't understand why. She'd just felt somehow that they were made for each other. Liz had been completely smitten, utterly besotted, had fallen deeply in love with Sam.

Liz's best friend, Judy, had tried to warn her off Sam.

Maybe he was forever overcompensating for being so delicate-looking, Judy had suggested in the slightly annoying 'amateur psychiatrist' mode she sometimes adopted, but whatever the reason might be for his outrageous behaviour the fact of the matter was that everyone knew Sam Craven screwed around like you wouldn't believe. 'His reputation is notorious for seducing women, then dumping them,' Judy had told her. 'The guy will ruin your life. He isn't worth it. You must see that.'

But Liz hadn't seen that because love for her had been blind. She'd been convinced that, while he may have been a compulsive pussy-hound before meeting her it would be different from now on. It had been lust with all those other girls. Sam was in love with her. That had made him a changed man, she'd convinced herself, launching herself wholeheartedly, recklessly even, into the affair. Sam had asked Liz a short time after they'd become lovers if she'd like to marry him and she'd said an immediate and ecstatic yes. The couple had duly wed – a quick Registry Office affair – and had spent an idyllic week on a Greek island where they'd made constant and energetic love, both in the grip of an overwhelming passion.

Then their brief honeymoon had been over and inevitably it had been back to real life – where all too soon, and all too predictably, Judy had said, Sam had reverted to type. 'A leopard doesn't change his spots,' Judy had warned at the outset and she'd been proved right with a vengeance. Sam had started to neglect Liz shamelessly and had embarked on a series of flagrant one-night stands and short-lived affairs. Liz had done her best to hold the marriage together but eventually Sam's unrestrained sexual excesses had become too much for her and she'd thrown him out on his ear one memorable day. She'd contacted her lawyer and started divorce proceedings on the very same day, insisting on reverting to her maiden name that same day too.

Liz had tortured herself with regret for a time after that. Why had she fallen for Sam Craven's oily charms, she'd wondered bitterly. He had never felt anything even approaching love for her. Why hadn't she seen that at the start? Why hadn't she heeded her best friend's dire warnings? Liz avoided Judy now, very rarely saw her. This was because she felt such a damned fool, couldn't face that 'told you so' look in her friend's eyes. Sam had effectively killed her friendship with Judy stone dead. The man was worse than a mere philanderer, much worse. He was a louse, a jerk, a complete fucking bastard. He had made a fool of her, treated her like dirt, made her a laughing stock. Liz hated him with a passion. Hatred is corrosive, though, and she'd felt she should fight it. Get on with your life, she had told herself. Forget that cock-happy son of a bitch.

But that had been over a year ago, the divorce well behind her, and Liz had found that she still couldn't forget and she certainly couldn't forgive. She continued to seethe inside, simmering with rage, festering with fury. She was like a volcano, on the surface calm but with a core of fire waiting to erupt. When these feelings became too powerful she found there was only one thing that would calm them, if only temporarily. That was to go out and take a leaf out of her hated ex-husband's book and fuck herself senseless on a one-night stand. And on that subject …

'… *arrived.*' Liz caught only the tail-end of whatever it was that Christine had just uttered.

'Sorry, Christine,' she said. 'I was miles away there for

197

a moment. What did you just say?'
   'I said that we've arrived.'

Chapter Twenty-nine

CHRISTINE TURNED THE DAIMLER off the road and brought it to a stop for a moment before a set of high wrought-iron security gates. She took a remote control from the glove-compartment and flicked a number into it, which opened the gates. She then swung the Daimler into the private drive beyond, which was lined with high trees and which led to a detached house set well back from view. The house was in darkness apart from a single light that was triggered by the sound of the car and which illuminated the entrance with a soft amber glow. Christine got out of the car and then Peter did likewise. Liz followed. She could feel a combination of tension and sexual excitement start to throb deep inside her.

As soon as they had entered the house, Christine switched on the downstairs lights and she and Peter led Liz into a big elegantly appointed living room. It contained various items of expensive-looking mahogany furniture and a sumptuous black leather couch. Several beautiful landscape paintings adorned its walls. One wall also held a gilt-framed full-length mirror. The room's dark wooden floor was highly polished and largely uncarpeted apart from a number of strategically placed throw mats of vaguely oriental design.

'Where were we, Liz?' Christine asked, a sardonic smile playing about her lips. 'Oh yes, you were rubbing

Peter's hard-on through his tight leather jeans and he was finger-fucking you ... until you came over all angst ridden and distracted, that is.'

'Sorry about that,' Liz said.

'No problem,' Christine replied. 'Would you like a drink?' she added, gesturing towards a well-stocked drinks cabinet.

'No thanks,' Liz said. 'I'm good.'

'Oh, I don't think you're *that*,' Christine laughed, seating herself on the black leather couch. 'And to prove my point, might I suggest that you carry on doing what you were doing with my husband in the car?'

And Liz did, standing right there in that elegant living room. She grabbed Peter by the waist and started kissing him again, putting her warm mouth and tongue to his. She kissed him hard and soon his tongue and lips were as ardent as hers. Liz could feel the heat building up in her sex, adding to the excitement she felt. She moved her hand against Peter's leather-covered erection once more, enjoying the pulsing feel of it. He reciprocated as his fingers stroked her, playing with her wet pussy so that she moaned urgently into his mouth, 'Finger-fuck me harder.' And he did, his hand rubbing all over her hot sex, his fingers working fast and hard over her clit, rubbing her all wet and sticky.

Liz stopped kissing Peter after a while and threw her head back, knowing how enticing she looked both to him and to his gorgeous wife. She knew how sexual abandon was painted all over her face, how it clouded her green eyes. Her breath was coming quickly, her pussy drenched and creamy as Peter's fingers plunged in and out of her and she rubbed and rubbed at his leather covered shaft.

Then Christine got into the act again, this time addressing Peter. 'Stop what you are doing, Peter, and take off your boots and socks,' she said, and he obeyed instantly.

'Now take off your top,' she added and he eased it up high and pulled it off, revealing a nicely toned physique.

'Unbutton those tight leather jeans,' Christine instructed next and he did so, his fingers trembling with excitement.

'Now take them off,' Christine added and Peter eased the leather jeans down over his cock. He then removed them and his shaft, already thickly inflated, sprang up violently. By the time he was completely naked it was rock hard, urgent with need. Liz noted excitedly that Peter was entirely devoid of body hair, had obviously shaved or waxed it all off. What a turn-on!

'Want to get naked too, Liz?' Christine asked, her eyes shining.

Liz didn't answer, simply pulled her tiny red mini dress over her head and kicked off her stiletto-heeled shoes. She was now as naked as Peter and, oh my, how she enjoyed being fully exposed in this way. She luxuriated in the intoxicating sensation of cool air on her nude body, feeling indescribably horny in her nakedness. She ached for that zipless fuck with Peter now, ached to do it right there and then in full view of his delectable wife.

But it was clear to Liz that Christine was the one who was calling all the shots that night. What did she want her to do now, Liz wondered. But Christine didn't seem to be in any hurry for her to do anything at present.

Instead she spoke again to Peter. 'Liz looks great buck-naked, doesn't she,' she said and he nodded lasciviously in response, feasting his eyes on the swell of Liz's breasts, on her large erect nipples, on her long shapely thighs meeting at the hairless mound of her wet pussy.

'Kneel before her,' Christine added and Peter knelt down in front of Liz, waiting to see what would be required of him next.

'Turn and crawl across the room,' Christine then instructed him. This order didn't faze Peter in the slightest, it goes without saying. But it certainly threw Liz. She looked down, her eyes wide in amazement, watching Peter do exactly as he'd been told, crawling on hands and knees to the other side of the room like a well-trained pet. It was extraordinary. It was also very exciting to her in ways she would have found almost impossible to articulate at that time.

'Now turn back round but remain on your knees,' Christine told Peter next and he obeyed. He made no further move until she motioned with a beckoning hand for him to return, and then he crawled on all fours back to his position in front of Liz.

'When I say the word I want you to use your mouth to worship the sex of the beautiful naked goddess standing above you,' Christine told him next.

Hearing herself referred to in this way made Liz flush with pleasure and she became even more sexually excited – intensely so. The heat in her sex was growing and growing. It seemed to permeate her whole body. She parted her thighs a little before Peter's face and waited expectantly for Christine to say the word.

'Worship her sex with your mouth now,' Christine said after an endless moment and Peter touched his lips to Liz's pussy. She felt soft tremors start to flow as his pink tongue moved slowly at first over the slippery lips of her sex. Then his mouth and tongue became more insistent, drinking her as he licked and licked at her pussy.

But Liz wanted more. Her nipples were as tight as rocks, her thighs quivering as she bucked and tried to move her sex more rapidly against the persistent licking of his tongue. She jerked her hips forward again and again towards the point of his tongue.

Liz began to moan and flush and shove herself down on Peter's mouth until the sensation was so heavy and intense that she knew she was about to climax. The pleasure tightened and then began to surge through her, as she shoved her sex down against his mouth again, his face glistening with her juices as he licked deep inside her.

And then it happened. Liz groaned deeply as she reached a climax that was absolutely delirious. Her whole body rippled with pleasure as wave after cresting wave of erotic bliss washed over her. It was by far the most intense orgasm she'd ever experienced. It was amazing. *Christine and Peter* were amazing.

What next, she wondered, shivering with anticipation. What was the next erotic delight this deliciously pervy pair had in store for her? She was soon to find out – and from Christine, the lady who clearly held all of the cards that night. She started to show her hand straight away. 'Lie flat on your back, Peter,' Christine said. 'Prostrate yourself before the naked goddess standing above you.'

And he did.

'Do you enjoy sucking cock, Liz?' Christine asked then, both of them looking at Peter's erection, which was sticking up like a flagpole.

'It's one of my favourite things,' she replied with a grin.

'Then why don't you start doing one of your favourite things,' Christine suggested, returning her grin. 'Try to avoid making him climax, though, if you can help it.'

Liz got down on her knees between Peter's thighs and leant forward, putting her arms either side of his waist. She parted her lips and closed her mouth tightly over the hot flesh of his cock, letting it slide in slowly. It tasted very good: meaty, tangy. Slowly Liz began to work her mouth up and down, cascading her tongue across the hard length of Peter's shaft. Then she built up momentum, his cock in her mouth becoming harder and more urgent all the time. Peter's breathing was quickening more and more until he was panting uncontrollably and seemed to be on the verge of climaxing. That wouldn't do at all, Liz decided – not after what Christine had said – and she stopped blowing Peter there and then before it was too late.

Liz withdrew his erect cock completely from her mouth, looked at the glistening flesh and the glans soaked by her tongue and the rivulet of fluid that welled from its cum-slit. After a suitable pause she looked at Peter's handsome face and he silently urged her to return to her task, his shining blue eyes filled with sexual longing.

Liz decided that he'd retreated from the danger zone sufficiently and that it was safe to go on. Opening her lips she took his hardness into her mouth again. She pulled it deeper in this time, pressing it all the way in, deep-throating him. At the same time Liz put a hand between her legs and began to masturbate, rolling her fingers first over her stiff clit. Then she rubbed her hand vigorously all over her wet sex and up inside herself, her fingers thrusting and thrusting. Her palm and wrist were soon soaked and she could feel pleasure spiking up through her fingers from her pussy as a result of her energetic self ministrations.

And as Liz frantically pleasured herself in this way, she kept on blowing Peter. She continued to take his length, letting her tongue lash the underside of it, moving her mouth up and down, the pace growing faster and faster still as he moaned with her movements. She sucked and sucked while finger-fucking herself furiously, penetrating her wet pussy with hard thrusts, her breasts jiggling, thighs quivering.

Delirious with the double pleasure of Peter's cock in her mouth and her own fingers working away feverishly at her sex, Liz arched her back ready for the climax she knew would soon be upon her. God, she felt juiced up, her crotch soaking, her hand drenched. She could also feel Peter's sexual excitement mounting towards the point of no return.

Mindful once again of Christine's request, Liz stopped sucking Peter's cock then. She took it out of her mouth, and started concentrating exclusively on her own pleasure. Faster and faster Liz masturbated until there was a roar in her ears and her pulse began racing wildly in her breast and she knew she was going to go over the edge again. Then her grinding fingers pressed hard on her clit so that she climaxed suddenly, her whole body shaking and shuddering in ecstasy.

Once her climax had subsided Liz drew back a little and smiled down at Peter, who smiled back in return. Liz's pussy was still as wet as could be and her hand was coated with sticky love juice. She held her fingers to Peter's face, touching his cheek with their tips before opening his lips. 'Lick them,' she said and he snaked out his tongue to obey. He sucked at her fingers, lashing his tongue over them until eventually she pulled her hand away.

Liz then turned again to look at Christine, that night's undisputed Mistress of Ceremonies, to see what she wanted her to do now. Would she perhaps ask her to go back to sucking Peter's cock, get her to maybe go all the way this time and finish him off with her mouth? She found that Christine was no longer seated on the leather couch but was now standing next to a mahogany cabinet by its side.

Christine gazed back at Liz for a moment, her blue-green eyes luminous. Then she wordlessly opened the top drawer of the cabinet. From this she took out a large black strap-on dildo complete with leather harness, as well as a bottle of lubricant. She placed each of these items on the top of the cabinet before closing the drawer. What exactly was she going to do next, Liz wondered excitedly. She couldn't wait to find out.

Chapter Thirty

WHAT CHRISTINE DID NEXT was to strip off her clothes very quickly. She did this with the utmost ease simply by sliding out of her flimsy black dress and removing her high-heeled shoes. Liz allowed her gaze to traverse Christine's body from top to toe. She thought she looked fabulous: with her lustrous dark hair and radiant complexion, with her glittering eyes and sensual lips. She loved her voluptuous body too. The woman was magnificent in her nakedness, Liz thought. She positively oozed sexuality.

At that moment Liz felt in pain with lust ... for Christine. She could feel her breath quicken and her nipples stiffen and her clit pulse with a hot insistent throb as she gazed at the other woman's lush wicked body. She'd never made love to another female in her life but she could certainly imagine making love to Christine. She could imagine tonguing her pussy, could imagine putting her fingers in her. She could imagine fucking her with the large strap-on dildo, could imagine Christine fucking her with it too.

She watched Christine buckle on the strap-on and take hold of the bottle of lubricant. 'Please stand up, Liz,' she said and Liz did, rising gracefully to her feet.

Christine then turned to Peter, saying, 'Get back on to your knees again and crawl to the centre of the room.'

Peter instantly obeyed, getting himself on to all fours once more and starting to crawl sinuously on his hands and knees across the room. Liz could tell by the way he crawled that he was getting an exhibitionistic thrill from it, no doubt just like he had the time before when he'd been sent crawling across the room by his gloriously dominant wife.

Liz could tell that Peter was delighting in the knowledge that she and Christine were watching him from behind. He moved languorously, knowing that every movement excited his audience of two. And that excited him also, Liz could see that. The fact that Christine and she were watching him was making his cock even stiffer. But he must be getting off on more than just the exhibitionism, Liz thought. He must really get off on grovelling on his knees like that at his wife's command.

'Assume the position,' Christine told Peter when he'd reached the centre of the room. He responded by pressing his face and chest to the polished wooden floor, lifting his behind high. His cock had begun to drizzle a silvery rivulet of pre-cum.

'Open yourself,' Christine demanded next, striding bare-footed towards him and motioning for Liz to do likewise. Peter obediently reached back with both arms and held the cheeks of his backside apart, presenting the pink opening of his anus to them both.

It was then that Liz suddenly remembered what Peter had said to her as they'd walked from the nightclub to Christine's Daimler. '*You* won't get hurt,' he'd told her with that telling inflection she thought she'd heard in his voice. So that was it: Peter was the one who was going to get hurt. He was going to be fucked in the arse with a large strap-on dildo. Liz held her breath as she waited for Christine to thrust the dildo hard into Peter's arsehole – so

208

hard that it would make him scream with pain, *just like she'd personally love to do to that despicable fucker Sam Craven ...*

But Christine, who had now doused the dildo thoroughly with lubricant, did no such thing. Instead she positioned herself behind Peter and slowly, gently worked the thickness of the dildo in and out of the opening of his anal hole a few times. She pushed it in a little further with each careful thrust, stretching his initially resistant sphincter. She continued to slide the dildo into him with carefully regulated pushes and pauses, easing it in slowly, letting the sensations build up gradually. Liz watched as the dildo finally spasmed all the way into him, that final motion making him grunt with satisfaction.

Peter put his hands back in front of him then and Christine began to sodomize him. As she moved inside him with the dildo, her strokes were at first slow and powerful but when she could tell he was ready they became fast and thrusting. Her magnificent naked breasts brushed his shoulders as she moved in and out with increasing vigour until she was riding him really hard, pounding right into him. Her rhythm was strong, each thrust going deeper into his anus, filling him, penetrating him, until he started moaning and shuddering convulsively with her movements.

At that point Christine stopped buggering Peter, although she left the dildo lodged in his anus. She turned to her side and smiled up at Liz, who was watching with rapt interest.

'I want you to make him come now please,' Christine said, and Liz thought, What does she want me to do – get on my knees and wank him off, crawl underneath there on my back and suck him to orgasm while he licks my pussy; what *exactly* does she want me to do?

Before she had a chance to ask, Christine said, 'Kneel down at the front of him and squeeze his nipples as hard as you can, really torture them.'

With that Christine went back to sodomizing Peter, pushing deep into his anus in a strong thrusting rhythm, making his pleasure mount. His pleasure mounted further still when his nipple torture began. And it *was* pleasure he was experiencing, Liz could see that from the ecstatic, slack-jawed expression on his face. *It was torture too –* Liz made damn certain of that as she squeezed at his nipples, imagining that they belonged to that fucking creep Sam. But she knew she could do more and she *wanted* to do more. Liz started to squeeze Peter's nipples extremely hard, her fingers closing with great force on the two rigid nubs of flesh and causing him to let out a whimper. He cried out more loudly when she increased still more the savagery of her squeezing and he pressed back so that Christine could thrust even deeper and harder into his anus.

Liz gave one final vicious squeeze of his nipples, twisting them also at the same time. And that had the desired effect. Peter began to tremble without control and then yielded to the ecstasy of release. He called out a wordless explosion of desire as his cock erupted, sending one thick spurt after another of ejaculate splattering onto the shiny dark floor beneath him. Liz stopped squeezing Peter's nipples then and moved her hands away from his body. At the same time Christine stopped fucking him in the arse. She stayed locked together with him for a moment before she withdrew the dildo from his open anal hole.

Christine looked at Liz and smiled seductively, fixing her eyes on hers. 'Want to stay the night, share my bed with me?' *My* bed, not *our* bed, Liz noted. By now she could understand much better the dynamics of Christine and Peter's relationship. Christine was clearly completely in charge, Peter totally under her thumb. Something else had clarified itself in Liz's mind too. She had thought that she'd been picking Peter up at that club tonight when all the time he'd been picking her up for his wife – who wanted her for both of them. The feeling, as far as Liz was concerned, was entirely mutual. She nodded her assent to Christine, returning her seductive smile.

Liz could feel her heart race and her pussy tighten. She wanted so much to share Christine's bed tonight. Never mind about staying the night, she thought as she ran her hands up over her stiff nipples – the hands that had just *tortured* Peter's nipples, the hands that would soon be pleasuring Christine in her bed, taking her again and again with amazing intensity. She didn't just want to stay the night, she wanted to stay period. This was where Liz wanted to be, here with this wonderfully kinky couple. She wanted this to be her home from now on, wanted it to be her life.

And that indeed is what came to pass – and so much more besides.

Chapter Thirty-one

ONE YEAR LATER

LIZ KNEW IT WAS bound to happen some time or other, knew that Sam Craven would turn up again like the proverbial bad penny. He'd begged to come and see her, when he phoned, saying it was crucial that they meet. He also informed her that he was jobless, had been made bankrupt about six months previously and that he remained stony broke. In fact he was so strapped for funds, he told her, that the only accommodation he could afford was a crappy rented bed-sit on the North Circular Road. In addition he claimed to be a changed man. And Liz agreed with him in that last assessment if by changed he was referring to the fact that he'd evidently lost his shallow job in marketing and gone through all his money and was currently on the skids. But beyond that, she was extremely sceptical. What was it that Judy had said? A leopard doesn't change his spots.

Christine had told Liz that under the circumstances she and Peter would make themselves scarce for a few hours. So it was into an otherwise empty house that Liz let her errant ex-husband, a man she'd not laid eyes on for over two years. Her first impressions were that he did indeed appear changed. He seemed sombre and subdued, very nervy too. His face was sheet-white, as if drained of all blood, his blue eyes had lost their sparkle and his long dark hair was no longer wavy but lank. For all that though, he'd still managed to retain his androgynous good looks and remained outstandingly attractive. Damn the man, Liz thought; she hated him like the devil yet she still couldn't help fancying the pants off him.

Liz waited for Sam to come through the front door and into the hallway before she closed the door behind him. The sharp sound of the door shutting seemed to startle him. He turned and looked at her with anxious eyes.

He really is in a terrible state, almost a nervous wreck, Liz said to herself without sympathy. He was about as much of a wreck as that jalopy he'd turned up in today. A couple of years ago it would have been some flash sports car or other. How the mighty had fallen! She led him down the hall and into the living room. The French window at the end of the room opened onto a beautifully landscaped rear garden, which was bounded by a high brick wall.

'You told me it was crucial that you see me,' Liz said, her expression as severe as the black leather trouser suit she was wearing. 'So, spit it out. What's this all about?'

'I'm desperate for you to take me back,' he said.

'So, what makes that crucial?' Liz asked, irritated.

'It's crucial to me, really crucial,' Sam replied urgently. 'You see, I can't bear to live without you, not any more.'

'Bullshit!'

'It's true.'

'Well, you're going to have to,' Liz said coldly, looking at him with distaste. 'If that's all you've got to say for yourself you're clearly here under false pretences, so beat it. Go on, push off.'

'Please, Liz,' Sam pleaded, a quaver in his voice. 'I

beg you.'

'I said, beat it.'

'Please don't send me away,' he said, suddenly breaking into a sob. 'Without you my life has completely fallen apart. It has no meaning. You're all I ever think about. You haunt my dreams, you …'

'Shut the fuck up!' Liz interrupted with a shout. He raised startled eyes to her, knocked sideways by this explosion of wrath.

There was a long silence that seemed to stretch until it might break. Then Sam ventured to speak again. 'I'm sorry for everything,' he apologized quietly. 'I'm deeply sorry for the way I treated you.'

'So you damn well should be,' Liz rasped, her green eyes ablaze. 'You made my life a complete misery when we were married, with all your incessant screwing around. I've found happiness this last year and there's no way I'm going to let you ruin it for me. You say that you're a changed man. Well, I'm a changed woman, a very changed woman.'

'I understand that,' Sam said quietly. 'You're living here in some kind of ménage à trois with a married couple, aren't you?'

'Yes,' she replied. 'And the emphasis is on the trois. There's no place for you, especially as it's a *sadomasochistic* ménage à trois.'

'Oh.' Sam's eyes widened with surprise.

'You hadn't expected that, had you,' Liz said with a note of triumph. Actually she hadn't expected it either – not the extent to which the relationship would turn out to be defined by sadomasochism or the depths of her own innate sadism, previously so deeply sublimated. It had been a staggering revelation to her. Also, as the maxim goes: When you've found the best, why bother with the

214

rest. Liz had given up on one-night stands when she'd moved in with Christine and Peter. And so had they – for exactly the same reason, they'd both assured her with transparent sincerity. But all of that was another story and not one she had the slightest intention of sharing with her despised ex-husband.

'No I hadn't expected that,' Sam said. 'I hadn't expected it at all. But …'

'But what?'

'But I still want to be with you.'

'No way.'

'Please make a place for me in your new life,' he pleaded. 'I'll agree to any conditions you make.'

'Any?' Liz said, giving him an unbelieving look. The guy must have taken leave of his senses, she thought.

'Any,' he insisted.

'Then you'd better hear what you'd be letting yourself in for,' she said, thinking that it was time to get all this foolishness over with and call Sam Craven's bluff.

'Go ahead, I …'

'Don't talk any more,' Liz told him sharply, contempt in her voice. 'What I have to say now is extremely important, so listen and learn. Let's be clear – if you speak out of turn, I'll punish you for it.'

Sam's eyes went wide again and he bit his lower lip. And although he really wanted to, he did not speak.

'A lot of marriages are a sham to some extent,' Liz said, her face cold. 'Ours was a *total* sham, wasn't it?'

Sam hesitated for a moment, not knowing whether what Liz had said demanded a reply or not. He guessed correctly that the question was a rhetorical one and said nothing.

'My relationship with Christine and Peter is not a sham in any way, it's the real thing,' Liz went on. 'But it's extremely unorthodox. You see, Christine and I are lovers and sadists and Peter is a masochist and our slave – a very devoted one he is too. He used to be solely Christine's slave but ever since I moved in she and I have shared his ownership. Now, be truthful, Sam. Do you honestly think you could fit into a set-up like that?'

'As a slave?'

'Of course as a fucking slave,' Liz replied with a snort of derision. 'What did you think? As a naked slave actually. It is very rare that Peter is permitted to wear any clothes. In fact basically speaking he is only allowed to get dressed if he has to leave the house, which he is seldom permitted to do. Today's very much the exception. I repeat, Do you really think you could live like that?'

'Yes I do,' Sam answered, the tremble in his voice not only revealing the extent of his nervousness but also belying the certainty of his reply.

'You're not frightened of all the *pain* involved?'

'N-n-no,' he stammered. Liz had never heard Sam stammer before. The man she remembered, self-confidence personified, would never have done so.

'Interesting,' she said.

'I'm sure I …,' he began, but silenced himself when he noticed the steely look she shot his way.

Liz turned and walked over to the black leather couch where she sat down. Sam followed her and made to join her on the couch.

'No,' she said, putting a hand out firmly to stop him. 'Kneel before me.'

Sam almost said something then, could barely contain himself, but again he bit his tongue. Once he was kneeling down he looked up at Liz, his face flushed with embarrassment. His eyes lingered on hers for a moment but he found that he could not hold her gaze and he quickly lowered them.

'You definitely still want to move back with me?' Liz asked, her voice emotionless.

Sam knelt rooted to the spot, his head bowed. 'Yes,' he whispered. 'I want that with all my heart.'

'And you accept the conditions that would be involved – the ones that I've just set out for you?'

'Yes.'

'I'd have to consult with Christine about this, of course.'

'Of course.'

Liz hesitated for a moment before saying, 'Actually, you know, I'm not sure I'm even prepared to *think* about talking to Christine about it. Why the hell should I?'

'Please, Liz,' Sam said, his voice pleading. 'I won't let you down this time, I swear it.'

'Hah!'

'I'm utterly sincere.'

Liz pondered again for a while and then said, 'You fully understand that if – and I stress the word *if* – I agree to talk to Christine about this and if she and I allow you to move in, you'd be a naked slave to both of us, like Peter.'

'Yes, I understand.'

'And you still want to go ahead?'

'Yes.'

'You're absolutely sure?'

'I'm certain,' Sam replied. 'So what do you say?'

'What do I say?'

'Yes.'

'What I say is this,' Liz responded. 'Take off all your clothes.' She smiled to herself as she watched Sam get to his feet to do her bidding, thinking that what she proposed to do to the miserable bastard after that would *really* call his bluff.

Chapter Thirty-two

SAM'S HANDS WERE SHAKING nervously as he undressed, making him fumble with his clothes. He stood facing Liz but remained unable to look at her, gazing down the whole time. His jacket came off first and then his shoes and socks. Then down came his slacks, falling to his ankles, and he stepped out of them. Next he undid the top buttons of his shirt and pulled it over his head. He was down to his briefs. 'Come on, get those off too,' Liz told him impatiently when he hesitated. 'It's not as if I've never seen you naked before.'

'That's true,' Sam acknowledged with a small smile.

'Anyway, you're going to have to get used to being naked if you get what you want and Christine and I agree to let you stay here as our slave,' Liz continued. 'Or are you having second thoughts about the whole idea? If that's the case just say the word and I'll send you on your way right now.'

'I'm not having second thoughts,' Sam assured her and duly removed his briefs, letting them fall to the floor quickly and stepping out of them.

'Turn full circle for me,' Liz told him next and as he turned his smooth, slender body his cock started becoming erect. By the time he had completed his circle it was at full mast and his face was flushed bright pink with shame.

'Do you find this humiliating?' Liz asked. 'I see that you are blushing.'

'Yes,' Sam replied. 'I do find it humiliating – very humiliating.'

'Then I'm forced to conclude that you enjoy being humiliated,' Liz said. 'That's one hell of a hard-on you're sporting there.'

'I deserve to be humiliated,' was all he said in reply.

'And you enjoy it?'

'Yes,' he said quietly, briefly meeting her eye and then flicking his gaze down to the floor again. 'I can't understand why but yes I suppose I must.'

'Get back on to your knees,' Liz said next, pointing to the space at her feet. Sam obeyed again, without question. She reached out and stroked his back, running her fingers lightly over his skin from his shoulder to his waist and back again. He shivered under her sensuous touch.

Then with one hand she yanked hard at his hair and pulled him closer, looking intensely into his confused blue eyes. 'You like being humiliated, it seems, but do you think you'll like what's going to happen to you next? Do you think you'll like being spanked?'

'I d-d-don't know,' Sam replied, his nervous stutter having returned.

'Have you ever been spanked before?'

'N-never,' he said, struggling to get his voice back under control. 'I've never been beaten in any way.'

'Do you think you deserve to be spanked?'

'After the way I treated you, I deserve to be hung, drawn and quartered,' Sam replied.

'That's as may be,' Liz said. 'But do you think you deserve to be spanked?'

'Yes.'

'Do you *want* to be spanked?'

Sam didn't answer straight away and Liz repeated herself, 'I said do you want to be spanked? Answer the question.'

'Yes,' he replied softly.

'Is that a truthful reply or are you just saying it because you think it's what I want to hear?'

'It's the truth,' he said, blushing furiously now. 'I don't understand why I want to be spanked – I really don't – but it's the God's honest truth that I do.'

'Then get over my knee this instant,' she ordered.

Sam obeyed straight away and bent over Liz's lap. The cheeks of his backside tensed and his erect shaft throbbed excitedly against her thigh as he anticipated the punishment he was about to receive, the punishment that he'd had to admit to Liz – and to himself – he *wanted* to receive.

Liz deliberately kept him waiting, though, and simply stroked the smooth cheeks of his rear for a while. Then: Smack! The harsh sharp noise announced that his spanking had at last commenced. Smack! Liz's hand came down again with another harsh spank. Sam yelped both of the times that Liz's palm collided with his backside. 'Silence,' she snapped. 'If I hear one other sound out of you while you receive your spanking, all of this will be off. I won't even contemplate talking to Christine about you being our slave and will simply send you packing – and for good.'

With that Liz returned to her vigorous task. There were a lot more hard smacks, when the crisp sound of hand on naked flesh resounded round the living room, Liz steadily increasing the frequency and hardness of her smacks. She continued relentlessly, following one spank after another in swift succession until the cheeks of Sam's backside smarted a fiery red. But he did keep absolutely silent, desperately anxious not to screw up with Liz – and crying out in pain inside instead.

And as Liz came towards the end of the heavy spanking she had inflicted on Sam, she thought, smiling to herself once more, well, I haven't called the bastard's bluff yet. But there again I've barely started.

Liz told Sam to get off her lap and stand up then, and once he'd done that she got to her feet herself. She looked him in the face, her expression menacing. 'That was merely a warm up,' she said. 'Now I'm going to beat the living daylights out of you ... unless you want to walk away. It's entirely up to you.'

'I don't want to walk away,' he said, although he looked positively terrified.

Liz strode over to a wall cabinet, opening it a little and extracting a leather-covered swagger cane. 'This should do some damage,' she said approvingly as she weighed the implement in her hands. 'Would you not agree?'

'Y-y-yes,' Sam replied, stuttering again, and Liz saw that he'd begun to tremble all over as well.

'Now, I want you to turn and face the couch,' she ordered. 'Lean over it with your arse in the air.' Sam obeyed without delay. 'Now spread your thighs,' Liz added. 'I want to see your arse-cheeks spread wide.' Again he obeyed immediately.

Liz then brought the tip of the swagger cane to his lips. 'Kiss it,' she urged.

Sam looked over his shoulder at her, his blue eyes full of questions. 'Kiss it, I said,' Liz repeated in irritation and he obeyed, turning his head back and touching his lips to the implement.

'Once again, I want absolute silence from you while you're being beaten,' she told him before moving the swagger cane and swinging it through the air in a vivid trajectory. Crack! The sudden pain that seared across Sam's backside was agonizing. Crack! Liz brought the implement down again with even greater force and it hurt even more. Further fierce strokes followed in swift succession and as the savage beating continued Sam desperately tried to contain the furious pain but to no avail. Liz beat his backside with remorselessly fierce strokes until it was criss-crossed with clear stripes. But Sam gritted his teeth and took his punishment, uttering not a single sound, determined with every measure of resolve he could muster not to foul up this one opportunity he had to at least have a chance to be a part of Liz's life once more.

Liz finally stopped beating Sam and examined with cruel satisfaction the red painful-looking stripes down each side of him from the first swell of his backside to his upper thighs.

'Get back on to your knees and turn towards me,' Liz said then and he did so while she remained standing where she was.

'All right, Sam,' she said, looking down into his anguished face. 'I'm prepared to talk to Christine about you becoming our slave. Of course, she may very well not like the idea, in which case that will be the end of the matter. But hey, if that's what happens at least I'll have had the satisfaction of giving you the thorough beating you so richly deserve. It's been a long time coming, *you absolute shit.*'

Chapter Thirty-three

LIZ SENT SAM AWAY soon after that with the instruction that he should return at the same time the following day. All he could do in the meantime in that crummy bed-sit of his on the Western Avenue was nurse his aching backside and pray that Liz would present his case in as favourable a light as possible to her lover Christine, and that she in turn would respond favourably. He didn't hold out much hope, though. Liz had made it perfectly clear to him in what miserably low esteem she continued to regard him.

When Sam arrived at the front door the next day, at first it was very much the recipe as before. It was Liz, looking as stern and unforgiving as she'd done the previous day, who let him into the house. It was Liz who ushered him into the living room, Liz who told him to strip naked and Liz who instructed him to kneel on the floor. But then Liz left the room in silence to be replaced immediately by another woman. And that woman was stark naked. She was also as stunningly beautiful as Liz, Sam thought, with her long dark hair, glittering blue-green eyes, sensuous lips, and gloriously curvy figure. He marvelled too at her fantastic breasts, with their stiff thick nipples, and at her smooth hairless pubic mound.

'C-Christine?' Sam whispered haltingly as the woman approached him, her hips swaying provocatively. Watching her made his mouth go dry.

'That's me,' she said, her face impassive.

'H-h-hello.'

'Liz won't be back for some time,' Christine said, ignoring his stumbling salutation. 'It's just you and me for a while. Anything you'd like to know?'

Sam tried to regain his composure and managed to go almost to the opposite extreme in the process. 'Yes – what have you and Liz agreed?' he asked urgently. 'Did you decide I could be a slave to you both?'

'Don't be so absurd,' Christine replied, looking down at him disdainfully. 'I don't know you from Adam. I need to get to know you before Liz and I make any kind of decision on your request. The only thing we've agreed so far is that she would put you at my disposal for a couple of hours today and that during that time you would be expected to do everything I tell you to do.'

'I see,' Sam said nervously. 'And then what?'

Christine did not answer the question but instead asked one of her own. 'Tell me something,' she said. 'How do you think things went yesterday with Liz? Do you think you did well?'

Sam shook his head ruefully. 'No, I don't think I did well at all, to be quite frank,' he admitted. 'I wanted to please Liz so much and took my punishment like a man. But I went away feeling that she hated me as much as ever.'

Christine sat down on the leather couch before his kneeling form. 'You say you took your punishment *like a man*, pretty-boy,' she said with a smile of amusement. 'But tell me this: did you enjoy it?'

Sam took a long moment to answer, as though the experience had been so bewildering that he needed time to fathom it out. 'I was excited by it,' he confessed, looking embarrassed. 'And I must say that came as a very big surprise to me, a revelation really. But I can't say I enjoyed the experience, no. Maybe if there hadn't been so much riding on it I might have been able to let myself go a bit. But uppermost in my mind was my frantic desire not to displease Liz.'

'I can understand that,' Christine told him, passing a hand through her lustrous dark hair. 'And how do you feel about displeasing me?'

Sam reflected for a moment and then gave her his answer. 'It's the same thing really,' he said. 'If I displease you, I also displease Liz. I don't want to do either. I want very much to please you both, serve you both.'

'And do you find the idea of serving us – being our slave – sexually arousing?'

'Yes, to be truthful,' Sam replied with a blush. 'I do find it sexually arousing.'

Christine leant forward until they were face to face. She gazed into his eyes. 'Do you find *me* sexually arousing?'

'Yes,' Sam said. 'I find you … irresistible.'

She lifted her head slightly then, parted her lips, and he came towards her. They touched lips softly, and tentatively he began to kiss her.

'Oh, I think we can do better than that,' Christine said. She parted Sam's lips, pressing his mouth hard with her own, taking control. When she pulled away she saw his look of confusion and fear.

'You think this is a trap, don't you?' she said with a laugh. 'Liz lets you out of her sight for five minutes and you're back to your old tricks, that kind of thing.'

'I don't want to let her down again,' he said. 'I'm desperate not to.'

'The only way you'll let Liz down while you're with me is if you resist my advances or otherwise fail to do what I tell you to do,' Christine said, her voice suddenly harsh. 'I've already told you what she and I have agreed. Now pucker up, pretty-boy.'

Christine kissed Sam again, pressing her hot mouth to his lips, pushing her tongue all the way in voraciously. She broke the kiss eventually and began to stroke her hands down his back. She then brought them round to his stomach and up to his smooth chest, stopping when her fingers closed over his stiff nipples. Sam held his breath as Christine squeezed them hard for a painful moment, her fingers like burning pliers.

'Come and join me on the couch,' Christine ordered next, fixing her eyes on his again. Sam obeyed immediately, getting up from his knees and sitting next to her on the black leather couch. They sat side by side, kissing again while Christine caressed his body as she liked.

'You're so hard,' she whispered, when her fingers found the tautness of his erection.

Sam's only reply was a low moan. He trembled when she began to masturbate him, alternating a light pressing with a firm grip, stroking and caressing at his hardness until he moaned constantly with pleasure.

'Do you want me to stop, pretty-boy?' Christine asked, breathing the scent of his sexual arousal.

Sam shook his head vigorously, but could not trust himself to speak.

'Well, *I* want to stop,' Christine said with a smile. 'I want to do something else.' She stopped masturbating him and instead leant down and brought her lips to his erect cock, which was now so urgent that a pool of moistness had appeared at its tip. Christine sucked that moistness away and was rewarded with a soft groan of pleasure from Sam.

She began to blow him in a regular rhythm then, kept on sucking and sucking until she felt his erection pulsing in her throat. She extracted his cock from her mouth then. 'Do you want me to stop, pretty-boy?' Christine repeated the question she'd asked him before.

'No,' Sam panted. 'Don't stop.'

'But, again, *I* want to stop,' she said, getting to her feet. 'I want some pleasure now. Lie down flat on your back on the couch.' Sam did as he'd been told straight away, his erection sticking up rigidly in the air.

Christine then climbed on to the couch. She began to sit astride his face, looking down into his eyes before positioning herself over his mouth, slowly sitting lower. She felt his breath on her inner thigh and then the hot touch of his lips. Silently, she reached down to pull her labia open, to show him what she wanted. Then she clarified it with words. 'Eat my pussy, pretty-boy,' she said. 'Don't stop until I tell you to.'

Sam began to probe Christine's sex with his tongue, sucking and licking her until she was soaking wet. Sam's face was shiny with her juice and he knew how excited he had made her. Christine closed her eyes to the pleasure that was now sweeping through her. It was a pleasure so strong that she knew that she was going to climax directly over his mouth at any moment and she groaned and sighed with the feeling.

Finally the pleasure exploded through Christine, as she shoved her sex down against Sam's mouth and her orgasm came, making her shudder convulsively until she shuddered at last to a halt. But Sam didn't stop. He kept using his tongue to spin pleasure on her sex in the aftermath of her mighty climax. Sam wasn't going to stop until *she* told him to. He was going to do exactly as he'd been instructed, like the good slave he aspired to be.

Chapter Thirty-four

'YOU CAN STOP EATING my pussy now, pretty-boy,' Christine told Sam eventually. She climbed off his love juice-soaked face and ordered him to get on to the floor in a kneeling position once again. Then she sat back down on the leather couch. 'What shall I do with you now, I wonder,' she said, pondering for a moment. 'I know, I'll give you a hand-spanking,' she decided. 'Get over my knee.'

When Sam had pulled himself prone across her lap, Christine paused to admire the sight. Across her knee, his naked buttocks were displayed perfectly. They had a harmonious shape, curving gracefully from the small of his back. She smoothed a hand along them, enjoying the feeling of his soft skin and the sight and feel of the bruises and marks still evident from the robust beating he'd received from Liz the day before. Christine could tell how sexually aroused Sam was too, it couldn't have been more obvious 'A certain part of your anatomy is throbbing away nicely against my thigh,' she said with a laugh. 'You're obviously still very turned on.'

'I am,' he acknowledged, letting out a shudder of excitement.

Christine then pulled the cheeks of his backside slightly apart to look at the dark button of his anus. 'You realise that if we accept you as our slave – our *sex*-slave –

Liz and I will regularly fuck you in the arse,' she said gleefully. 'Do you want us to do that to you – subject you to regular strap-on anal sex?'

'Well, no, quite honestly,' Sam replied with a gulp. She had to be joking, hadn't she? *Hadn't she?*

Christine changed the subject. 'Is there anything you want to ask before I start spanking you, pretty-boy?' she said.

'Am I allowed to make a noise?' he asked. 'Liz didn't want me to yesterday. She told me to be completely silent while she was beating me.'

'That was Liz and that was yesterday,' Christine said. 'Today it's yours truly who's going to be chastising you and as far as I'm concerned you can make as much noise as you like. Also I can assure you that if Liz hears any cries of pain from you coming out of this room she won't mind a bit, quite the reverse in fact. I'm sure she'll be delighted.'

Having cleared up that little matter, Christine raised her hand all of a sudden and brought it down forcefully on Sam's backside. The sharp slap was so hard that it left a distinct red mark on his flesh and did indeed make him cry out with pain. She spanked him a second time, lifting her hand high and then bringing it down swiftly to make contact with his rear, leaving another red mark on his flesh and making him cry out again. Christine delivered a third heavy stroke, which smarted even more painfully. It made Sam cry out more loudly this time and left a deeper red mark on the cheeks of his backside.

Christine smacked Sam again and again over and over, until his backside was patterned a deep red and his cries were echoing round the room – cries, Christine noted, that had steadily become moans of erotic pleasure.

She stopped spanking him then but held him in

position over her knee. 'I asked you before whether you thought you'd like being regularly fucked in the arse by me and Liz and you said no,' she reminded him. 'Would you like to change your answer by any chance?'

'No,' Sam gasped. 'I certainly wouldn't.'

'That's a pity,' Christine said. She raised her hand again and resumed the spanking, harsher still this time, beating hard flat strokes against his punished flesh. Sam wailed and cried in response to this ferocious spanking, trying to wriggle free but to no effect as Christine held him firm over her lap.

Still holding him in position, she stopped spanking him again. 'Would you like to change your answer about being fucked in the arse, pretty-boy?' she repeated.

'No, no, no,' Sam cried.

'*Most* disappointing,' Christine said. She suddenly pushed him to the floor roughly, telling him to get onto all fours.

'Wait there,' she added before rising to her feet and striding a few steps to a mahogany cabinet at the side of the couch. She pulled open the top drawer and took out a black dildo strap-on and its harness along with a bottle of lubricant. When Christine had done the self-same thing the first night she'd met Liz a year ago Liz's reaction had been one of obvious sexual excitement. It was very different with Sam today. His erection was now rapidly on the wane and he was looking up at her in horror as she buckled on the harness. His terrified eyes were fixed like glue on the black dildo now jutting from her crotch and which she had begun to lubricate.

'Tell me you want me to fuck you in the arse, pretty-boy,' Christine said tauntingly, adding a little more lubricant to the black shaft. 'Go on, say it.'

'No,' Sam repeated yet again, crawling backwards,

moving away from her.

'Get back here,' Christine demanded angrily, her eyes flashing. 'I told you quite clearly before to wait where you were. What the fuck do you think you're doing?'

Sam hesitated, but realised before it was too late that he was on the verge of screwing up totally here, blowing everything. He began crawling back on his hands and knees until he had returned to his previous position. 'I'm sorry,' he said, chastened.

'Sorry you may be but I'm going to have to punish you for that transgression,' Christine said and strode towards the same wall cabinet from which Liz had extracted the swagger cane the day before. She took out a heavy leather flogger from the cabinet and made her way back towards Sam who was still on his hands and knees in the place she'd left him although he was now trembling constantly with fear … and something other than fear: intense sexual excitement. His cock had become hugely erect again, Christine noticed with wry amusement.

She raised the flogger and brought it down hard across the cheeks of Sam's backside, imprinting a pattern of red lines on his already punished flesh. He cried out with pain, prompting her to quickly beat him a second time, the leather snapping hard on his aching backside. There were more angry red imprints and another cry of pain. A third, fourth, fifth and sixth strike followed in swift succession; more angry red lines, more cries of pain. There then followed strikes seven to twelve. It was somewhere towards the end of that last ferocious onslaught that Sam's cries of pain transformed themselves into loud moans of pleasure.

Christine forced him to the floor then with a bare foot. Sam lay face down, his heavily chastised backside smarting furiously and his shaft throbbing fit to burst against the polished wood beneath it. Christine knelt down between his spread thighs, watching him squirm with erotic abandon against the floor.

'I'll ask you one more time, pretty-boy,' she said, leaning forward and whispering into his ear. 'Do you want me to fuck you in the arse?'

There was a long pause, pregnant with unbearable sexual tension. 'Yes!' Sam cried out finally. 'Yes! Yes! Yes! Yes! Yes!'

'... is the right answer,' Christine announced triumphantly as she mounted him, pulling his waist to her and forcing the dildo into his anus in one pitiless thrust. It made Sam climax in an instant, screaming out his release like a demented being as cum burst out of his cock, liquid and sexual, onto the hard floor beneath him. Liz would have heard that piercing scream, she was bound to have done. *Anyone* in that house would have heard it.

Chapter Thirty-five

ON THAT OCCASION IT was Christine who sent Sam off with instructions to return at the same time the following day. She and Liz would deliberate in the meantime about his request to be their sex-slave, she told him.

'And will you tell me the outcome when I arrive?' he asked.

'No we won't.'

Sam's heart sank. 'But why not?' he asked in dismay.

'You seem to forget something, Sam,' Christine replied. 'There are three people in the ménage you're so anxious to join: Liz, myself, and my husband Peter. It would not be appropriate to make a decision on this without involving Peter. To give you one obvious scenario, what if you two guys turn out to hate each other on sight?'

'But why should we?'

'True,' Christine acknowledged. 'But you don't *know* – none of us do.'

'I take your point,' Sam agreed reluctantly.

It was therefore into the same elegant living room that a day later Sam was ushered by, this time, both Liz and Christine. The two women looked stunningly beautiful – and stunningly dominant too – in what they had on. Christine was dressed in a skin-tight black leather cat-suit, complete with leather gloves and she also had on long high-heeled boots. Liz was wearing an identical outfit except hers was dark red, not black, and of shiny rubber latex, not leather. Sam could feel himself stiffen at the sight of his ex-wife and her lover in these amazing outfits, could feel his heart beat stronger and his palms go damp.

Sam saw that there was a handsome dark-haired man kneeling upright in the middle of the room and that he was naked: his body tight and lean and, Sam also observed, completely hairless. He observed too that he had a long thick cock, which was semi-hard. 'This is slave Peter,' Liz said. Peter smiled over at Sam, his blue eyes shining, and he smiled back. Well, it certainly wasn't hate at first sight, Sam said to himself. He thought Peter looked pleasant and engaging. He was an undeniably sexy sight too, stark naked on his knees in the centre of the room with his completely shaven body and a half hard-on.

'Undress, Sam,' Liz ordered and nervously he began to obey. He kicked off his loafers first and pulled off his socks. Then he unzipped his denim jeans and tugged them down, revealing that he'd been naked underneath and that his big cock also was partly tumescent. Sam pulled his jeans off completely and finally removed his top, exposing his smooth bare torso. With his long wavy hair – the lankness now all but gone; with his long-lashed eyes and full lips and delicate features; with his slender arms and waist and the smooth musculature of his narrow chest; with his pronounced stiffly erect nipples ...with all of that he gave the appearance of a pretty, flat-chested girl. He did from the waist upwards anyway!

'Kneel down,' Liz instructed once Sam had stripped completely. 'I mean *right now*, not tomorrow,' she added sharply when he failed to get to his knees straight away, and he quickly knelt down.

'Sorry,' he said, giving her an ingratiating smile. She

responded to this with one of her frostiest stares. She clearly still hates my fucking guts, Sam thought despairingly.

Christine spoke next, taking a seat on the leather couch and addressing her kneeling husband. 'Peter, crawl smartly over to me,' she said. 'Show Sam just what a good slave you are.'

She did not have to wait a second for her order to be obeyed. Immediately Peter bent down onto all fours and crawled hurriedly towards her, keeping his head bowed the whole time. As soon as he had arrived at Christine's feet she reached down and began to touch him, caressing his lower back and the curve of his backside. Christine then wetted the middle digit of one of her leather-gloved hands with a gob of spittle and inserted it into Peter's anus, starting to slide it slowly in and out.

Sam watched intently, fascinated by the way Peter let himself be invaded by Christine in this manner without betraying a flicker of emotion. Instead he merely waited patiently for the next order he would receive from her.

And it was not too long in coming. Christine stopped fingering Peter's anus and barked out an instruction. 'Adopt the position,' she told him and he stretched, pushing his backside higher and his face and chest down. Christine then began to caress his rear again, smoothing her hands over its firm cheeks.

Sam had been gazing at all this so intently that he had not noticed Liz slip silently out of the room. He noticed her return though, noticed particularly what she now had attached by means of a dark leather harness to the crotch of her skin-tight red rubber cat suit. It was a long black strap-on dildo and she had already liberally smeared it with lubricant.

He watched as if spellbound, his wide eyes focussed

on the shiny black phallus, as Liz strode towards Peter. He kept watching as she positioned herself behind the slave in order to sodomize him.

And it soon became obvious to Sam that Peter liked it, liked being fucked in the arse. He groaned softly when Liz eased the black dildo into his anus. He groaned again as she worked it in and out slowly. She was careful to build the pleasure steadily with the slow, steady penetration. Then Liz began pushing the dildo hard into Peter's anus, making him cry out with undisguised delight.

Sam could feel his face burning, embarrassed by the sudden urgent desire to be where Peter was. He wanted to have Liz fuck *him* in the arse with the dildo, wanted it so badly.

Or if not Liz ...

At that point Christine, as if reading his mind, rose from the couch. She went to the mahogany cabinet and extracted from its top drawer the strap-on dildo she'd used on him the previous day, along with the bottle of lubricant. 'Crawl next to Peter,' she told Sam, strapping on the harness and dousing the dildo with lube.

Sam crawled lithely into position beside Peter, feeling the heat of the other man's body now that they were so close together, both of them massively erect. Their eyes met for a moment and all that he could see was the look of unadulterated pleasure in Peter's blue eyes as Liz continued to pound into him.

Then it was time for Sam to be sodomized also as Christine pressed on his upper back so that he bent down with only his pretty behind in the air. She then pushed the hardness of the dildo into his anus, forging deep into him. Christine gripped Sam by his long hair and started buggering him slowly but soon quickened the pace, fucking him expertly with the black dildo. As she speeded up her thrusts, his excitement grew, a mixture of pain and pleasure. By the time she was really pumping into him, he could feel lust rushing through him and he groaned and grunted unrestrainedly with the feeling.

Christine stopped pulling Sam's hair in due course, putting her palms on his backside instead, but she did not reduce the vigorous force with which she was sodomizing him. He moaned with desire at her movements as she used her strap-on dildo on him, entering and re-entering his anus faster and faster. Christine was fucking Sam really hard now, making him gasp with pleasure and move his body with each stroke, pushing himself back on the dildo as she hammered him to the depth of himself. He felt totally, *wonderfully* degraded.

He looked over at Peter then, gazed into his shining blue eyes and the two men smiled at one another once more. There was no doubt about it: Sam and Peter were bonding.

Liz and Christine smiled at each other too, neither of them breaking rhythm as they continued pounding into their charges, one of whom was a sex-slave – *their* sex-slave; the other a desperate wannabe.

Chapter Thirty-six

FAST FORWARD A DAY and there they all were in that elegant living room once more. Christine and Liz were standing with their backs to the couch, dressed once again in their skin-tight cat-suit outfits complete with gloves and long high-heeled boots – Christine's outfit black and leather; Liz's dark red and rubber latex. They were wearing their black strap-ons again too. Sam was kneeling naked beneath them, his trim form now shaven clean of what little body hair it had possessed. Liz had told him to do this when he'd left the previous day and he'd been pleased to obey her. Peter was also kneeling naked, but somewhat apart in the centre of the room, in the exact spot that Sam had first set eyes on him the day before.

'Have you made a decision yet?' Sam asked, looking up at Liz and Christine with an earnest expression on his face.

'We are still undecided,' Liz said coolly.

'You undoubtedly have an awful lot to learn,' Christine put in with the same cool tone. 'To be quite frank with you, we are both doubtful whether you are capable of learning some of the lessons that need to be absorbed in order to be a good slave.'

'I've shown I can take punishment,' Sam replied. 'Surely that's the main thing.'

'That comment merely reveals the depths of your

ignorance,' Liz said scornfully. 'Obedience − complete unquestioning obedience at all times − to Christine and to me is what would be required of you as our slave. *That* is the main thing.'

'I've proved I can be obedient in that way,' Sam said, trying to sound confidant. 'For instance I shaved off all my body hair like you told me to.'

'Big deal!' Liz retorted. 'You hardly had any in the first place.'

'But surely I've proved I can be obedient,' Sam persisted. 'Another example …'

'I − *we* − beg to differ,' Christine interrupted. 'We have already encountered instances of resistance, reluctance and tardiness on your part. Do you accept that?'

'Well, yes, but …'

'So, what you have just been claiming doesn't hold water,' Christine cut in again. 'Agreed?'

'Agreed,' Sam admitted.

'You are going to have to be punished for making such a false claim,' Christine said. 'You do accept that, don't you?'

'I do,' Sam agreed with a sigh, capitulating completely before he dug himself even deeper into a hole of his own making. 'I accept what you say and that I need to be punished.'

'That's something, I suppose,' Christine acknowledged.

'But not much,' Liz said, fixing her piercing green eyes on Sam. 'You *like* being punished, you *like* pain. You've already made that obvious. So, I don't think that your willing acceptance that you need to be punished takes us much further forward at all.'

'That's a fair comment,' Christine said.

'I can do better when it comes to showing obedience to you,' Sam assured the two women, looking from one to the other of them urgently. 'I can do much, much better and I will.'

'But can you go all the way? Can you show complete unquestioning obedience to us at all times?' Liz asked. 'Are you sure you are *willing* to go all the way?'

'I am,' Sam replied, looking up at her earnestly.

Liz gave a faint smile. 'That very much remains to be seen,' she told him. 'It's easy to say such things. Actions speak louder than words.'

'And talking of actions,' Christine said. 'It is now time for that punishment I spoke about.'

'That's right, Sam – the punishment you *want*,' Liz added sarcastically. Then she turned away from him and looked over at Peter, saying to the kneeling slave, 'Go to the wall cabinet and fetch the red leather paddle for me, Peter. Also bring the bottle of lubricant from the cupboard.'

As Peter got to his feet and hurried to his task, Liz gazed down at Sam who was now on his hands and knees. She knew what was going through his mind. He knew he was about to be beaten and that he was almost certainly going to be buggered too. And he wanted those things, *craved* them. She could see his excitement. It showed on his face and in the thick erection of his cock, hanging stiffly between his thighs as he knelt on all fours and awaited his punishment … and his pleasure.

Peter handed the red leather paddle and the lubricant to Liz and returned to his former kneeling position in the middle of the room. Liz put the bottle of lubricant on a side table, readily to hand. She lifted the paddle up high and paused for a moment. She smiled a sadistic smile and then brought the implement down in a swift arcing movement to land on Sam's backside. The noise from the stinging blow filled the room, the sound of hard leather on soft flesh echoing louder than the sharp exhalation of Sam's breath. The red imprint of the paddle had marked his backside, leaving an oval imprint on his naked flesh. When Liz brought the paddle down a second time Sam's erection flexed noticeably, the excitement he felt growing stronger. Several more sharp blows from the paddle served to deepen the red flush across his backside, each stroke making him breathe harder and faster as it increased his sexual arousal.

Sam's face was down at ground level now, his reddened backside raising even higher, presenting a rounded fleshy target on which Liz could continue to inflict her hard punishment. He responded to each harsh stroke of the paddle with a gasp of breath that was both pain and pleasure.

Liz stopped beating Sam, putting the paddle to one side, and smiled enigmatically. It was already clear that Sam was a sexual masochist – although neither of them would have guessed that fact when he'd first tried wheedling his way back into her life a few short days ago, any more than he would have guessed that she'd turn out to be the thoroughgoing sadist that she undeniably was. But being sexually masochistic was nowhere near enough, of itself, to make him good slave material. In fairness to the sorry bastard, though, Liz conceded, it *was* a start as was the enthusiasm he had quickly developed for receiving strap-on anal sex. But no; obedience, that's what Christine and she wanted from a slave, complete obedience. And with that, of course, went complete subservience.

'Suck Christine's *cock*,' she told Sam with heavy emphasis on the last word as Christine took up position in front of him. 'Worship it with your mouth.' Sam did as he'd been told unquestioningly, raising his head from the ground and wrapping his lips around the black dildo that Christine was now waving in his face. Christine leant back at first and let him suck and lick, lashing the dildo with his tongue. Then she leant forward and grasped his hair, forcing his face up and down on the dildo, making his mouth work harder, deeper.

'Now lick Christine's boots,' Liz told Sam next. 'Worship them with your lips and tongue.' Christine's high-heeled leather boots were long, tight and narrow-tipped and were polished to a fine shine. Sam again obeyed his instruction without question, withdrawing the dildo from his mouth, dipping his head once more and pressing his lips to the shiny leather of Christine's boots. He licked and lapped at them with his sinuous wet tongue until he became almost completely lost in the action.

Then he felt Liz move the tip of her strap-on dildo, now slick with lubricant, between the heavily beaten cheeks of his backside until it was resting directly over the tightness of his rear hole. She brought her red latex gloved hands to his arse-cheeks, pulled them widely apart and pushed the dildo into his rear opening. Sam gasped with pleasure-pain as the cool, hard object penetrated him fully. He then returned to licking Christine's high-heeled boots – this time like a man possessed.

As Sam licked and licked at the shiny leather, Liz began thrusting the dildo in and out of his anus harder and harder. It was making him more and more excited – incredibly aroused. The hard flesh of his erection was now smeared copiously with pre-cum fluid which had worked itself from its glans. Sam felt excited beyond words, thoroughly elated; this was fucking *great*.

That was when Christine moved her boots away from

Sam's lips. She then pulled his head up by yanking at his hair again. 'Now, Liz and I want you to suck my husband's cock and want him to suck yours,' she said. Peter had moved from the centre of the room, Sam noticed, and was now kneeling by her side.

Sam was shocked immediately out of his sense of elation. He gazed up at Christine with a look of horror on his face and he could feel his stomach turn. 'B-b-but I'm not gay,' he stammered.

'Are you *sure* you aren't, pretty-boy?' Christine asked, her voice taunting.

'Yes I'm sure,' he insisted, aware that throughout this exchange Liz had not for a moment stopped thrusting into his anal hole with her strap-on.

'It doesn't matter,' Christine said. 'Don't forget, Sam – total unquestioning obedience, that's what we are looking for from a slave. Now get on with it, you two – suck each other's cocks.'

At that point Peter slithered on his back under Sam and fastened his lips to his erection, immediately starting to suck it up and down. Sam reciprocated, telling himself that he had no other choice. Soon the two men's mouths and bodies were moving with their own rhythm as Liz continued to sodomize Sam with great vigour. And as Sam carried on doing what was expected of him he couldn't help wondering if there could possibly be anything more demeaning for a heterosexual man like him to be required to do than to suck another man's cock and have him suck his.

It was Peter who climaxed first, his seed spurting from his cock into Sam's open mouth. Sam sucked the fluid from Peter's hardness and, assuming this too was required of him, reluctantly swallowed it down as the other man's cock pulsed in his throat.

Liz was still pounding in and out of Sam's anal hole, pushing against the redness that stung his viciously paddled backside. She pressed down on Sam's body, pushing the dildo deeper still into his anus as Peter beneath him carried on sucking his cock, bringing him ever closer to climax.

Finally Sam closed his eyes tight and shuddered to orgasm, ejaculating thick spurts of cum into Peter's mouth. The taste of the other man's spunk was deep in his own throat as he continued being penetrated anally by Liz. She kept on filling his anal hole as she pushed the dildo deep into him. Liz, it was clear, would finish buggering him when she damn well felt like it.

As for Sam, he may have finished in the sense of having climaxed but he wasn't finished *per se*. Indeed for the first time since he had embarked on his mission to be a part of this incredibly deviant ménage he was starting to feel that he was in with some sort of a chance. After all, if what he'd just done didn't show obedience he didn't know what in hell's name did.

Chapter Thirty-seven

'WELL, CHRISTINE, WHAT DO you make of *that*?' Liz asked as she at last withdrew the dildo from Sam's gaping anus. Christine was standing by the leather couch and was in the final stages of unbuckling and removing her strap-on harness from her leather-covered form. Peter was by then back on his knees beside her.

'I think it was outrageous,' Christine replied, her tone affronted. 'It was a disgrace.'

Sam, who remained on all fours with Liz behind him, looked over at Christine in alarm. He had imagined that the two women would have been delighted at his display of obedience. What had he done wrong, for God's sake?

Liz spoke again to Christine, 'You distinctly told these two to suck each other's cocks – not to suck each other *off.*'

'I have to say that I blame Peter entirely,' Christine said. 'He knows perfectly well how literal we are in our instructions and he chose to ignore that on this occasion. Also he climaxed first of the two of them *and* he carried on sucking Sam's cock until he'd climaxed too. He was undoubtedly the one to blame in my opinion.'

'I'd be the last person in the world to make excuses for Sam,' Liz said. 'But in this case I'm inclined to agree. I assume you are going to punish Peter or do you want me to do it … or shall we perhaps both do it?'

'I'll punish him,' Christine said. 'In fact I'm going to do it right now.'

'Good,' Liz said firmly.

Christine looked down at Peter. 'How do you feel?' she asked.

'Scared, Mistress,' he replied, sounding it. Sam sympathised with Peter's situation; he couldn't fail to be sympathetic. He was also interested in his use of the term 'Mistress' in his reply to his wife. This was some kind of slave-speak, Sam presumed and he really liked the sound of it, he couldn't deny. But what interested him most of all was what Peter *hadn't* said. What he hadn't said was that he was sorry – very, very sorry – for committing the cardinal sin for a slave: that of disobedience. Something didn't sit right here.

'I'm glad you're scared,' Christine told Peter. 'You've got every reason to be scared. I'm going to use the *studded* paddle on you. Go and get it out of the wall cabinet.' She made no reference to Peter's apparent lack of contrition at disobeying her, Sam noticed. Why? It made no sense when one considered the importance she and Liz placed on a slave's total obedience at all times. No, something definitely wasn't right here, not right at all.

Christine picked up the black leather paddle that Peter now handed to her. Sam could see that it was in a different league altogether to the red paddle that Liz had used earlier on him. It was of markedly thicker leather for one thing and for another was heavily studded with ferocious-looking metal studs. Sam could see that Peter would have every reason to be scared, knowing that this was the disciplinary implement with which he was going to be punished.

Christine sat down on the couch. 'Get over my knee,' she said curtly, taking Peter's arms and pulling him across her lap. In seconds, his backside was raised high, its muscular cheeks offered for punishment. Peter glanced back towards Sam then. His gleaming blue eyes met his and lingered. He seemed to be trying to tell him something with that lingering gaze but what was it? Sam wondered if what Peter was trying to tell him without words was that this was some kind of deception devised by Liz and Christine to test Sam further. He'd better be seriously on his guard, he decided. He didn't want to fail this test, whatever it proved to be. It could well be critical.

Peter turned away suddenly just as Christine brought the studded paddle swinging down in a smooth curved path to smack down hard on his backside. It connected with his flesh with a loud Thwack! that echoed around the room in a sharp report.

A second harsh stroke followed the first, Christine bringing the studded paddle down even harder on his rear. This time the sharp Thwack! was followed by a moan of pain from Peter. Harsh stroke followed harsh stroke in quick succession and agonized moan followed agonized moan from Peter. Soon a pattern of deep red was imprinted on his backside, the colour of the punishment standing out starkly against his skin.

Christine's punishment of Peter continued relentlessly and he began to writhe, squirming over her lap as she inflicted endless hard blows on his backside with the metal-studded paddle. But Peter's writhing did not equate exclusively to pain, Sam could see that. Instead he had begun lifting himself, raising his punished backside higher to receive his beating. Peter moved to the rhythm of the punishment Christine was inflicting on him, offering himself, opening his body to the strict chastisement and then moaning with pleasure-pain when the studded implement touched its fire to his flesh.

Christine eventually stopped beating Peter and pushed him to the ground so that he was lying flat on his front, his erection pressed to the dark wooden floor. She kicked his legs apart and then turned to the kneeling Sam. 'Crawl over to Peter and position yourself between his legs,' she commanded and he did, trying as hard as he could not to let his nerves get the better of him.

'Look at these marks,' Christine continued, using the studded paddle to point out the punished marks it had imprinted on Peter's rear, which was flushed the deepest red.

'Now put your lips to those marks and kiss them, Sam,' she went on. And he did. Leaning forward on his knees with his backside in the air, Sam began pressing his lips to the red flush of Peter's punishment, feeling the heat of his pain.

'Now lick his punished arse,' Christine said and again Sam did as he'd been told, moving his wet tongue in silent exploration of the smarting pain that Christine had inflicted on Peter's backside.

'Now open up his arse-cheeks.' Sam obeyed again, lifting his head slightly and using his palms to stroke the firm reddened flesh before parting the cheeks to gaze at the pink tightness of Peter's rear hole. Sam thought he knew what was coming next and he was right.

'Lick his arsehole,' Christine said and Sam knew that he had no option but to obey. *This* was the test. This was what Peter's bogus transgression and Christine and Liz's equally phoney outrage at it had been devised to lead up to. When you are a heterosexual male could there be anything more demeaning than to be required to suck another man's cock and have him suck yours? Sam had asked himself that question when these acts had been forced on him earlier. The answer was that yes, there was something more demeaning than that and he'd just been told to do it.

Sam eased his face forward to lick Peter's anal hole, grimly determined not to be found wanting in this latest 'test'. As he did so he became aware of his own arse-cheeks being prized apart and felt something hard and familiar push against his anus. Liz was evidently going to sodomize him again with her strap-on dildo. And that is exactly what she did as Sam resolutely got on with doing what he knew he had to do.

Chapter Thirty-eight

FAST FORWARD ANOTHER DAY. Sam was alone with Liz in the elegant living room with which he had become so familiar of late. She was seated on the leather couch and was again wearing her red rubber latex cat-suit outfit, complete with gloves and long high-heeled boots. Sam was naked and on his knees in front of her. He was in for yet another set of 'tests', he assumed resignedly.

'Christine and I have made a decision,' Liz announced out of the blue. 'We have decided to allow you to be our sex-slave …'

Sam's face lit up. 'Thank you, thank you so much,' he gushed.

'You didn't let me finish,' Liz said, her voice impassive. 'It will only be for a short trial period of five days, which will start the day after tomorrow.'

'I still thank you from the bottom of my heart,' Sam replied in the same gushing tone.

Liz went on impassively, 'As our slave you will only be permitted to address Christine or me if we invite you to speak. Do you accept that?'

'Yes,' he replied eagerly. 'I accept that without question.'

'Fine,' Liz said. 'That rule can apply with immediate effect. And here is another rule you are expected to adhere to as of right now: when you talk to either

Christine or me you must always address us as 'Mistress'. Do you accept that too?'

'Yes, Mistress,' the eager supplicant replied. 'Again I do so without question.'

Then Liz dropped her bombshell. 'It is only fair to tell you that Christine, who I originally thought would be most reluctant to come to any such an arrangement, has turned out to be considerably more enthusiastic about it than I am. In fact she had to use all of her powers of persuasion to get me to agree to it at all. You see, for reasons you're fully aware of, I find that I still harbour *considerable* feelings of hostility towards you.'

'Listen, Mistress...' Sam began to say.

'Quiet,' Liz said sharply. 'I've just told you that you are only allowed to speak to me when I invite you to. I'll not allow you to speak out of turn again. Is that clear?'

'Yes, Mistress,' Sam replied nervously. 'Sorry, Mistress.'

'Apology accepted. I'm glad you understand,' Liz said, with a smile that did not reach her eyes. She added sarcastically, 'Now, may I have your *permission* to go on?'

'Y-y-yes, Mistress,' Sam stammered, thoroughly disorientated by the way this exchange was going.

'I go back to what you have been told before,' Liz went on. 'As a slave to Christine and me you will be expected to be obedient to us at all times. You will be punished constantly when you *are* obedient and that will bring you pain but it will also bring you pleasure – a heady combination you have clearly already become addicted to. If you are disobedient, however, you will also be punished but in a manner that will be *most* disagreeable to you.' Liz paused to smile at his obvious discomfort and then went on. 'Obedience is the watchword, no matter how distasteful what you are ordered to do may be to you at times. I hope you fully understand that.'

'Am I allowed to speak now?' Sam asked hesitantly.

'Did I invite you to speak?'

'No, Mistress.'

'Then you have answered your own question, haven't you,' Liz laughed softly, delighting once more in his discomfort.

'Yes, Mistress.'

'I'll let you off this time but make sure it doesn't happen again or I'll subject you to a punishment you definitely won't like,' she warned with chilly calm. 'Do you understand?'

'Y-y-yes, Mistress,' Sam replied, the nervous stammer having returned again to his voice.

'To continue,' Liz said. 'During your brief trial period you will be able to leave any time you want, night or day, if you don't like our rules or you don't like the way you're being treated. The choice will always be up to you. But be aware that should you make such a choice you will never be allowed back. Equally, if you transgress our rules or are otherwise disobedient you can expect to be punished most unpleasantly at best or be summarily and *permanently* ejected at worst. And don't think that we won't do that. Speaking personally, I'll be looking for the slightest excuse to get rid of you during those five days,' she warned. 'You do realise that, don't you?'

'Yes, Mistress,' Sam replied quietly, trembling with emotion. 'I realise that only too well.'

'I may of course be mistaken,' Liz smiled in a way that showed him that she very much doubted that she was. 'But I don't believe that you are going to be able to hack it here for more than a day or two of your trial period, which means that I'll very soon be rid of you for good.'

Sam desperately wanted to say something now, something that might make Liz think better of him, have some faith in him. But he knew that he had not been invited to speak, so wisely held his tongue.

'Is there anything you'd like to say to me or ask me?' Liz then said. 'And I don't want to hear any bullshit from you about being a changed man, asking me to trust you, empty words like that. They cut no ice with me.'

Sam paused for a few seconds to think, his mind of necessity sent off on a different tangent. Then he said, 'This is a bit prosaic, Mistress, but I've been wondering … eh …'

'What have you been wondering?' Liz said impatiently.

'I've never seen anyone else in this house apart from you, Christine and Peter, Mistress. I've never met a maid or anyone like that. I don't understand how things work. Will I be responsible with Peter for the upkeep of the property, the housework and so on?'

'Not during the trial period certainly,' Liz replied. 'And after that – in the *highly unlikely* event that you pass muster – to only a very limited extent. I won't go into any great detail now because it wouldn't be appropriate but essentially everything major on that front happens here on one day of the week only: tomorrow in fact, which is why your trial period won't start until the following day. It is an arrangement that Christine already had successfully in place before she and I became lovers and one which we have continued with. Food and other provisions that we order online are delivered here then as well as any other deliveries. A team of cleaners, helpers and gardeners come in on the same day too. While all that is going on Peter stays secreted – indeed locked – inside a place where he has to spend a lot of time anyway, a place that he has been made responsible for keeping scrupulously clean and tidy. You will share that cleaning function with him in the remote eventuality that you end up a member of our household.

'Every time Christine and I need to give the house a veneer of normality Peter is locked in this place, which incidentally is always warm ... a bit like Hades. So any time there's a particularly cold snap Peter is locked in there. Any other time it suits Christine and me, which it does frequently I might add, he finds himself in there – as will you while you're with us. Would you like me to show you the place I'm talking about?'

'Yes, Mistress,' Sam replied. He was highly intrigued by what he'd just heard and also more than a little frightened.

Liz rose from the couch in one fluid motion, strode towards the living room door and then turned to look at him. 'Get up off your knees and follow me,' she commanded.

Chapter Thirty-nine

SAM FOLLOWED LIZ'S CAT-SUITED form out of the living room, along a corridor and down a flight of stairs. At the end of the stairs was a heavy door with a key in it, which Liz turned before pushing the door open. She ushered Sam into the room beyond, flicking on its dim wall-lights as they entered.

Sam immediately began to cast his eyes around the dark cavernous basement area in which he now found himself, seeing that it was decked out as some kind of dungeon. Its equipment included a St Andrews cross mounted against one of the black walls, a horse, a whipping bench, and a metal spreader bar with steel manacle attachments at either end, which hung from the high ceiling by chains. Along the length of one wall there was a rack of dark wood upon which hung a large collection of disciplinary instruments, including straps, riding crops, tawses, whips and paddles.

Sam's eyes widened in apprehension as he took in the rack of disciplinary implements and turned to look again at the rest of his surroundings. But he felt more than apprehension, he felt mounting sexual excitement too. He could feel his cock begin to harden and throb.

'This dungeon is where you will receive much of your punishment from now on,' Liz announced. 'Does the idea of that excite you?'

'Yes, Mistress,' Sam replied hesitantly, looking into her gleaming eyes. He could feel the colour rise to his face and his cock stiffen further, pulsing with more insistence.

'I can see that it most certainly does excite you,' Liz said, her gaze straying to his erection. 'Now, turn back and face the rack of disciplinary instruments.'

Liz stopped behind Sam when he'd turned to look at the row of implements and, after slowly peeling off her latex gloves and putting them to one side, she put her hands on his back. She began running her fingers sensually over his smooth skin, following the contours of his upper body. It felt wonderful to Sam, making him sigh softly.

'Christine's always calling you pretty-boy and she's right,' Liz breathed into Sam's ear as she continued to stroke her hands gently across the smooth skin of his back and then on to his slender arms. 'You're a long-haired pretty-boy,' she added. 'From behind you could easily be a nude girl with a nice boyish figure, and you feel like one to the touch as well. It turns me on, I have to say. Disciplining you today – giving you your first dose of punishment in this dungeon – is going to be a sheer pleasure for me. Is it going to be a pleasure for you too, pretty-boy?'

'Yes, Mistress,' Sam whispered through trembling lips.

'Are you quite sure?' Liz asked, her voice suddenly gloating. 'I'm *really* going to hurt you this time, you know.'

'Y-y-yes, Mistress,' he stuttered, his eyes fixed on the array of disciplinary implements that lay before him as he wondered which of them she was going to use on him to 'really hurt him'.

Liz strode to the front of Sam then, glancing at his

slim, smoothly muscled chest and pronounced nipples and eyeing once more his powerful erection. 'At the front you look like a girl too – a pretty girl with a nice little flat chest and wearing a big flesh-coloured strap-on dildo,' she smiled. 'That's right, isn't it, pretty-boy?'

'Yes, Mistress,' he said, smiling nervously back at her.

Liz turned away from Sam, took a couple of further paces and put her hand to one of the disciplinary implements on the rack. It was a thick leather tawse and looked particularly fearsome. 'Does this frighten you as it should?' she asked, pulling it out from its place on the rack and turning to look at him again. 'Does it frighten you a lot?'

Sam swallowed hard. 'Yes, Mistress' he admitted, his blue eyes glazing over with fear.

'And yet it excites you as well, is that not so?' Liz said, letting her fingers linger on the glossy surface of the tawse and her gaze linger once more on Sam's powerful erection.

'Yes, Mistress,' he said, his voice trembling. 'I am frightened and excited at the same time.'

'Go and stand in front of the St Andrews cross with your face to the wall,' Liz ordered, pointing at the wall-mounted cross. 'Once I have strapped you to the cross I intend to chastise you with this tawse. I promised you that when I subjected you to your first punishment in this dungeon it would really hurt. This tawse is the implement I intend to use on you to achieve that effect.'

Sam's eyes locked onto hers for a split second and then he turned away nervously and padded towards the wall-hung cross. In his trepidation and his excitement, though, he hugged something to himself that Liz had said to him when she'd been gently stroking his back and arms. This woman who professed to have retained such strong feelings of hostility towards him had said that he turned her on. Well, she'd *sort* of said that anyway.

Liz wasted no time in strapping Sam to the St. Andrews cross. She bound him there, face forward and in a spread-eagled position, his wrists and ankles tightly secured to its leather-covered surface. She also wasted no time in commencing his discipline, using the heavy leather tawse. The quick-fire snapping sounds as its thongs connected for the first time with his backside echoed through the dungeon. She hit him again straight after that, bringing the sturdy leather implement down hard on his flesh and making Sam cry out in pain.

'Silence!' Liz demanded harshly, bringing the tawse down a third time onto its target. Strokes four and five landed in quick succession after that, the sharp percussive sound of heavy leather thongs snapping against Sam's reddened backside filling the dungeon.

On and on Liz beat Sam, his agonized face turned to the wall as he suffered in silence each savage stroke of her punishment. She'd said she was going to really hurt him this time and she hadn't been exaggerating. He winced in silent anguish, his expression shielded from her view.

After numerous further vicious strokes, all of them delivered with deadly precision, Sam momentarily forgot himself. He sighed audibly just the once, the short gasp of pain escaping from his lips despite himself.

'I said silence!' Liz reminded him, her voice even harsher. 'You'll have to suffer the consequences if I hear another sound out of you.'

She continued beating him remorselessly as he bit into his lip to keep himself quiet. It was the only way he had to stop himself not so much gasping as screaming out in agony.

Liz paused briefly to caress Sam's backside, to feel the burning heat that suffused his flesh. He turned to her briefly at that point, a look of pleading in his agonized blue eyes.

'Soon,' she said by way of a response, the single word whispered almost languorously as she brought her arm back to recommence the savage punishment. 'Soon,' she repeated as she brought it back again.

Soon, Sam started to say the word to himself over and over again like a mantra. But Liz certainly did not stop beating him soon. She certainly did not reduce the momentum of her beating soon either, far from it. But soon Sam didn't care because soon was indeed when it happened. Soon was when the livid pain he was experiencing translated itself into something else: pure pleasure. Soon he started moving with her rhythm, lifting himself in his bonds, pushing his rear back to meet each stroke. Soon he was accepting his chastisement with delight as its ecstatic heat began to radiate through his being. Soon was what Liz had said and soon was when all of this happened.

Liz paused to caress Sam's rear again and he pressed it back against her softly stroking fingers and sighed inwardly with pleasure and anticipation. And this was not anticipation that his punishment would soon be over. Oh no, Sam didn't want it to be over. What he wanted was that it would soon recommence, more savagely than ever. Liz did not disappoint, suddenly snapping the tawse down extra hard on his punished rear with a brisk jagged motion. Sam found it exquisitely agonizing.

Liz upped the ante even further then, raised the stakes still more, her strokes growing even stronger as she made sure that every inch of Sam's backside was patterned red – and that he grew ever closer to the orgasm she felt certain he would not long be able to restrain. And she was right. Sam was ready to burst, nearly ready to come. His whole body was shaking in his bonds. His throat was parched, his heart beating like a drum and as for his cock ...

Liz timed it just right. Letting the tawse drop to the shiny dark wooden floor of the dungeon, she gave Sam another instruction. 'Come for me now, pretty-boy,' she ordered, adding quickly, 'but remember – not a sound.'

And Sam did come – hugely. A sharp tremor started in his shaft and rose all the way to his head before spasming right through him and returning to his erection. That was when he reached the peak of erotic delight, his semen bursting out and spraying warm and silky onto the leather cross to which he was so securely bound. Sam's climax raged and raged then, keeping him at that peak for a brief eternity of erotic bliss, and the whole of the time he was aware of himself crying out repeatedly in ecstasy ... inside his head.

Chapter Forty

SAM HAD ONLY THAT moment stopped hyperventilating. The experience he'd just been through had been amazing, awesome, incredible. He was immensely impressed – partly at himself at having been able to keep completely silent under such extreme circumstances – but primarily at Liz. How had she been able to do those things to him? How had she been able to do them without allowing herself even the smallest verbal clue from him? How had she known when the acute pain she had been inflicting on him would turn to agonized ecstasy? How had she been able to make him climax that way? How had she known the exact time to tell him to climax? It was as though she was able to read his mind, control it even. It was frightening but it was also unbelievably exciting.

Liz unbuckled the straps that held Sam to the St. Andrews cross. 'Kneel here,' she ordered, pointing to a space on the dungeon floor at her feet. Once he was in position she added, 'You realise that Christine and I will have total power over you while you remain our sex-slave, don't you?'

'Yes, Mistress,' he replied, his face turned up to her.

'And does that frighten you?' she asked, looking down at Sam with eyes that seemed to see right through him.

'Yes, Mistress, it does frighten me,' he admitted, unable to turn away from her gaze.

'That's as it should be,' she said with a faint smile. 'It works to your advantage too, can you see that?'

'No, Mistress,' Sam admitted, his expression confused.

'If you are frightened it means that you are more likely to be obedient,' Liz explained. 'And only by always being obedient will you have a hope in hell of succeeding during your trial period as our slave, which – while brief – is going to be exceptionally challenging for you. *Now* you understand the point I was making, don't you?'

'Yes, Mistress,' Sam agreed with a shiver.

'Do you understand why you are on your knees in front of me?' Liz then asked.

'Because you told me to,' Sam replied, looking up beyond her cat-suited body to her beautiful face. 'It shows my obedience to you.'

'That is so,' she said with another faint smile. 'But it is also symbolic. It shows that you are beneath me, that your true place is at my feet, worshipping me. Do you accept that?'

'Yes, Mistress,' he said.

'Show me that you accept it. Show me that you worship me by licking my boots,' Liz ordered and Sam immediately bent forward and began to lap at her high-heeled boots. Just like the time he'd been ordered by Liz to lick Christine's boots Sam found the activity intensely demeaning, yet, at the same time, it stirred an excitement in him that made his cock stiffen once more.

'That's one of the ways you can worship me,' Liz said, pulling at his long hair to make him kneel up. 'But there are more ways, and you will learn some of these during your trial period *if* you last the course. And if you are serious about doing that the golden rule you must always remember, which I'll spell out for you one last time, is that *complete* obedience at all times on your part to

Christine and to me is required of you. Do you fully understand that?'

'Yes I do, Mistress,' Sam replied, resolving to stick to that golden rule like a limpet.

'Now, I see that there are parts of the St. Andrews cross that are covered with your spunk,' Liz said. 'Lick it all off for me.'

Sam gave a sharp intake of breath and remained rooted to the spot for a moment. Liz wasn't really expecting him to …

'Do it now and make a good job of it,' she snapped and, trembling, he obediently crawled into position and set to his unwelcome task. For some reason that he couldn't fathom, though, his cock remained hard the whole time he was doing it.

Chapter Forty-one

Liz was satisfied that Sam had licked the St. Andrews cross completely clean of his cum although he was continuing to lap at its leather covered surface. She presumed correctly that he was waiting for her to tell him to stop and she could see – how could she miss it? – that he still had a powerful erection.

'All right, that's enough. Stand up and face me,' she said, her voice cold. Sam stopped licking the cross, got to his feet and turned towards Liz whose next action at first seemed to give the lie to the chilly tone she'd used when addressing him. She began to run her fingers gently through his long wavy hair. Sam thought this might be an indication that she was pleased with the way he'd carried out his last task, humiliating as it had been. He was quickly disabused of this optimistic notion when she then tightened her fingers, grabbing handfuls of his hair so that her knuckles pressed hard against his skull. She pulled his head down, making him get back onto his knees.

'Ah!' Sam cried out, his face twisting into a grimace of pain.

'Were you trying to say something?' Liz said, bringing her face down to meet his.

'No, Mistress,' he replied, breathing hard as he looked into her shining green eyes. 'It was a cry of pain.'

'Good,' she replied, gripping his hair even harder. 'A

cry of pain is acceptable on this occasion. But you are not permitted to speak as such unless directly invited to, as I have already told you. That standing instruction *has* sunk in, has it?'

'Yes, Mistress,' Sam panted.

'I'm glad to hear it,' Liz said with a cruel little smile. Sam cried out loudly as she pulled at his hair again, the pain like sharp daggers in his head.

'God, how I like to hurt you,' Liz said with relish, jerking his head back suddenly, making him cry out even more loudly this time. 'I always knew I'd enjoy hurting you, getting my own back after the fucking disgusting way you treated me during our marriage. But I didn't realise quite *how much* I'd enjoy hurting you. Mind you, you've proved to be a surprise yourself, and I'm not referring to the fact that it turns out you're as much of a masochist as I am a sadist. Do you know what I'm referring to?'

'No, Mistress,' Sam replied, still wincing with pain.

'Well, put it this way,' Liz said. 'Who would have thought my notorious Lothario of an ex-husband would have turned out to have such a gift for sucking cock? I certainly wouldn't have guessed that. I might have guessed it from your appearance, pretty-boy, sure, but certainly not from your record with the ladies.' She began pulling Sam by the hair again, this time until he was flat on his back on the dungeon floor. 'Now, suck the heel of my right boot, *cocksucker*,' she ordered. 'Imagine that its Peter's big stiff cock you're sucking.'

Sam began pressing his lips to the red heel, sucking the hard, shiny dagger into his mouth. His heart was pounding, throbbing violently in his chest as he did as he'd been told to do. Sam pictured himself sucking Peter's hard cock. He told himself that he was doing it not because he wanted to, God forbid, but because he had no choice in the matter. He was doing it because Liz had *told* him to. The idea filled him with a perverse delight that caused his shaft to stiffen further, becoming rock hard.

Liz pulled her boot away from Sam, its high heel wet with his saliva, the smear of his lips on the shiny red latex. 'Get to your feet again, cocksucker,' she told him.

When Sam was standing once more, Liz began to stroke his bare chest, her long fingers tracing whirling patterns over the silky smoothness of his skin. He uttered a shrill cry of pain when she caught hold of one of his stiff nipples between finger and thumb. He shifted forward to try to lessen the pain but she responded by pulling the pronounced nub of flesh even harder. Liz let go for a second and then grabbed the other nipple and pulled hard, making Sam cry out again. When she released him his chest was marked with dark red around the nipples, which ached with intense pain.

'You just wait until I *clamp* these,' Liz remarked, flicking her fingers across his nipples casually. 'Then you'll really know what nipple torture is all about, won't you?'

'Yes, Mistress,' he said, shivering with pain.

'Now, back onto the dungeon floor with you,' Liz said, grabbing Sam by the hair once more and directing him backwards until he was once again lying flat on his back on the ground at her feet.

She stepped over him then, planting her high heeled boots on either side of his head. Once in this position she unzipped and removed the central panel of her red latex cat-suit, revealing to his awe-struck gaze the wondrous sight of her hairless pussy and the rounded cheeks of her backside.

'Worship my sex,' Liz ordered as, with her back to

Sam's gaze, she squatted down on her heels on either side of his head, her pussy hovering above his mouth. He breathed in deeply, inhaling the musky scent of her excitement. The lips of her sex were slightly parted, offering a glimpse of the paradise beyond them, which was all wet and gleaming and slick. Gently, Sam touched his lips to Liz's sex, kissing her softly, pressing his tongue into the folds of her pussy. He traced the dark petals of her labia with his tongue, moving it back and forth slowly. He worked it deeper and deeper into her pussy with each stroke until she was soaked with love juice and groaning with pleasure.

'Lick harder,' Liz demanded then and Sam began spearing her sex with his tongue, pressing in deep to brush against its moisture-soaked walls. He pushed his tongue in and out, pushing his face right against her backside, eating from her pussy directly. Her juices soaked him, wetting his mouth, his lips, his face. He sucked harder, wanting to devour the very centre of her pleasure.

'Lick harder still,' Liz ordered as she squatted down more firmly, trapping Sam's head between her thighs. And he did not falter, his mouth sucking and licking feverishly at her pussy. Liz began to use her fingers fast and hard on her clit then, rubbing frenzied circles around the stiff bud as Sam mouthed her wet open pussy. He could sense the urgency of her pleasure. She was moving faster and faster, grinding down on his face. Her juices were pouring into his mouth now to be sucked and savoured there until he knew – and she knew – that she was about to climax. And then she did, the muscular spasms ripping through her deliriously as she cried out her pleasure and pushed down even harder onto his face.

*　　　　*　　　　*

267

Sam had felt close to being smothered to the point of suffocation when Liz had climaxed and he hoped she would climb off his face after that. But she didn't. 'Worship me here now,' Liz said, using the palms of both hands to squeeze open the cheeks of her backside to reveal the puckered orifice of her anus.

Gathering up his resolve, Sam obeyed immediately and traced his tongue from the opening of her dripping sex back to the anal hole that she was now demanding that he pleasure. He pushed his mouth against her rear crack and his tongue against her anus. He began licking the tight ring of muscle slowly, lavishing her arsehole with the wetness of his tongue until she squirmed.

But it clearly wasn't enough for Liz. 'You're not licking hard enough, pretty-boy,' she announced in a harsh tone. 'I'm going to have to punish you for that.' She dug her high heels into Sam's shoulders suddenly, making him cry out from beneath her thighs. He cried out a second time when she grasped his nipples again, squeezing tightly, sending sharp jags of pain through his body.

Sam tried to ignore the pain by focussing all his attention on licking Liz's anal ring as hard as he could, his mouth pressed firm against the cheeks of her backside. She ground herself down against his mouth as his tongue penetrated in and out of her tight rear passage. And as it did, Liz began to moan and gasp her pleasure, which was as real as the pain she was continuing to inflict on Sam's nipples with her tightened fingers.

'Harder still,' Liz ordered and Sam obeyed, pressing his mouth deeper into her anus, sucking and licking lustily while doing his utmost to ignore the pain that spasmed from his nipples as a result of her pincer-like grip on them.

Eventually Sam forgot all about the pain he was in. It didn't matter. All that mattered to him was the pleasure he was giving to Liz as his tongue flicked hot and hard at her anal hole. He mouthed and kissed and licked every inch of her rear opening, his tongue licking its magic over her arsehole. His body moved with her pleasure as her quivering thighs gripped his head and her backside pressed down on his face. And all the while her fingers carried on torturing his nipples mercilessly.

Finally Liz pushed herself down onto Sam's face with force, so that his tongue sank even deeper into her anus. At the same time she squeezed his nipples as savagely as possible, causing him to utter a strangled cry of pain that fuelled her own pleasure to just the right degree. Her groin began to spasm then and her whole body started to shake as her climax raged.

Liz said nothing for a short while, her heart still pounding from her orgasm. Then she spoke, 'That was quite an experience,' she said, giving Sam's nipples one last ferocious squeeze. 'Yes, quite an experience – Having my small arsehole pleasured by the biggest arsehole I've ever met in my life.'

Chapter Forty-two

LIZ CLIMBED OFF SAM'S face then and, leaving him flat on his back on the floor, strode out of the dungeon. She slammed the heavy door shut behind her but didn't lock it. Sam lifted himself up on his elbows. He looked down at his bare chest and saw the red marks around his nipples, which still smarted horribly. He lifted a buttock and gazed back at the red marks there too, the ones Liz had inflicted on him with the vicious tawse, and which smarted like blazes as well. But the pain Sam was suffering was a strange sort of pain, one with which he was becoming more and more familiar. It was a pain that felt like pleasure. He could taste a faint trace of his own ejaculate from when he'd licked clean the St. Andrews cross, mixing in his mouth with the taste of Liz's pussy and of her anus from when she'd ridden his face.

Sam's erect cock pulsed responsively as he thought of lying under Liz and worshipping her pussy with his mouth until she'd climaxed ecstatically and of doing the same to her tight anal hole until she'd shuddered to another ecstatic orgasm. Worship her sex and worship her anus, that's what Liz had wanted him to do. And worship was the right word because she was his Mistress and he was her slave. Her *slave*. He loved the idea of it, loved the idea of being Liz's slave, who existed only to please and serve and obey her.

Sam couldn't wait to start showing her how well he could serve her. Before long Liz's hatred for him would evaporate, he told himself with a sudden absurd surge of optimism, and she would be proud, so proud to call him her slave. Sam hoped that Liz would return to the dungeon very soon so that he could start really proving himself to her.

But when the dungeon door creaked open it was not Liz who entered But Christine and Peter, both of them as naked as he was.

'Get onto your knees, pretty-boy,' Christine ordered and he scrambled into position.

'Did you enjoy your first session in the dungeon?' she asked him.

'Yes, Mistress,' Sam replied.

'Liz has just been telling me that she had you licking her arsehole,' she said. 'Did you enjoy doing that?'

'Yes, Mistress,' he replied, feeling the cheeks of his face start to prickle.

'You recollect licking Peter's arsehole, don't you,' Christine said. Jesus, how would he ever forget *that* experience, he said to himself with a shudder.

'Yes, Mistress,' Sam answered, his face now burning with embarrassment.

'You had a hard-on as stiff as the one you're currently displaying while you were doing it. So I assume you enjoyed doing that as well,' Christine said, adding, 'Am I correct in my assumption? Make sure you are absolutely honest in your reply or you'll live to regret it.'

Sam didn't answer. He felt panicked, could feel the beads of sweat forming on his skin. While he'd been licking Peter's arsehole, Liz had been sodomizing him. That was why he'd had the hard-on. But what he'd been forced to do with his tongue hadn't exactly detracted from the experience, if he was honest. And Christine had just told him to be absolutely honest in his reply. Even so, he couldn't get the words out. It was so difficult.

'Answer my question,' Christine said, her voice angry.

Sam was trembling. Why did he have to answer the question? Had he been alone with Christine it might have been different, but there, in front of Peter, it suddenly seemed too much to ask.

'Answer the question, pretty-boy, or you'll have to take the consequences,' Christine warned him, her voice rising higher.

'Yes, Mistress,' Sam said finally.

'Yes, Mistress, what?' Christine persisted. 'Yes, you enjoyed licking Peter's arsehole. Say the words.'

'Yes, Mistress, I enjoyed licking Peter's arsehole,' Sam admitted, wishing like mad that Peter hadn't been there to witness his shameful admission.

'And you enjoyed it too when you sucked each other off, didn't you?'

'Yes, Mistress.' He looked briefly in Peter's direction and then swiftly averted his gaze. This was all so unbelievably embarrassing.

'I think I deserve an apology for your slow response to that first simple question I asked, don't you?' Christine said.

'Yes, Mistress,' he whispered miserably, trying not to think of Peter standing so close. 'I'm sorry, Mistress.'

'Stand up,' she told him sharply and he immediately obeyed. 'Step forward a little now,' she added, and he did as ordered, standing several feet before her, head bowed. He held his hands limply at his side, but his cock was anything but limp.

'Peter, stand in front of him,' Christine ordered next and a strong feeling of inevitability swept through Sam.

She was going to make the two of them engage in some sort of homosexual act again, he was certain of it. It was bound to happen. There was no way he could stop it now. And curse his cock. Why was it still erect? Sam felt frightened, confused, embarrassed and – fuck it – aroused.

'Put your hand on Sam's cock,' Christine ordered Peter and he started to squeeze Sam's hardness, his fingers curling around the base. 'Start wanking him off,' Christine added and then continued to issue a regular flow of orders, 'Keep up a regular rhythm. That's it; good, good. Now a bit faster.'

Sam's breathing had become ever more laboured, the excitement and the self-disgust and the confusion making his head swim and his heart race. He wished Peter would stop what he was doing … he wished he would carry on doing what he was doing … he wished he would stop …

Christine walked past Peter and stood behind Sam, putting her fingers to his back, letting her long nails slide across his smooth skin. She brought her mouth to Sam's ear and whispered softly, 'Would you prefer it if I was handling your genitals? I'm quite happy to do that, you know.'

Sam closed his eyes for a moment in relief. 'Yes please, Mistress,' he panted and Peter let go of his erection, moving aside to let Christine take his place.

'Do you know something, pretty-boy,' Christine smiled with unconcealed delight as she cupped his balls in her fingers. 'I think you might just have made the wrong decision.' With that she tightened her fingers around his scrotal sac, looked directly into his eyes, and squeezed.

Chapter Forty-three

CHRISTINE DIDN'T SQUEEZE SAM'S balls too hard or for too long. She didn't need to. The experience was excruciating, an explosion of crimson agony that made him scream. 'In future, when I ask you a question I expect a prompt reply,' Christine warned, when his screaming had ceased. 'If I don't get one, a simple apology from you will not suffice, as I have just demonstrated. Do I make myself perfectly clear?'

'Yes, Mistress,' Sam whimpered, still shivering with pain.

'Follow me,' she ordered then, taking him over to the section of the dungeon where the metal spreader bar with steel manacle attachments on either end hung by chains from the ceiling. She told him to raise his arms and then manacled his wrists to the spreader bar. After that she picked out a black-and-red braided leather whip from the rack of disciplinary instruments that lined the wall.

Sam readied himself for the vicious flogging he knew he was about to receive, tensing his body and gritting his teeth. The sharp pain burned like a flame to his flesh as Christine's whip came crashing down. He barely had time to catch his breath before her second strike landed. Again, the pain swept through him as the braided flogger landed explosively on his rear. Sam could feel the heat burning on the cheeks of his backside, the skin raised and

274

imprinted with the pattern of the whip's braided thongs.

On and on Christine berated his rear with the savage whip until he closed his eyes, feeling that he was unable to endure the severity of his punishment any longer. But he had to, because still she went on, whipping him so vigorously that he felt the breath knocked out of him with each strike. Sam's backside ached, the smarting pain of each impact merging with the ones that had preceded it and seeping through his body. He tried not to think of anything, tried not to see himself being so brutally chastised by Christine, tried not to imagine her eyes focused on his backside reddening further with every savage strike from the braided whip, tried not to think of the excitement that made his cock throb harder and harder.

'Peter,' Christine directed suddenly, bringing a stop to the rhythm of her ferocious strikes to Sam's rear. 'I want you to suck Sam off. Oh, wait a moment,' she added mockingly. 'I was forgetting, Sam, you're not gay, are you. Would you prefer it if I were to bring *my* lips to your cock instead? I'd be happy to oblige. I've done it before and you obviously enjoyed it that time. So, would you like *me* to suck you off?'

'No thank you, Mistress,' Sam gasped. No fucking way, he thought. After what she'd done to his balls a few moments ago he wouldn't put it past her to bite his dick right off!

'As you wish, pretty-boy,' Christine laughed.

There was a delay momentarily as Peter crawled into position. Sam looked down, past his cock with its bead of pre-cum fluid coating its slit, and into Peter's shining blue eyes. He looked up at him, his face as flushed as his own. Sam felt ashamed and humiliated and degraded as he also felt the dark feelings of arousal that went with those

275

emotions, and which were measured by the hardness of his erection. He closed his eyes again, unable to watch as Peter's lips closed around his glans, his mouth working to suck away the pre-cum moistness that beaded its tip. Sam groaned softly as Peter's mouth worked up and down his shaft with gentle firmness. He gasped as the sensations Peter awakened with his lips merged with the burning of the marks that covered his punished rear.

Christine then began to beat Sam once more, bringing the black-and-red braided whip down harder than ever. Each time it landed, the intense pain caused Sam to jerk forward, which had the effect of pushing his cock deeper into Peter's mouth. The pain grew stronger and stronger, as the pleasure increased that Peter was working on Sam's cock with his busy lips and tongue.

Sam felt as though his body was on fire, the sharp hot spears of pain on the cheeks of his backside reaching a peak. He could hold back no longer and with a strangled cry he climaxed massively. The seed exploded from his cock into Peter's mouth, flooding thick waves of cum onto his tongue and down his throat.

Christine stopped beating Sam at that point. Peter stopped sucking his cock too. He remained on his knees before him, strands of semen trickling from his lips. Sam stood back shakily in his bonds, gasping for breath. He looked down at his cock, smeared with spittle and semen but still erect despite or no doubt *because* of the pain from his punished backside.

And he suddenly felt filled with determination, his whole being suffused with it, permeated by it. Liz might hate him, and God knows he'd given her every reason to feel that way about him, but he loved her. He loved her more than he could ever once have thought possible. Sam loved Liz for herself and he loved her for the profound effect she'd had on him since he'd arrived back in her life, no matter how unwelcome that arrival had been to her.

For Liz he had already accepted the most extreme of punishments. For her he had allowed himself to engage in acts of the utmost degradation. For her he had allowed himself to be subjected to the most abject humiliation. He had done it all for her. He would do anything for Liz. He would do anything to get her back.

Sam felt his heart beat faster. He was going to show Liz what a good, no *excellent* sex-slave he could be to her and Christine during his trial period. And in doing that he was going to make her love him again. He had already endured such a lot towards that goal but there was obviously much worse in store for him when he moved in the day after tomorrow. Well, fuck it, he said to himself defiantly. He could handle whatever perversions were forced upon him during those five make-or-break days. He could cope with whatever pain, no matter how extreme it might be, that was inflicted on him during that time. It was his one and only chance to get Liz back and he wasn't going to mess it up. He *was* going to get her back.

Chapter Forty-four

CHRISTINE LED PETER OUT of the dungeon on his hands and knees then, leaving Sam to pursue his thoughts further. He reckoned he'd got the message loud and clear now. If he wanted to survive the rigors of his forthcoming trial period – and he wanted that more than anything else in the world – he must answer any question thrown at him by either Liz or Christine promptly and with total honestly, and must comply with everything they told him to do, no matter what it might be, absolutely without fail.

Sam understood very well that the trial period was going to be extremely difficult for him but he promised himself again that he would give it his very best shot, put all he had into it – and then some. He knew that Liz did not have high hopes for him at all, and indeed was just waiting for him to fail. But he was absolutely determined to prove her wrong. In doing that he would be able to rebuild the loving bond that had once existed between them and that he and he alone had wilfully torn asunder to be replaced by deep regret on his part and bitter hatred on hers.

'Hello there, Sam,' a quiet voice said. 'It's just you and me for the time being.'

Sam turned suddenly. He had been so lost in his thoughts that he had not heard Peter come padding back into the dungeon.

'Hi, Peter,' Sam said, turning to face him properly. He added hesitatingly, 'Look, I'm really sorry about the oral sex and everything just now.'

'There's no need to be sorry,' Peter replied simply. 'There was nothing you could have done about it anyway, and I didn't mind at all. I enjoyed it actually.'

'You did?'

'That's right,' Peter confirmed. 'It's left me dead horny, though,' he added, darting a look at his own erection – and at Sam's. 'I'll need to spank the monkey very soon if I don't get some other form of relief.'

'Well, that's honest,' Sam laughed.

Peter looked at him directly. 'Tell me, did you enjoy me blowing you just now?' he asked. 'One honest answer deserves another.'

'I guess I did,' Sam admitted with an awkward smile. 'I found it extremely embarrassing at the beginning, that's for sure – almost as bad as that time we were made to suck each other's cocks. But I was turned on too, especially as I was being beaten at the same time. I ended up – as you of all people would know – having one hell of an orgasm.'

Peter smiled and then said haltingly, 'Talking of that, I wonder if you could …' he didn't finish the sentence.

'You wonder if I could what?' Sam asked.

'Oh, nothing.'

'Come on, what were you going to say?'

'Obviously you don't have to do this if you don't want to,' Peter whispered. 'But I was wondering if you could give me a quick hand job, finish me off.'

'Sure, why not,' Sam shrugged, aping Peter's earlier display of insouciance. It wouldn't involve disobeying Liz or Christine, that was the main thing. So, if it was what Peter wanted … He brought his hand to Peter's erection and began to push his fist up and down.

It was then that the dungeon door crashed open. 'Is this what you get up to when I leave you unsupervised,' Christine demanded, standing naked in the doorway. She looked angrily at the two startled men in front of her who quickly sprang apart. 'Were you behind this, Peter?' she asked, her eyes narrowing with suspicion.

'Yes, Mistress,' he admitted. 'I felt so horny that I got kind of carried away. You see ...'

'That's enough!' she snapped angrily. 'I don't want to hear any pathetic excuses.'

'How about you, Sam,' she said. 'What have you got to say for yourself?'

'Sorry, Mistress,' he said, shaking fearfully. 'I really didn't realise I was doing anything wrong.'

'A likely story,' Christine snorted. She eyed both men contemptuously. 'Get on your knees, the pair of you.' They obeyed without hesitation, dropping down to the dungeon floor immediately like a couple of felled logs.

Christine glared at the two men for a while longer, her eyes shining. She then strode to the rack of disciplinary implements and picked out a heavy leather flogger. Turning and stepping forward, she planted her feet wide and pointed to the space in front of her.

'Peter,' she said, giving him a cold stare. 'Crawl over here.'

Sam could sense, almost taste, the fear and excitement that was surging through Peter as he crawled along the shiny dark wooden floor to Christine. 'You're a complete pain-slut nowadays, aren't you, bitch?' she hissed once he was in position, glaring at his exposed body and steely hard-on. 'You'll do anything to get yourself punished.'

'Yes, Mistress,' Peter replied with a shiver just as she brought the whip down, landing a heavy blow on his backside. He squealed and cowered as she laid several more blows to his rear, marking his skin red with the thongs of the whip. On and on Christine belaboured Peter's rear with savage blows. She struck again and again, using her full strength every time. Each one of her blows was a flash of pure pain that made Peter cry out more and more as the full effect of the whipping spread through his body. Each time the heavy leather flogger landed it brought another jolt of agonizing pain and another cry from him. Christine kept on beating Peter in this ferocious way until he began really bellowing in pain, screeching like a banshee. Only then did she stop beating him although she continued to hang onto the whip.

She began to masturbate instead, plunging the fingers of her other hand noisily into the wet parts of her sex. She then reached down and parted Peter's buttocks, revealing the tight rear orifice of his anus. She spread her wetness over his anal hole, lavishing it with her lubrication.

Christine stroked Peter's backside several times before suddenly pushing the pommel of the whip with which she'd recently beaten him with such savagery deep and hard into his anus, making him groan loudly with pain. She then began sodomizing him with the smooth pommel, entering and re-entering his anus, forging deeper into him each time. She made the implement move faster, making Peter cry out with pain each time she plunged it in and out.

'You're a complete pain-slut who loves to be fucked in the arse,' Christine said as she moved the implement faster still. 'Isn't that what you are, bitch?'

'Yes, Mistress,' he panted.

Sam watched, horrified and fascinated by Christine's violent penetration of Peter's body. He felt the excitement in the air, the tension rising as Peter's cries of pain started to become unbridled cries of pleasure. He began rocking himself back, moving with the hard rhythm of Christine's movements as she plunged the pommel in and out of his anus.

'Come for me now, bitch,' Christine demanded at last. With that Peter gave a strangled cry of pleasure before shuddering convulsively, rope after rope of creamy cum shooting out of his cock and splattering onto the dark shiny wood of the dungeon floor beneath him.

Peter stayed still for a few seconds, remaining on his hands and knees. Sam watched as Christine removed the whip handle from his anus and threw the flogger to the ground. She pushed Peter's head down and he pressed his lips to her bare feet, kissing them gratefully.

Christine looked over at Sam then, her eyes gleaming with cruelty. 'Your turn next, pretty-boy,' she said.

Chapter Forty-five

AFTER A FEW MOMENTS Christine instructed Peter to stop kissing her feet. 'Wait there on your knees, bitch, and watch Sam suffer now,' the naked dominatrix told him before striding towards the rack of disciplinary implements. Sam trembled with both fear and anticipation as he saw Christine turn from the rack and advance towards him with a substantial wooden paddle in her hand. 'Stand up,' she said. 'Then go and bend over the whipping bench.'

Sam got into position over the bench, its smooth leather surface cool against his erection. He awaited his punishment as Christine touched him with the flat surface of the wooden paddle, stroking it tantalizingly along the curves of his naked backside. 'You want this, don't you, pretty-boy,' she said.

'Yes, Mistress,' Sam replied, and it was true. He could feel it in the hardness of his cock pressed tight against the whipping bench, the head slippery with silvery fluid that leaked copiously in his excitement.

'Every stroke will hurt like fuck,' Christine promised. 'But you *still* want it, don't you.'

'Yes, Mistress,' Sam said. He moved his legs slightly apart and closed his eyes, ready for the punishment to begin. There was a sharp snap of sound that echoed through the dungeon, an explosion of pure pain that made his backside burn. Sam had no time to recover as she brought the solid wooden implement down again. He tensed and jerked forward as it snapped down on his naked rear.

The smarting sensation spread like wild fire, permeating Sam's punished flesh and then deeper into his being. Another harsh stroke landed, slicing through the air to land flat on his backside. It brought another explosion of pain followed by a gasp that Sam could not hold back. The next blow landed even more furiously, forcing him hard against the whipping bench so that his shaft rubbed wetly against its smooth leather surface.

Sam lost count of the strokes eventually. He lost sight of everything until his mind was focused purely on the remorselessly savage punishment that Christine was inflicting on his rear with the wooden paddle. The hot pain became blurred with pleasure, agony and ecstasy combined. The strokes fell like fire on the reddened cheeks of Sam's backside, adding to the heat that blazed through his body. His erect cock rubbed deliciously against the wetness he had smeared on the leather surface of the whipping bench.

Then the paddling stopped all of a sudden. 'Peter, hand me the heavy leather flogger I used on you,' Christine demanded and Sam braced himself for a savage whipping. But it did not happen. Instead Christine pressed the head of the whip's pommel against his anal hole and pushed it in with one decisive thrust. This sudden brutal invasion of Sam's anus hugely intensified the burning pain to the cheeks of his backside and it only took another few rapid thrusts of the pommel into him by Christine for the sensation to peak into a gigantic orgasm. His body quivered and jerked ecstatically as he jetted a thick stream of semen onto the leather of the whipping bench.

Christine removed the whip handle from Sam's anal hole. 'Stand up,' she commanded and he obeyed, looking at the slippery pool of cum now smearing the leather surface of the whipping bench.

'Lick that up and swallow it down,' Christine demanded and Sam leant forward and began to do as he'd been told. He could feel his face burning with shame as he licked up the thick droplets of cum until they'd become a creamy pool in his mouth. He let all this cum fill his mouth and then swallowed it in one gulp.

'Now lick up and swallow Peter's cum,' Christine ordered, gesturing towards the profusion of fluid that had squirted earlier from Peter's cock onto the shiny dark wood of the dungeon floor. Sam got onto his knees and crawled to the location, his head lowered, determined to lick up and swallow it all. He had to swallow all that cum just like he was going to have to swallow every ounce of his pride if he was to win Liz back.

Sam felt thoroughly degraded as he continued doing what he'd been told to do. But it was odd. At the same time he could feel his cock twitching to hardness once more. The truth was that Sam was discovering that he loved being degraded like this, really loved it. He wished Liz were there to witness the sight but doubtless Christine would report back to her, he told himself. She would report back to Liz the reason for his punishment too, he realised, and that definitely wasn't good news. Sam began to lose his erection as quickly as it had returned.

Chapter Forty-six

AFTER HIS FAUX PAS the day before last, Sam feared the worst from Liz when he arrived, small suitcase in hand, for what would be the start of his all-important five-day trial period as a sex-slave to her and Christine. His fears seemed to be confirmed when she opened the front door to him, wearing the same severe expression she'd worn the very first time he'd arrived at that door. She was wearing the same severe black leather trouser suit too.

'Ah, here comes the man who seems to think it's perfectly all right to wank off another slave without permission,' Liz said, her voice as unfriendly as the lack of welcome in her eyes.

When they entered the living room Liz told Sam to strip off all his clothing. By the time he was naked he was shivering with a mixture of trepidation and excitement and his cock was hard. But Liz hardly deigned to notice the state he was in, retaining the same glacial demeanour she'd had since she'd let him in. Then everything changed.

'I think I'll get naked too,' Liz said and it was that statement that seemed to Sam to make all the difference. The chilly atmosphere that had hung in the air around Liz since his arrival subtly altered, and Sam could feel an electric charge of sexuality begin to emanate from her. As Liz removed her clothes, every movement she made, every gesture was sexual. She undressed deliberately slowly and sensually, which he watched with growing arousal. Then, when she was completely nude, she put her high-heeled shoes back on, smiled a vulpine smile at Sam and began to caress him.

'You're such a pretty girly-boy slave,' she whispered seductively, letting her fingers travel over the silky-smooth skin of his neck and chest and stomach. He said nothing because he had not been invited to and he didn't make a move for the same reason. He simply stood and delighted in his submissiveness to her as she caressed his body.

'I want to use you for my pleasure,' Liz announced then, turning and walking towards a solid table at the side of the room and leaving him standing where he was. He watched excitedly as she bent across the table and parted her thighs, thrusting out her backside.

'Come over here and worship my pussy with your mouth, pretty-boy,' Liz demanded over her shoulder and within seconds Sam was under her, kissing and tonguing the wet slit of her sex. He sucked and licked intently, lapping at the opening of her body, seeking the pulsing of her clit with his tongue. Her pleasure mounted and she moaned softly, pushing her hips back. She was balancing on the points of her heels as Sam buried his face deeper still between her thighs.

'Now worship my arsehole in the same way,' Liz demanded and Sam shifted his attentions, pressing his tongue deeply into her rear hole instead and making her cry out blissfully in orgasmic delight. Her climax made his cock stiffen even more, until he was teetering on the edge of ecstasy, his tongue continuing to pleasure her anus until at last she told him to stop.

'I want you to worship my pussy again now, pretty-boy' Liz ordered, swivelling round and pushing Sam's face to her sex, before curling her legs over his shoulders. Her high heels snaked down his body, pressing painfully into his flesh as he brought her to another climax, his tongue deep in her pussy. Liz pushed herself further up then, sitting on the edge of the table and bringing her high heels to the front of Sam's body.

His orgasm came a moment later as she dug both her heels against his throbbing erection. The sharp pain combined with his intense sexual excitement made him shoot his climax all over her high heeled shoes.

Sam didn't need to be told what to do next. He began to lick and kiss her shoes, sucking away and swallowing his sperm as if such an activity was second nature to him, which of course it now was.

Sam thought that Liz might show him to his room after that, let him unpack and get settled in. But he was wrong. Instead, kicking off her high-heeled shoes again so that she was completely naked, she told him to leave his suitcase in the living room and follow her. Liz then took him down to the dungeon. Sam thought it would be empty when they got there but again he was wrong. Peter was there on his own, kneeling naked on the floor. He said nothing but gave Sam a friendly smile, which he returned.

Liz turned to Sam. 'I am going to really test your ability to show obedience now,' said the naked dominatrix, her voice cold. 'If you fail this test you needn't bother unpacking. That will be the end of that – you'll be out of my life for good.' She then strode over to the rack of disciplinary instruments from which she extracted a stiff black leather strap. Sam assumed she intended to use it on him or on Peter or on both of them. Once again he was wrong. Instead Liz walked back to

Sam and placed the heavy implement in his hand. He looked back at her blankly. What did she expect him to do with it?

'Peter got you into trouble by getting you to play with his cock the last time you were in here, didn't he, Sam,' Liz said.

'Eh ... yes, Mistress,' he replied falteringly.

'Would you like to punish him for it?'

'No, Mistress,' Sam replied, his eyes widening in alarm. He was horrified at the thought. If he'd discovered anything about himself in these last few extraordinary days it was that he was an out-and-out masochist; there wasn't an ounce of the sexual sadist in him. 'Mistress Christine has already punished Peter for what happened,' Sam added, trying desperately to wriggle off the hook. 'She punished both of us.'

'I know that full well,' Liz said. 'But it was really Peter's fault, not yours. So, I repeat my question: would you like to punish him for it?'

'Absolutely not,' Sam said. He couldn't think of anything worse.

'That's what I thought,' Liz said. 'And that's exactly why I want you to do it. I want you to show me how obedient you are by beating Peter with the strap. You are to give him a dozen strokes – hard ones too; don't hold back. Understood?'

'Yes, Mistress,' Sam replied unhappily.

Liz then addressed Peter. 'I want you to count out each of the strokes for me,' she said.

'Yes, Mistress,' Peter replied, looking frightened.

'Now lean across the horse over there,' Liz ordered and he padded nervously across to the horse and bent himself across it.

'Off you go, Sam,' Liz said. 'And don't forget – beat

him really hard.'

Sam got into position and, gripping the strap tightly, brought it down hard, stinging Peter's rear harshly. 'One, Mistress,' Peter gasped as his backside registered the pain.

'That wasn't hard enough,' Liz announced.

You could have fooled me, Peter said, or rather thought.

'You're going to have to do better than that, pretty-boy,' Liz added.

Sam swiped down harder the second time, putting greater energy into the movement of his arm. Peter gritted his teeth as the strap landed, slapping hard on his rear-cheeks. 'Two, Mistress,' he panted.

'Still not hard enough,' Liz insisted.

Sam brought the strap down as hard as he could this time, putting his weight into the movement so that the strap smacked down with a harsh sound that echoed through the dungeon. Peter inhaled sharply as the pain pulsed through him. 'Three, Mistress,' he whimpered.

'That's more like it,' Liz told Sam. 'Make all the rest of your blows at least as harsh as that last one.' And that's what Sam did. He didn't have the slightest choice in the matter since Liz had made it horribly clear that if he failed this obedience test that would be the end of all this. And that would be the end of him.

'Four, Mistress,' Peter cried as the lash made painful contact with his backside again.

'Five, Mistress,' he gasped, when the fiery touch of the strap landed once more on his reddened skin.

'Six, Mistress,' he cried out at the next hard impact of the strap across his backside, which was now burning fiercely with pain.

There followed six more strikes, each delivered by

Sam with such power that they made Peter cry out every time as pain – and pleasure – washed through him.

After the twelfth strike, Liz took the strap from Sam and told Peter to come away from the horse and turn round. When he did so the extent of his sexual arousal was self-evident. He had a huge erection, which was covered in smears of pre-cum.

'Now you *do* have permission to wank Peter,' Liz told Sam. 'Bring him off into your hand.'

In no time Sam's fingers found Peter's cock and he began to work it up and down insistently, making him shudder with desire. Peter climaxed quickly, the intense sting of his behind connecting to the pleasure throbbing through his shaft as he jetted thick spurts of cum into Sam's hand.

Sam thought he knew precisely what Liz would want him to do with all that cum. This time he wasn't wrong.

Chapter Forty-seven

SAM HAD WORKED OUT a simple plan for getting through his trial period, which he'd always known was going to be extremely tough – something his session in the dungeon being forced to discipline Peter had already amply demonstrated. He had decided that each day he would respond with total obedience to every difficult and tormenting challenge Liz and Christine threw at him. When he was alone at night in his bedroom, however, he'd take a break from all that. He'd relax, get a good night's sleep and recharge his batteries ready for the challenges ahead of him the next day. Liz and Christine had other ideas, though. The pattern was set on Sam's first night

Although no such requirement was made of Peter, who was in a bedroom down the corridor from his, Liz and Christine insisted that Sam keep the door to his room wide open. They in turn kept ajar the bedroom they shared, which was immediately across the landing from him. The two women then taunted Sam throughout the night with their noisy love making, the torment made worse by their instruction to him that under no circumstances should he even touch his cock, never mind masturbate.

As Sam lay in bed, there were times when he was sorely tempted to start stroking his erection but he remained obedient. As he listened to Liz and Christine's loud moans of pleasure as they made passionate love, his mind filled with images of what they were doing. No matter how hard he tried to sleep, their constant cries of pleasure forced him awake, his stiffly erect cock aching for release.

The two women seemed to Sam to be insatiable and their multi-orgasmic efforts drove him to distraction. His erection became painful and overpowering feelings of sexual tension began pulsing through him, making him breathe hard and leaving him on the edge of orgasm. It was only when Liz and Christine had finally drifted off to sleep and all was silence at long last that Sam was able to calm down sufficiently to sleep too. But as he slept he also dreamt a dream that was not only highly erotic but also deeply unsettling.

In the dream he found that he was no longer the pretty-boy that he'd always been. No, Sam had become a pretty *girl* and was making love to Liz who was naked apart from a tiny black leather thong. Sam was wearing a flesh-coloured strap-on dildo and had nice little breasts, which Liz was teasing, flicking her pink tongue against their hard nipples. While she was doing this, Sam's hand began to slide as if of its own accord down between Liz's thighs. It passed over her mons and then down to stroke the lips of her sex, which were concealed by the covering of the miniscule leather thong.

Sam's fingers pressed harder and harder against the leather thong, pushing the material in against Liz's pussy lips. She moaned softly and parted her thighs so that her sex bulged against the tight strip of leather that Sam was stroking. All the while Liz continued to feast on Sam's nipples, her mouth teasing each rigid nub in turn.

Sam's fingers eased back and forth between Liz's

thighs for a while longer and finally slipped under the tight leather thong and into her moist pussy where they circled and circled, rubbing her even wetter.

Liz lifted her face and smiled at her lover then. It was such a raunchy smile, such a *loving* smile. Her hitherto flinty eyes were soft now, filled with desire. Then Liz put her lips to Sam's. The kiss was wonderful. It was joyous. It felt just perfect.

Liz broke the kiss eventually, breathless. 'Keep on finger-fucking me under my thong but do it harder, slave,' she ordered and Sam obeyed immediately, grinding down on her lover's stiff clit before putting three fingers into her pussy, plunging in and out of all the wetness within.

Liz pushed Sam's fingers away eventually and turned over, rolling on to her front before pulling herself up onto her hands and knees. She reached back and began easing her tight leather thong down slowly.

Sam ran her hand up and down the flesh-coloured strap-on dildo jutting from her own smoothly shaven crotch as her eyes fixed on what Liz was doing. She'd pulled her leather thong all the way off now, the thin strip of sodden material at last discarded.

'Let's sixty-nine each other with me sitting on your face, slave,' Liz said and Sam obediently got into position under her. Sam moaned softly as Liz sat astride her face, pressing her backside over her mouth. Liz then fastened her own lips tight on her lover's 'cock' and began working them up and down. Liz sat lower and Sam's tongue moved at first slowly over the slippery lips of her sex and then faster and faster still. She was drinking lustily from her pussy now, licking deep inside her as Liz herself sucked and sucked at Sam's strap-on.

Liz then swivelled round and straddled Sam's thighs. She let the thickness of Sam's dildo impale her, as she slid down on it, her pussy tight and dripping wet. Sam moaned with Liz's movements as she ground her hips down, feeling the heavy push of the dildo inside her dripping sex.

Next Liz climbed off the strap-on and off Sam. She swung round on to all fours again and wiggled her backside, knowing her lover was able to see all the juice oozing out from her pussy lips and admire the puckered orifice of her anus. Liz insisted that Sam kiss and lick her rear and then her anal hole. And she of course obeyed.

Sam spread her loving kisses over the smooth cheeks of Liz's backside, her lips pressing between them and then moving down to lick at her anus at first long and slow and then faster and faster, making her burn with pleasure.

Liz was moaning loudly as Sam's tongue worked ever faster. 'Fuck me in the arse now,' she cried out finally, reaching back and pulling the cheeks of her backside wide apart so that she was completely open, exposed. And Sam did as she'd been told, entering Liz with the flesh-coloured strap-on, pushing it in and out of her tight anus.

Liz made Sam move the dildo faster, and as she did this both of them were breathing heavily, their bodies shaking. Continuing to jerk the strap-on frantically in and out of Liz's anus, Sam reached to the front of her Mistress and slipped two fingers into her pussy. And that did it – for both of them. When Liz cried out her climax, Sam climaxed too, her fleshy dildo spurting out thick waves of cum at the ecstatic moment of release.

Chapter Forty-eight

FLASH FORWARD A DAY and Christine and Sam were standing together in the living room, their naked bodies bathed by the afternoon light that was streaming in through the French window. Sam's backside was a rosy red from the harsh spanking Christine had just finished giving him and he had a medium hard-on.

'Follow me,' Christine said suddenly, turning on her heels and heading out of the room. Her voluptuous naked body in motion looked *so* enticing. Sam followed quickly after her. They did not go down the stairs and into the dungeon as he'd expected, but up the stairs along the first floor corridor and into a shower room. 'Kneel down,' Christine ordered when they'd entered one of its cubicles, and Sam immediately dropped to the tiled floor. He could feel his cock become harder, his excitement mounting as he wondered what was going to happen.

Christine stood right in front of him in the confined area, her bald pussy in his face, and she spread her thighs. 'Open your mouth wide,' she demanded and he obeyed instantly. 'Now drink.' The stream of translucent fluid that then jetted out from her crotch poured straight into Sam's mouth... And it had the oddest, the most surprising effect on him. It didn't diminish his excitement as he would have expected but made it grow stronger.

'Peter hates water sports,' Christine said, still urinating

into Sam's mouth. 'But I can see that you're different.' And she was right. His cock had become rock hard and he could feel himself grow dizzy with pleasure as his mouth trapped and sucked down the fluid that continued to pour from Christine's body. How demeaning this was, how degrading, how utterly depraved, Sam said to himself as he wallowed in his golden shower. What he was experiencing right now on this, only the second day of his trial period must *surely* be the ultimate submission for him, Sam thought. But he'd got it wrong again. He couldn't have got it more wrong.

Flash forward another day. This time it was Liz standing in the living room with Sam. He was completely naked as usual and Liz was almost so, wearing only her black strap-on dildo, which she had harnessed to her crotch. 'I want you to do something for me,' she said, opening a cupboard drawer to her side and taking out a bottle of lubricant of a kind he'd not seen before. 'Apply this all over your body.'

'Yes, Mistress,' Sam replied. He proceeded to coat himself with the lube before handing the bottle back to Liz who placed it back inside the cupboard drawer. She replaced it with another more familiar looking bottle of lubricant, which she put on top of the cupboard.

Liz then dipped back into the same drawer. 'Put these on,' she said. 'The lube you're now coated with will help you to slide them onto your skin.' She handed Sam a black rubber latex singlet and a pair of g-string panties, also of black latex. He donned the skin-tight items, feeling incredibly excited. The only way he could accommodate his erection in the rubber panties was to let the material hold it upright against his stomach.

'Does that feel good?' Liz asked, closing her fingers

around the shiny latex of the g-string that now covered Sam's hard-on. She began running her hand up and down its length.

'Yes, Mistress,' he whispered hotly. He liked the feel of the rubber latex that pressed tightly against his thick shaft and he liked even more what Liz was doing with her fingers.

She then stopped stroking his cock and took out a couple more black latex items from the cupboard drawer. 'Put these on now,' she said, handing him a pair of stockings and a long pair of gloves. Sam's upright cock swelled further and flexed in the rubber trap of his panties, arousing his excitement even more as he began to put on the latex stockings. They felt delightful as he pulled them on slowly over his small feet and up to the top of his well shaped thighs. The long latex gloves, which went several inches above his elbows, felt delightful too and matched the stockings to perfection.

'Turn and look over your shoulder at yourself in the full length mirror,' Liz ordered, and Sam did. His long wavy hair cascaded down his slender neck, his skin was smooth and glossy and so was all that tight shiny black latex adorning his lithe body: the singlet pushed in his narrow waist, making it narrower still; the long elegant gloves made his small hands look almost dainty; the g-string panties emphasized the curved, lubed cheeks of his pert backside; and his stockinged legs looked wonderfully feminine. From the back he looked like an extremely sexy young woman, erotically attired in tight black rubber. At the front he was acutely conscious of his manhood. The tactile sensation of the g-string panties pressing on his upright cock made him intensely aroused and he could feel a steady stream of pre-cum fluid trickle into the latex.

'Now put this on,' Liz said, dipping into the drawer

once again and handing him a black latex mini-skirt. Sam slithered the small clinging garment on over his hips. He felt a surge of pure excitement at the idea of being dressed as this deliciously erotic girl, an excitement that made his erection press even more insistently against the tight latex panties and trickle yet more pre-cum into them.

'You don't need to put anything else on. I'll do the rest,' Liz said then, reaching for her handbag and the make-up kit inside it. She took out a lipstick, popping the top off, and carefully applied a subtle layer of colour to Sam's full lips. She then used a little of her mascara to thicken and tint his long eyelashes.

'Believe me,' Liz said, standing back to admire her handiwork. 'You look just like a beautiful rubber-clad slave girl now. How do you feel?'

'Amazingly turned on, Mistress,' Sam whispered, hardly able to contain his physical excitement. The idea of being an incredibly sexy slave girl was even more intensely arousing than the powerfully erotic *dreams* of being one he'd had the last two nights in a row after listening to Liz and Christine making noisy love together for hours on end in the bedroom across the hall from his own.

'I'm going to call you Samantha from now on,' Liz said, her green eyes sparkling. 'Say your new name for me, slave.'

'Samantha, Mistress,' Sam replied softly, even more excited by the idea. Sam's, correction, *Samantha's* erect cock oozed more wetness into her black latex panties.

'Want me to fuck your tight little pussy?' Liz asked, fixing Samantha with her most seductive gaze.

'… Mistress …' she gasped, barely able to speak.

'Then take off your pretty panties and get onto all fours,' Liz said. 'I want to take you from behind.' She

299

reached for the bottle of lubricant and smeared a liberal amount of it onto her black strap-on dildo.

Samantha pulled down and removed her latex g-string and got into position on the floor on her latex covered hands and knees. Liz got into position too, eased the back of Samantha's mini skirt out of the way and started to enter the rubber-clad slave girl with her strap-on. She made her gasp painfully as she slid the dildo in, penetrating into her narrow passage. Liz pushed as far into her as the dildo would go, pressing it deep inside her orifice. Liz began to move in and out of Samantha, slowly at first but then faster. She created a smooth rhythmic motion that left her moaning with pleasure and moving in time with each thrust into her tight hole.

Samantha began to move with increasing urgency, opening herself more and more so that Liz's dildo could go deeper, faster. Liz responded by fucking Samantha harder and harder, making her moan even more. She caused her finally to cry out loudly with blissful ecstasy as she brought her to an earth-shattering climax. Samantha shuddered uncontrollably in delight as the orgasm spurted from her hard cock in liquid profusion, her tight hole spasming around the strap-on dildo pressed deep inside her.

It was the most ecstatic, the most exquisite of releases, sheer bliss. But it was also something else … It was in effect the end of Sam Craven's trial period. That's right, already over the halfway mark though he now was – so near and yet so far – Sam was to all intents and purposes finished. He was dead in the water; he just didn't know it yet. Samantha didn't know it either.

Chapter Forty-nine

THREE MONTHS LATER

SAMANTHA COULDN'T HAVE PINPOINTED exactly when it was that the truth hit her, the realisation that Sam Craven wouldn't have been able to win Liz back in a million years, never mind in five short days. Liz loathed the man like the very devil for the despicable way he'd treated her when they'd been married and she would always feel that way about him. She'd feel that way about Sam no matter how much he grovelled to her, how deeply he humiliated himself for her, how hard he tried to get her to change her scathing opinion of him. As for Samantha, though, she was something else, *someone* else. Liz felt very differently about Samantha, very differently indeed. She had been as happy to welcome her as a permanent member of the household as had been Christine and Peter after they too had had the opportunity of making the acquaintance of the lovely young woman.

Samantha realised that the sadomasochistic ménage in which the four of them now lived would be regarded by many people in the 'vanilla' world as perverted in the extreme. But what did they understand, with their narrow minds and blinkered, conventional ideas? Samantha didn't care what such people might think. All she knew was that living the way she now did made her happier than she'd ever been in all her life. She could have wished for no other fate. She felt that this was what she had been born to be: the slave in both body and spirit to Liz and Christine. She loved it when the two women told her what they wanted her to do, loved it when they told her what, if anything, they wanted her to *wear*.

They had told her that they didn't want her stark naked today or in rubber latex but in black leather. And that was what she was wearing: the high collar – an appropriate symbol of her enslavement to them, the tight long-sleeved top with the little breast pads subtly built-in, the kid-soft gloves, the backless g-string cock-corset into which she had buckled her erection, the ultra-short flared skirt, and the shiny stiletto-heeled shoes. Samantha loved wearing stiletto heels. She found that they caused the muscles in her backside, thighs and calves to tauten and gave her a delightfully feminine gait. She had great legs too, even if she said so herself.

It was the strangest thing but dressed in skimpy fetish outfits like this made Samantha feel even more naked than when she was completely unclothed, which she often was too. She guessed it was because such kinky feminine attire left her completely exposed, laid bare as the person she truly was.

Samantha stood and studied herself in her bedroom mirror, which was a large three-sided affair, and she liked very much what she saw. She surveyed the person in the glass with half-closed eyes, the reflection before her that of a long-limbed, smooth-skinned, leather-clad beauty. The porcelain-white face, framed by long dark hair that was wavy and lustrous, looked lovely; the eyebrows were thinned down to fine dark lines, the sparkling blue eyes were exotically rimmed in black, and the lips – moist and parted – were outlined in the glistening red lipstick Liz

302

had chosen for her, which was particularly becoming.

Samantha ran her small leather-gloved hands lingeringly over her black leather outfit as she posed for herself in the mirror, in love with her own body as it appeared before her. The high slave's collar made her neck look even more slender; the tight top not only gave her a nice little bust but also cinched in her waist perfectly; and the extreme miniskirt showed off the glimmering paleness of her thighs and helped give the illusion that most of her height was in her beautifully curved legs, an effect that was further enhanced by her stiletto-heeled shoes. Breathing deep of the perfume-scented air – her perfume, which was musky and understated, had been chosen for her by Liz as well – she turned away from the mirror. Samantha sashayed towards the door, her body moving with a natural sway of the hips. She was going to go downstairs and join her three lovers in the living room.

And there the three of them were in that elegantly appointed room. Christine and Liz were naked apart from the black double dildo strap-ons they both had harnessed on – with one end lodged excitingly inside the sex – and the thigh-high black leather boots with spiked heels they were also wearing. Peter was naked and erect and was bent over the leather couch where he was being whipped by the two dommes in unison with heavy leather floggers. Their strokes fell harshly on both sides of his rear, marking his flesh with vivid lines. Peter writhed under the hard blows that fell across his backside, the sharp pain of impact merging with a suffused red glow that seeped through his body. He felt pre-cum wetness pour from the glans of his erect cock, the fluid excitement leaking so copiously that he felt close to orgasm. Then, before it was too late, the two women stopped beating him.

At that moment, as if on cue, the door opened and Samantha came in. 'Ah, there you are, slave,' Liz said. Her tone was curt although the gaze she gave her across the room was filled with unmistakable affection. She added warmly, 'Love the outfit, by the way. You look extremely sexy.'

'Thank you, Mistress,' Samantha replied in delight, her voice a husky whisper. She gave a small curtsy and felt her shaft strain against the buckled leather of the cock-corset. The feel of the constricting strips of leather was tantalizing on the sensitive flesh of her cock.

'I want you to give me a blow job while Mistress Christine beats your arse,' Liz said, rubbing her fist up and down the hard black erection jutting from her body. 'Now get down on your knees, crawl over here and get to work.'

Samantha could feel her heart thumping with excitement and fear as she crawled towards Liz on all fours. Her leather micro-mini skirt was lifted high at the back, exposing her naked rear in the backless g-string. She felt feverish with desire, anxious for the harsh love and punishment she knew she was about to receive.

Samantha arrived before Liz and closed her lips around the dildo instantly, beginning to trace its length with her tongue. She could see the other end to the dildo, which was pushed deep into Liz's pussy. Samantha moved up and down, sucking and licking vigorously at the hardness that filled her mouth. And she waited in excited trepidation for the inevitable...

The first stroke of Christine's flogger landed hard on her backside, whistling through the air to impact on her soft flesh with a loud report. Samantha could not cry out in pain; she could only suck harder. The heavy whip came down again. She winced, moving forward as the fire touched her flesh once more. She sucked harder still, closing her cheeks around the stiff shaft of Liz's strap-on. When Christine's flogger came down again Samantha felt the echo of the sensation in her corseted cock, pain turned to pure pleasure. Then Christine suddenly stopped beating her and put the whip aside. She lubed up her strap-on dildo next before handing the lube to Peter. 'I want you to fuck Samantha while I do the same to you,' she told the kneeling slave.

'Yes, Mistress,' he replied excitedly. He smeared his erection with lubricant and started to crawl towards Samantha.

Liz spoke next. 'Keep on blowing me while you're being fucked, Samantha,' she said, adding emphatically, 'Neither of you two slaves is allowed to climax unless you are given permission.'

Samantha kept on sucking Liz's strap-on while also using both of her leather-gloved hands to hold the cheeks of her backside open as Peter positioned himself so that the head of his cock was pressed into place. Christine positioned herself similarly behind Peter. When she was ready she pushed down against the punished cheeks of his backside. She forced herself into him and at the same time he forced himself into Samantha.

There was a sharp pain that made Samantha gasp into the dildo she was sucking, but it was nothing to the thrill of being fucked. She closed her eyes as Peter's cock slid all the way into her, his hardness lodged deep inside.

While Samantha could make very little noise because her mouth was wrapped around Liz's strap-on dildo, Peter was able to make as much noise as he liked. And he did, moaning and crying out as he was fucked by Christine with a hard swift rhythm … and as he did the same to his fellow sex-slave.

Samantha in the meantime was in seventh heaven. She saw herself as she was: a beautiful, desirable young woman who was sucking one lover and being fucked from behind by another, taking the hardness that was being plunged into her just as he was taking the hardness being plunged into him by her other lover. Samantha had never known such sexual delight, such erotic bliss. She found that she couldn't hold out a second longer and felt her tightly corseted cock exploding, its creamy liquid bursting out in spasms.

Oh dear, Samantha sighed to herself when her orgasmic trembling had finally stopped. She had been expressly told not to climax unless given permission to do so but had forgotten herself in the passion of the moment and disobeyed that instruction. She was bound to be severely punished for her disobedience and deserved to be. I don't know, Samantha said to herself happily, I can be *such* a bad girl sometimes. I really am the end.

Mistress of Torment
Alex Jordaine

When dark fantasy turns to darkest reality...

Self-bondage addict Paul is submissive to the core but craves constant hard discipline. A chance meeting with an old friend brings him within the thrilling orbit of top professional dominatrix Mistress Nikki and the ultra-sadistic Mistress Alicia.

An erotic novel with strong BDSM and Femdom content.

ISBN 9781906373825, price £7.99

First Spankings – True Spanking Initiations
Peter Birch

Accounts of real spankings given to real women! From the occasional bit of fun to tales from the most dedicated enthusiasts, the detailed stories include well known names from the genre of spanking erotica, many personal friends of the author, and confessions from around the world. It's an enthusiast's book, no question, but if you're curious about what really makes the kinky girls tick, then this is a must for any erotica shelf.

Peter Birch has been spanking girls for thirty years now, and has collected stories from the thirties to the noughties. This is the very first encyclopaedic erotica collection of erotic punishment given by boys to girls, and given by girls to girls, even in public. And one thing is guaranteed: every single confession is a genuine account of a woman's first experience of going over the knee.

ISBN 9781907016271 price £7.99

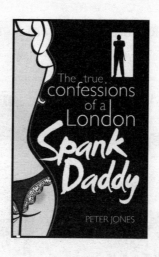

The True Confessions of a
London Spank Daddy
Peter Jones

Discover an underworld of sex, spanking and submission.
A world where high-powered executives and cuddly
mums go to be spanked, caned and disciplined.

In this powerful and compelling book Peter Jones reveals
how his fetish was kindled by corporal punishment while
still at school and how he struggled to contain it.
Eventually, he discovered he was far from alone in
London's vibrant, active sex scene.
Chapter by chapter he reveals his clients' stories as he
turns their fantasies into reality. The writing is powerful,
the stories graphic and compelling.

Discover an unknown world…

ISBN 9781906373320 Price £7.99

More Spanking Titles from Xcite Books

9781905170937 £7.99

9781906125837 £7.99

9781906125899 £7.99

9781906373702 £7.99